NEST EGG

ALOHA CHICKEN MYSTERIES: BOOK 1

Josi Avari

Want to know about new releases, free books, and fabulous prizes? Sign up for my newsletter!
josiavari.com
and connect with me on facebook

Also by Josi Avari

The Aloha Chicken Mysteries

Nest Egg (Book 1)

Hen Party (Book 2)

Hard Boiled (Book 3)

Hen Pecked (Book 4)

Home to Roost (Book 5)

Sunny Side Up (Book 6)

Three French Hens (Book 7)

Empty Nest (Book 8)

Bad Egg (Book 9)

Chick Flick (Book 10)

Chicken Out (Book 11)

Egg Nog (Book 12)

Love Birds (Book 13)

Spring Chicken (Book 14)

Over Easy (Book 15)

Walking on Eggshells (Book 16)

Fly the Coop (Book 17)

Love Nest (Book 18)

AND INTRODUCING TWO NEW COZY MYSTERY SERIES!

The Word Witch Mysteries

Spell it Out (Book 1)

The Desperate Strangers Travel Club Mysteries

Stranger on the Seine (Book 1)

This is a work of fiction. Similarities to real people, places, or events are entirely coincidental.

Nest Egg

First edition. March 8, 2019.

Copyright © 2019 Josi Avari.

Written by Josi Avari.

Cover art and illustrations by Richard Lance Russell

See more at richardrussellart.com

Chapter One

It shouldn't have been such a surprise for Saffron to see a chicken in a pot.

But the chicken was alive, and the pot was filled with straw, and the sound the chicken was making made Saffron doubt that anyone had told it that Uncle Beau had left the Hawaiian house it was nesting in to her.

The door was slightly open and had been for some time. None of the doors were locked, Saffron had discovered, and it was a good thing because the lawyer had said there were no keys to the house. When Saffron had inquired incredulously how that could be, he'd explained that nobody in the sleepy little island town of Maika'i ever locked their doors anyway, and Uncle Beau had likely lost the keys long ago.

She was standing just inside the back doorway, the bright tropical morning reaching its warm fingers into the dingy interior of the house. Saffron took off her ever-present sunglasses. She had just driven up from Honolulu, and the turquoise and white of the ocean, the vibrant pink of the flowers on the trees lining the long driveway off the main road, and the flashes of golden sand she'd seen driving along the coast still danced in her head. The vibrance outside made starker the dusty browns and grays of the cluttered house.

Color was an extraordinary experience for Saffron. She saw more colors than most people, and in different ways.

She never understood, for example, why people said she had red hair. When she looked in the mirror, she saw strands of orange and gold. She saw some that were wine colored and some nearly yellow. All together, they made up a shining copper that was as foreign to her idea of the red of an apple as it was to the green of the grass.

Her mother, who had passed away a few years ago, had been one of the few people who realized that Saffron had a unique eye for color. She had learned it early on when she'd enrolled her daughter in free painting classes at the local youth center. The endeavor hadn't gone well, because the teacher had insisted that the students use green for trees and blue for skies and gray for buildings regardless of what color they actually were. Saffron knew the sky in a hundred shades of pink and violet, the trees in blues and browns and creams. She couldn't bear to misrepresent them by reducing them to a single color.

The self-portrait she'd been told to do for the class was a disaster, too. She looked in the mirror and saw her skin as peachy-salmon, a color not encompassed in the basic crayon box. It was brushed across the cheeks with cherry and across the forehead with pale azure. Her freckles were a hundred shades. The teacher had argued that all she needed was a tan crayon and a brown one, and Saffron had been forced to hoard her colors and blend them as best she could. She spent five times as long on her portrait as anyone else. So the teacher had kicked her out. Sometimes Saffron liked to say that she was an art school dropout.

That's why she kept her sunglasses handy. They helped dull the colors so that she didn't see things so differently than other people. It cut down on awkward conversations. Now, without them, the dingy interior of the bungalow was a still-life of muted golds and reds, pinks and browns. They were a relief to her eyes. The color in the verdant island outside was a shock after coming from the gray of Washington DC.

The chicken in the pot wasn't the only chicken in the kitchen, either. Another scrawny bird scrambled out of Saffron's way as she pushed the door open. He was a young rooster, with long legs and bright orange pointed feathers laced with pale gray tips falling across his back like a costume. He scuttled over to the far side of the room as Saffron took a look at the sprawling bungalow her uncle Beau had called home.

Saffron tried not to panic. This place was not her style. She tugged a bottle of hand sanitizer out of her purse, a nervous habit, and smoothed it on her hands as she tried to force herself to venture farther. She tucked the bottle back into the small pocket in the lining of her purse that was designated for it and turned her face back to the open door. She took a tremulous breath of the sweet morning air.

Saffron's purse wasn't like other purses. She didn't toss everything in at random. She carried nothing she didn't need, and everything she needed had a place. A wallet inside held her checkbook, cards, and cash. Her driver's license was in a side pocket, lip gloss and powder in another pocket. There were no errant sticks of gum, no lidless pens, no unidentifiable crumbs at the bottom. It was, like everything in her life, perfectly organized.

She had her purse, a suitcase, and an envelope from the lawyer. Inside it was a sheaf of papers that made up a comprehensive insurance document complete with photos of all the valuables in the house after her uncle's death. She hadn't looked through it yet, but the front page said that she was to verify that the items were, in fact, in the house when she took possession of it. Now she saw that checking what was there would be a significant task. She tried to breathe.

The suitcase she'd carried onto the wide lanai held exactly one week's worth of tops, skirts, jeans, shoes, and matching jewelry all rolled into neat cylinders and stacked for easy access. Her rental car was devoid of soda cans or stray receipts, as pristine as when she'd picked it up.

Atop the shock of seeing the true state of the place, she was jetlagged from the 5 hours she'd lost flying to Hawaii from Washington DC, and the humidity had already undone her sleek and straightened hairstyle. The natural waves of her strawberry curls were beginning to assert themselves. Though she'd carefully touched up her day-old makeup before she'd exited the plane, the humidity had misted every available patch of skin, and she could tell her careful mask was disappearing. She felt as askew as this place looked. There were piles everywhere: old crates and boxes, once-damp aloha shirts draped out to dry, and books and photo frames stacked on every available surface.

This was chaos. Saffron didn't do chaos. Her event planning business back in DC was called *Every Detail Events*, and she had a reputation for events where even the smallest particulars were taken care of. Her apartment, her life, had been the same way. It had come to define not just her business, but also everything else.

She closed her eyes a moment and pictured her 700-square-foot studio apartment in the Yardley building back in DC. Or what used to be her apartment, anyway. She'd sold her lease before coming here, hoping to make enough on the sale of this place to buy a chic office space back in DC with an apartment above. Right now she missed The Yardley. Her flat there had been all steel and glass and sanitizable surfaces. She had opted for tile instead of wood, a leather sofa, glass end tables, and steel countertops. Nothing but the feet of her sparse furniture touched the floor. She had decorated in charcoal gray, black and white because they showed dust the best and it could be removed quickly. Décor was timeless, not seasonal: two hand-blown glass vases in a rich blood red were the only art she had allowed in. Back home she employed a house cleaning service weekly and scrubbed the apartment herself nightly. Before Reggie had left, he had told her, "I just need a little more chaos in my life," as he tried to explain to her why their relationship wasn't working for him. She had responded, "I don't do chaos."

Yet here she was, and opening her eyes she saw that there was no other word for this place. This was chaos upon chaos. In addition to the obvious hoarding, it looked as if someone had rifled through some of the boxes lately. She supposed the lawyer would have had to uncover her contact information somehow.

The dust here was unlike the dust in DC. Back home, it

collected in sharp, black grit on the tops of side tables and chair rungs. Here, it clung soft and heavy to nearly every surface, vertical or horizontal. In addition, a fine moss grew on the windowsills and vines snaked in through the windows, which her uncle had apparently left slightly open.

Something else had been left open. Saffron reached out and touched a tile from the backsplash that looked to be hanging away from the wall. It swung easily, and she pulled her hand back in surprise as she saw, behind it, a perfect little compartment. Saffron pushed the tile back to the wall, where it disappeared into the mosaic pattern of the backsplash. Intrigued, she tapped at it again, but this time it didn't budge. It took two minutes of playing with it before she found that the key was to push in on the top left corner. It gave under her fingers and then sprung open. She inspected it and discovered a catch and a hinge. It was a secret compartment built into the wall.

An empty secret compartment. Saffron pushed it closed and turned back to the disaster that was the kitchen.

"So much for moving to paradise," she said to the chicken.

Not that Saffron had ever lived with the misconception that Hawaii was paradise. Her mother, Abigail, had made sure of that ever since Saffron's father left. She had been almost certain that he'd come back to Hawaii, and she'd taken every opportunity to tell Saffron what an unpleasant place it was.

Since her father had never come back, and since he'd never made any effort at contacting her, Saffron assumed he was dead. Part of her hoped he was, since the thought of him out in the world somewhere, living his life while she suffered through her mother's loss alone made Saffron desperately angry.

Last year, Saffron's boyfriend Reggie had repeated history and run off to Hawaii, too. He had chosen a promotion in the Honolulu office of his medical supply company over the promotion he was offered in the DC office. Though he'd been sure he could convince her to move there, he couldn't, and that had effectively been the end of that relationship. She hadn't contacted him since he'd left the mainland, and she wasn't looking him up now. She was glad that they'd had absolutely no contact for the last year. That made it easy to avoid seeing him for the short time she was on the island. She didn't even have his contact information anymore.

Saffron had no desire to stay any longer than it would take to tidy this place up and sell it. She'd really only come because of a vague curiosity about what might be in those boxes. When the realtor had sent her some photos of the place, she'd seen her father's name—Slate Skye—on the corner of a page sticking out from a crate.

So she'd come to see what other secrets the house might hold. But she hadn't had any idea it would be this big a job.

Of course, it had been nearly a year since Uncle Beau had died, and the place had been left wild in his absence. Even before that, it appeared, Uncle Beau had been living pretty wild himself.

According to Gilbert Simmons, the lawyer who'd handled the will, Saffron was the only family Uncle Beau had left. Uncle Beau had married when he was young, but his wife, Saffron's aunt Ila, had died in a car accident with their young son just a few years after the wedding. Uncle Beau had never brought anyone into his life again.

Saffron wanted to turn around and get out of there, hop a plane, and go straight back to DC. But her apartment at the Yardley was gone, probably carpeted and redecorated in mustard and teal by the chipper young Midwest couple she'd sold her lease to. There was no place to go back to. Besides, she could do this. She'd cleaned up many a venue before the perfect wedding: the abandoned warehouse in the Union Market section of DC came to mind. She'd transformed that eyesore into an enchanted garden in three weeks. She could do this.

The first step was to remove the livestock. Saffron approached the young rooster on the floor, wondering how to get him out of the house. She reached for him, but he effortlessly flapped out of the way. She chased him around the kitchen table, which was laden with papers and boxes and crates. He observed her with one beady eye.

Saffron decided to slow down. Maybe if she didn't look so eager, he'd forget she was coming after him. She walked away, then circled back around the table as he got interested in some spilled cereal and began scratching and pecking at the floor. That was encouraging. Saffron paused, noticing that under and behind all the clutter was a pretty standard kitchen setup: stove with chicken, sink, dishwasher, microwave. But there was something odd. There were two refrigerators: one near the door and one back in the corner by the table. The one by the table was avocado green, and the other was a relatively new stainless steel model. Both were unplugged and their doors propped open.

The rooster's scratching drew her attention again, and Saffron moved toward him. She sidestepped around the table, keeping her eyes toward the stove but maneuvering closer to the bright little bird.

As she neared, he took an easy step or two away from her but didn't flee too far. As she closed the distance, his spindly legs suddenly went into overdrive, and he sped away like a roadrunner with a couple brisk flaps of his wings for extra speed.

"This is what they mean when they say something is as useless as herding chickens," she told him. "Now, come on. We're not both going to stay here."

The rooster chose that moment to let out a strangled sound, not a clear cock-a-doodle-doo like she'd heard cartoon roosters make. There was a note of defiance in it. Saffron looked at him. "You really can't stay if you're going to make sounds like that. I need some sleep."

Maybe she could lure him close, then catch him. Scooping up a handful of spilled cereal, Saffron crouched down and held out her hand.

"Here, chick, chick," she said, "here, boy."

Reggie had been the proud father to a dog—a brindle boxer named Rocky—and this had always worked with him. Of course, he hadn't had much to hide behind at the Yardley. When Reggie and Rocky visited Saffron's apartment, there'd barely been enough room for the three of them.

The chicken seemed completely uninterested in the food. He wandered away from her—back around the table—and leaped onto Saffron's luggage, where he started pecking at the Union Jack sticker from her trip to create the perfect London wedding last spring. The door stood open behind him. Maybe she didn't need to catch him just now. Instead, Saffron ran at him, throwing her arms up, scattering the cereal as she did so.

The rooster let out a surprised "bawk!" and flapped off through the open door onto the wide lanai that wrapped all the way around the farmhouse. Saffron slammed the door with a feeling of accomplishment.

Now she was met with a quandary: should she keep cleaning or get some rest? The hen was sitting quietly now, and though it would have to go, her redeye flight was catching up with her.

Investigating the house, she found that there were three bedrooms, a living room, two bathrooms, and the kitchen—all filled with stuff. Only two spaces were cleared enough to be of much use to a human being: half the futon in the living room and a narrow area on the bed in the master bedroom where Uncle Beau must have slept.

Saffron herself could never close her eyes on that bed. She'd have to clear it first.

Saffron went back to her luggage in the kitchen and pulled a bottle of orange juice from her bag. "It's going to be a long day," she told the chicken in the pot.

THOUGH SAFFRON HAD HEARD a lot about sea turtles and monk seals, chickens were the most visible wildlife in Hawaii. Saffron scattered a little flock of roosters on her way through the parking lot of the town's small hardware store, Coconuts and Bolts.

She was wearing a broad sun hat that she'd picked up, and she stopped to smooth on some sunblock. Her peachy skin had taken on a definite rosy hue since she'd gotten here, and she didn't want it to go all the way to tomato. She'd had enough sunburns in her life to take the precautions to avoid them.

Cleaning supplies were expensive in Hawaii. In the store's home-care section where Saffron found some cleaner, buckets, gloves, and scrub brushes, prices were sometimes twice what she would have paid back home. But there was no way around it. The bungalow had to be cleaned.

She also found a set of pillows and hideous blue sheets printed with surfboards. There were plush towels printed with pineapples, and she picked those up as well. She was hauling it all to the front when she heard a warm voice behind her.

"Bathing chickens out on the egg farm?"

Saffron turned to see a square man with a lined face the color of kukui nuts. His teeth were white and straight, and his eyes creased like seashells at the corners. His white beard, neatly trimmed, softened the strong line of his jaw. He wore a red and white Hawaiian shirt.

"Excuse me?" she said.

"You're the girl taking over the Hau'oli ka Moa egg farm, right?"

"I'm the one cleaning it up to sell it," she said.

The old man's face clouded, then cleared, "But you'll be staying while you clean it up, eh?"

She nodded.

"And you'll want to get top dollar for it."

"Naturally."

"So you'll want it cleaned pretty well. I've seen it. That's a big job there."

It made Saffron's head hurt to think of it, "I know." She said, edging toward the checkout. In DC, you didn't have to talk to people in the store.

"Used to make a lot of money, that farm," the man said.

"Hmmm. Doesn't look like much now."

"That's cause the chickens are out and everything's dirty. Nobody wants to buy dirty eggs. You'll have to wash up the place and make sure those chickens get back in their pens and get their baths too. Then you'll have people lining up to buy Hau'oli ka Moa eggs again."

"What does that mean, anyway?" Saffron had seen the words on the sign when she'd pulled up to the farm.

"The Happy Chicken," the old man said, and cast his bright smile toward her. It was hard not to like him, even with her head pounding. "I'm Mano. Aloha."

Saffron knew that she was supposed to say *aloha* back, but it felt pretentious somehow, as if she were using something that didn't belong to her. Instead, she just said, "I'm Saffron. Nice to meet you." She couldn't shake his hand, because her arms were full of cleaning supplies, but she gave him the best smile she could muster, "thanks for the information. I'll try to get the chickens gathered and everything cleaned up. Would you mind telling people that the place is for sale?"

Mano nodded, "I'll let them know. Good luck out there. Big job." He paused a moment, "do you want some help?"

Saffron had always been suspicious of people who wanted

to help. "No, I'm fine," she said, "thanks anyway." She turned and got to the checkout before he could offer again.

THERE WAS something cathartic about clearing off the bed. Saffron was astounded at the sheer number of empty egg cartons Uncle Beau had stacked there. It took her several trips to carry them to the hallway, where she stacked them atop several other piles. Beneath them were boxes of books and photo frames.

Lifting the heavy boxes to the floor and stripping off the dingy blankets and sheets, she was pleased to find an almost new mattress and a beautiful koa wood bedframe. She wiped the dust from it and traced the glossy, curling grain of the wood with her fingers. Carved into it were pineapples, coconuts, and banana leaves.

She'd had a wall-mounted stainless steel headboard back at the Yardley. There had been no place for dust to collect, and her bedroom had been just big enough to walk around the bed to the narrow closet. This place was different. The bungalow was sprawling and earthy. She could picture it tidy and decorated, a Hawaiian home anyone would love to have. This bed alone would bring two or three times as much as one of the fancy wedding dresses she'd helped brides pick out back home.

Her mouth turned bitter with a rush of anxiety. Every Detail Events was being run by her assistants Trish and Clark in her absence, and several important events were coming up. That's why she needed to get this done quickly. She needed to get back to her life. She calmed her panic by reminding herself that she was here *because* of her business, not in spite of it. According to Rose, her real estate agent, the money from this sale would be enough to pay for the new office space at the Veridian, in one of the most lush districts of DC, a standing ad in DC Bride, and a brand-new van to ferry decorations and food to the venues. She'd driven her sedan in DC rush hour with a six-foot dressmaker's dummy wrapped in tulle sticking over her shoulder and very nearly brushing a three-tier Remi Callaghan wedding cake, and she was not doing that again. The extra capital from this sale had the potential to solve those startup problems and launch her into the top event planners in DC. She tried not to think about the fact that this time last year, she'd been expecting to plan her own wedding. It had been penciled in for next weekend, but that was before Reggie went to Honolulu.

She vacuumed and scrubbed, hauled and cleared until the master bedroom and bath were shining and bare. The wood floor shone warm and sleek under the wide windows. She'd even cleaned the wood fan blades. The tawny tones of the wood throughout the room made the place feel welcoming. She spread the surfboard sheets on the bed and stood back to admire the room. Her efforts had paid off. It was an oasis in the sea of clutter.

It was dark outside now, and Saffron wandered to the kitchen and ate a handful of macadamia nuts from a can she'd bought at the airport. Glancing through the cupboards, she saw plenty of boxes, cans, and bags, but she didn't trust any food in here. She wished she'd stopped at the bright little Paradise Market she'd seen on the town's main street.

The chicken in the pot clucked her annoyance at Saffron's intrusion. Saffron was too tired to put her out right now. She simply didn't have the energy for another chicken roundup. All she wanted was sleep.

"All right, all right, one more night of freeloading for you," she told the chicken as she switched off the light and stumbled from the kitchen. "But I'm getting you out of here tomorrow."

She felt like she could breathe properly in the tidy bedroom. In fact, she could almost forget the catastrophe outside the bedroom door, and she was so tired she almost forgot she'd been hungry.

Saffron pulled off her grimy clothes and unzipped her suitcase. On top were her soft gray pajamas and her toothbrush. She went into the little master bath and brushed her teeth. She stripped off the remaining smudges of her makeup and dabbed at her face with the soft pineapple towels. Saffron slipped into the surfboard sheets.

In her dreams, she was chasing chickens. It was a noisy squawk from the kitchen chicken that woke her in the middle of the night and made her sit up. Saffron pushed the fog of sleep from her mind and listened.

Footsteps. Someone was walking in the house.

The wavering beam of a flashlight jittered away the shadows in the hallway. Saffron squinted against the splashes of color the beam revealed in the darkened hall.

"Who's there?" Saffron called. The light disappeared, and Saffron looked around for something to defend herself with. She heard the creak of the floorboards as the intruder retreated. She jumped up and moved to the bedroom door, where she snapped on the bedroom light and then, reaching around the door frame, the hall light.

Saffron's chest was tight with fear. She'd lived in DC her whole life and never had a break-in. She'd been here for bare hours, and someone was in her house.

The back door screeched, and Saffron stepped quickly down the hall to see if she could catch a glimpse of the fleeing perpetrator.

By the time she reached the door, though, and closed and locked it, she could see no one outside under the wan yard light through its grimy glass.

The kitchen didn't seem so ominous now that the lights were on. The hen on the stove was making a soft, insistent thrumming sound. Saffron recognized it as a warning. For the first time in her life, Saffron understood why people kept pets. It was nice knowing that there was another living creature with her.

Nothing in the kitchen seemed disturbed. Saffron walked through into the living room. That was where the burglar had concentrated. She could see streaks in the dust where his fingers had gripped a box or peeled back a flap. One box had been upended on the single remaining space on the futon, its contents scattered and vaguely sorted. She wondered how long the person had been in the house before she'd woken up. The thought made her squirm.

Still, an empty house full of stuff was bound to draw thieves. They probably didn't even know she was here, and even the little changes she'd made would be hard to spot amid the flotsam and jetsam of Uncle Beau's life. The intruder had fled through the back door, which looked out on the yard, the little cottages, and the steep mountainside beyond the farm, so he probably didn't see her car sitting out front.

She sat on the floor next to the futon and looked at the contents of the dumped box.

It seemed to be a conglomeration of old military items. There were brass pins with eagles and crosses, colored bars, ribbons. There was a cloth-covered canteen, a field manual for a rifle regiment, and a set of dog tags. Saffron recognized her grandfather's name on them.

Everything was worn and faded. Nothing stood out as particularly valuable. But it did seem there might be missing items. There was a shadowbox laying face down on the futon. Its back had been popped off and left beside it. The display surface was black velvet, badly faded except for one spot. Saffron could clearly see the shape of a knife with a thick handle and a curved blade. There was a paper tag pasted to the velvet that read, "The Knife that Saved My Life in Germany." It must have belonged to her grandfather when he fought in World War II. He'd left from this very island after the Pearl Harbor attack. So the thief had taken at least the knife and maybe more. The box was much bigger than it needed to be to hold these few bits of memorabilia. Saffron shivered as she ran her finger along the edge of the knife's silhouette. The intruder had probably been carrying this when she shouted out and scared him away.

Saffron looked around. She had no way of telling if anything else had been taken. The daunting mountains of Uncle Beau's possessions cast heavy shadows in the glare of the overhead light, and Saffron shrugged. The burglar didn't know it, but he was probably doing her a favor carting some of it away.

Saffron made a call to the emergency dispatcher.

"Maika'i City Services," said a woman's voice, "what is the nature of your emergency?"

"Someone's broken into my house," Saffron said.

"Is the intruder still there?" The woman's words weren't rushed, and her tone conveyed no urgency. Rather, she seemed interested in the story.

"No," Saffron said, "I think I scared him off."

"Did you know the person?" the woman asked.

"No, I don't know anybody here," Saffron supposed she had, technically, met one person—Mano—but that didn't seem relevant.

"Would you like an officer to respond?"

"Don't they just do that anyway?" Saffron found that she was already peering out the window, expecting to see flashing lights approaching from the main road.

"See, we only have the one officer here," the woman said, still conversational, "and Maika'i is the safest town on the island, so we don't really have to dispatch for every call." Was she chewing gum? Saffron winced. "Officer Bradley can come out in a while," the dispatcher said, "but he's on another call right now—a domestic thing over at Rod Peters' house," Saffron wondered if the woman should be telling her this, "and he probably won't be back for an hour or so, but I can send him your way when he comes back."

Saffron stuttered out her agreement and tapped her phone to end the call. If this was the safest town on Oahu, Maika'i City Services seemed to have little credit to take for that.

Chapter Two

Light was beginning to touch the sky over the sea outside the front windows, but it was still very early. Saffron returned to the bedroom and tried to go back to sleep, but even though her arms ached and her vision was blurry with fatigue, her mind would not shut off and allow sleep to return. She kept seeing that figure, knowing that he'd been in the house while she slept. In addition to the fear, she was also still on DC time, and she felt as awake as if it was two in the afternoon.

She figured she might as well go through some of the boxes while she waited for the sun to catch up with her. The hall outside the master bedroom was stacked with boxes and crates and piles she'd emptied from the room yesterday. She switched on the lights and started with a beautiful old crate that had "Juicy Pineapple" woodburned into the side of it. She could have used it for a trendy cakestand at a vintage wedding event. Inside was a stack of books, everything from "Getting Started with Landscaping" to an early edition of "Gone with the Wind."

She set them aside. She'd have to check and see if any of them were worth selling. If not, they'd make great centerpieces, especially for a booksy wedding.

The next crate held more books, and the third was filled with photos in frames. A much younger Uncle Beau held a baby in the top one, and as she went down, she saw more of his life. His wedding, his service in the Navy, his childhood.

She flipped the last frame over. It was an exquisite silver creation, ornate and interwoven. In its center staring out at Saffron were the eyes of her father. The young Slate Skye stood with Uncle Beau and her grandparents on the beach, a line of waves breaking in the water behind them.

The boys were not yet ten years old, their wide eyes and bright smiles unlike the men she remembered.

Her father had left when Saffron was a toddler. Her only memory of him was his goodbye, as he leaned down over her crib and kissed her on the forehead. The memory was colored with the electric blue of his eyes, a color she had only seen a few times since—once on a tropical fish, and once in a lightning-lit night sky.

And she had only come to know Uncle Beau when he was

old. He'd come to her mother with cash for her medical bills, and though not even that could save her, it had lessened the stress for them considerably. Uncle Beau had visited regularly until the end, six years ago, and then she hadn't heard from him until his attorney called with the news.

Saffron slid the photo back into the box and piled the other frames back on top of it. Some things, Saffron felt, should stay buried.

A ragged blast of sound from the porch made her jump. The rooster had apparently spent the night out there and was letting her know that day was dawning. He crowed twice more just to be sure she was up. Saffron was ravenous. She headed for the kitchen and was all the way there before she realized there'd be no cooking today. The kitchen needed cleaning, and there was still a chicken on the stove.

The nest the hen had made in the pot looked soft and tidy. In fact, right then the hen was carefully tucking an errant straw into the nest, weaving it carefully back under another so the end didn't stick out. Saffron couldn't help but like her. They shared a love of neatness.

Still, it wasn't neat to have a chicken living on the stove. "You've got to go," Saffron said, moving over to open the door. Maybe she could scare it out like she had the rooster.

Only he was there waiting like a salesman. Saffron closed the door before he could come in. He crowed again.

She'd have to grab the chicken and put her out. She approached the pot, eliciting a low warning trill from the hen.

"Don't get sassy with me," she said, "I own this house. You're just squatting."

The hen tipped her head and, incredibly, seemed to grow larger. Saffron stepped back.

"You know, the last time I was this close to a chicken, it was at the Bombay Club in DC, and it was in my chicken tikka masala."

This didn't seem to bother the hen. Her trill had now become more rapid, and the low sounds blended into each other and made an unnerving growl.

"And you look like tikka, too. You're the same color. And believe me, I know color." Saffron studied the hen. Saffron's unique color vision was paired with a remarkable color memory. Saffron carried in her mind a catalog of every color she'd ever seen and could match tints she saw to ones she'd seen years ago. The shimmering orange of the hen's feathers, the way they seemed made up of reds and golds and a hint of violet, was a perfect match for the rich tikka masala sauce back in DC. "In fact, that's your new name. I'm calling you Tikka." She thought this might intimidate the hen, but it just pulled its head closer to its body and swelled even more. Saffron shifted her weight from one foot to the other. The hen, round and full, had the most remarkable feathers. They were a vibrant golden orange, with stark black edging. They came to a rounded point and made her look like she was wearing armor. Saffron was growing less confident about picking her up.

The rooster crowed outside. Saffron glanced through the window and saw him perched on the railing of the lanai, swiveling his rusty head to stare at her through the window. The steel blue points on his feathers rippled across each other like chainmail.

"You want a name, too?" Saffron called to him. "I'm calling you Curry." The rooster didn't seem intimidated, either. In fact, he ticked his head up and down as if nodding approval.

"You can't stay here," she said, turning her attention back to Tikka. "Nobody's going to buy a house with a chicken living in it." Saffron backed away, trying to think. Maybe she should have taken the old man up on his offer to help.

The hen quieted as Saffron retreated.

Saffron froze. As the hen settled down, another sound was

clear. It was a high squeak, insistent and delicate. Mice? No, this was much too constant. It was coming from the pot.

And then she realized. "Tikka, you old rascal," she said, "you've got a baby in there."

No wonder the hen was so reticent to vacate. Saffron stilled and waited. When Tikka seemed sure that she was no longer threatened, she shifted slightly. The fuzzy black head of a chick peeked out from under her mother's wing. It was the chick that was making all the noise now.

Tikka tucked the little ball of fluff back under her wing and shifted again. Underneath the hen, several more eggs were visible. Tikka tucked her head under herself and brought it back out, nudging half of the empty shell the chick must have come from out of the nest. She repeated the process and pushed out the other half. The shells fell to the stovetop with a hollow sound.

The hatch must have just begun.

"Well played, Tikka," she said. "I certainly can't move you right now, can I?"

The rooster crowed from outside again.

"You're not coming back in," Saffron called to him. She moved away from the hen and grabbed her caddy of cleaning supplies from the sink. "At least we can keep your babies from hatching in a filthy kitchen," she said.

Saffron filled two garbage bags with old cans and boxes of food. She ran three loads of dishes through the dishwasher and scrubbed the cupboards until her knuckles hurt.

It was in the top cupboard that she found the second hidden compartment. Behind the teacups, a sliding wood panel was built back into the wall. She never would have seen it if she hadn't been scrubbing an ages-old ring left by a dried-up bottle of molasses. The agitation shook the panel just loose enough to make a hairline crack revealed by the strong light Saffron had set up to see into all the corners. Carefully, she slid back the panel. At first, she could make out nothing in the small, dark space, but she adjusted the light, and the lumpy outline of a black velvet bag appeared.

Saffron could tell as soon as she hefted it that there were coins inside.

She moved to the newly-scrubbed table. Tikka watched her with interest as she poured the clinking treasure out onto the table. Four gold coins slid out, along with two old US passports. The coins, each showing a woman's head surrounded by stars on the front and an eagle made from a shield on the back, were marked 1898. The passports belonged to her grandparents.

As she cracked them open, a little note fell out of her grandmother's:

Beth,

Just a little mad money to get you home for a visit. Come whenever you have the time, and bring our precious grandsons.

It was signed by Lulabelle Hardy, Saffron's great-grandmother on her grandmother's side. She thought about the distance between Minnesota and Hawaii, and how her grandmother had come with her grandfather here when he came to work for the fruit companies. From what she understood, that had only lasted a few years before he bought his own farm and built this house.

Saffron knew what it felt like to miss your mother. She had, suddenly, a new appreciation for her grandma Beth, out here in the islands. She wondered if she'd ever seen her mother again. The ties of family had to stretch pretty far without breaking back in those days.

Saffron didn't know how much the coins were worth, but she suspected they were valuable. She put them back in the bag and stowed them where she'd found them. This house was full of surprises.

When the kitchen was clean and the boxes had been moved

into the living room for later sorting, Saffron made her way outside.

She blinked at the explosion of color that greeted her. DC's overwhelming color was gray. Gray monuments, gray streets, often gray skies. Here, the verdant green almost hurt her eyes. There were deep greens composed of azure streaks and gold sheens, neon greens with overtones of magenta and lemon, dusty greens that held bronze and bluebell tones. Everywhere she looked, layers of plants were growing: cerulean grass on the ground, knee-high bushes, emerald shrubs the size of houses, and above it all, towering palm trees with clusters of coconuts that seemed impossibly high.

Saffron slid her sunglasses on. There was only so much color she could stand. The farm was alive with chickens. They were scratching in the grass, rolling in the sand, and chasing each other around the yard. Their feathers came in every color, and within those colors, more colors: black with violet and turquoise overtones, tangerine with shimmering aqua and splashes the color of sunshine. Looking at their plumage was a treat to Saffron. Still, she felt the old twitch of annoyance at something out of place. She wanted them in their pens, as the old man had said, clean and useful and most of all contained. She walked toward a group of them, and they scattered. As she had learned with Curry, rounding them up wasn't going to be easy.

A flash in the undergrowth drew Saffron's attention. She walked toward it and crouched where she could peer into the bush. There she saw the smooth, ovoid shapes of several eggs, resting in a depression filled with dried grass and leaves. It was a nest. She supposed there were many such caches of eggs throughout the property. One more reason the chickens should be in their pens. This nest was so well camouflaged that she would never have seen it if she weren't looking at just the right angle. Gathering eggs to sell from dozens of such wild, hidden nests would take forever.

Flowers grew on many of the trees and bushes. The whole place smelled sweet, and the fresh breeze from the ocean on the other side of the house left Saffron feeling rejuvenated.

A police cruiser came nosing into the driveway. Saffron walked around the house and met the officer as he climbed out of his car. He was a stocky man with a square jaw, early fifties. He had a weathered face that had seen, Saffron could tell, a lot. The officer held his face taut, with a callous indifference evident in the set of his mouth. His nametag said *Bradley*.

"Had a call about a break-in?" he said. His voice was flinty.

"Right. Someone was in my house last night."

"Your house?"

Saffron felt defensive. "My Uncle Beau left it to me. I just got here from DC yesterday."

"Ahhhh," Bradley breathed a long, exasperated sigh, "I see." Saffron wondered what he saw, but the officer didn't expound. "You want to take those glasses off?" he asked. His tone was authoritative, so Saffron obliged.

Without her sunglasses, she could see the blue tinge to his jaw, where his beard would be if he weren't clean-shaven. She felt more confident, somehow, when she could fully assess her surroundings with her full range of color vision. She looked him in the eye.

"They take anything?" He didn't seem to want to use any more words than he had to.

"Maybe?" She tried to explain, "I'm not sure. I just got here, and this is my uncle's stuff, and—"

"So nothing that was important to you?"

"Well, I don't think so. Maybe some of my grandpa's army stuff," Saffron was going to continue, but Bradley cut her off again.

"Did you engage the intruder?"

Saffron shook her head. "No, he ran off when he figured out I was there."

Bradley shrugged, "Probably local kids. This place has been vacant a long time, and they mess around, you know?"

Saffron felt he should be a little more concerned, "I know kids can be mischievous, but—"

"Look, miss, I am the only officer here. I know out in Washington there's whole fleets of personnel ready to swoop in whenever somebody disagrees with their neighbor or has a hangnail, but I have been out all night dealing with people whose lives depend on me showing up to stop their abusive husbands from sending them to the hospital. You get why I'm not that worried about some kids daring each other to go into an abandoned house? I'm looking around, and I'm just not seeing any immediate danger here."

There was nothing more to be said. "I guess I just wanted to make a report so you'd know somebody is breaking in on your beat."

"I appreciate that. But in the future, don't call unless you're in real peril. You're not in DC anymore."

Saffron didn't say anything as she slipped her sunglasses back on and watched him climb back into his cruiser. He flipped a U-turn in the yard. Last night's incident suddenly seemed less threatening and more absurd, and she supposed she was at least glad to be feeling angry now instead of afraid.

The heartbeat of the ocean came to her in the sound of the steady waves on the beach ahead. From where she was standing in the yard, she could see the blue curls of its reaching swells. She let the sound calm her.

Framing the view of the ocean was a long, zigzagging line of palm trees, unbroken except for a thirty-yard stretch that gave a perfect ocean view from the picture window in the living room behind her. The golden sand of the beach cast a happy glow around the scene.

Saffron let her gaze follow the treeline south, where, just a couple hundred yards away, the trees grew thick at the base of an enormous lava rock point that protruded hundreds of feet out into the sea. The waves broke against it in a violent spray, foam chasing them back out before they rushed tirelessly to batter the point again. Saffron wondered absently how long it would take for the water to wear it away.

Not ready to go back in yet, Saffron wandered down the driveway to the back of the house. A vast lawn separated the main bungalow from three little cottages where the workers on her grandfather's farm used to live. She wasn't surprised to find that Uncle Beau had filled them with more stuff. They were little square buildings containing a couple bedrooms, one bath, a small living room, and a kitchen. Wide, screened lanais held dusty wicker furniture and made an extra outdoor room in the back of each cottage, and open lanais framed the fronts.

These, apparently, had been closed up much longer than the main bungalow. The cottages were sealed up, and most of the furniture and boxes inside were covered with sheets.

Beyond them lay the egg house. Saffron knew what it was because there was a finely carved tiki-style plaque above the door that said "Egg House." It was a long, low building that stretched a hundred feet away from the front doors. Pens on either side of the center aisle had roosts and nest boxes along the corridor. The pens led out to long, grassy paddocks accessed by tiny doors raised and lowered with pulley systems accessible in the central aisle.

At the door end, where she had just come in, Saffron saw work areas on both sides. A hand-cranked conveyor belt ran behind each nest box and carried the eggs to the work areas, where stacks of egg trays sat as if they'd been used yesterday. Both work areas had sinks, and in the left basin of each sat a square apparatus with spiral bristle brushes and spray faucets.

Saffron played with one of them for a moment, trying to

figure out what they were for. One side had a circular crank that she could spin to make the brushes turn. When she switched on the water, it sprayed a fine mist over the brushes. The bristles curved around at about two-inch intervals, just the size for an egg to travel along them.

An egg washer! This would spray and scrub the eggs as you spun the wheel. Saffron switched off the water and smiled at the ingenuity of whoever designed this place.

The work area also held a feeding system for each side. There were places to load bags of feed and crank them up to a raised bin, where it looked as if the apparatus tipped them and poured the feed into the bin. A pipe, intercepted by another crank, protruded from the low right corner of the bin and connected to other pipes that went into feeders in each pen. Saffron assumed that turning the crank would send feed shooting down the pipes and into the feeders.

The building was overgrown and empty, but in better shape than the house by far. Saffron decided to work on tidying it up for a while. As she began, some of the chickens from outside started to wander in and scratch in the center aisle.

"No you don't!" she said, "you're not coming in here without your bath!"

She chased them out and finished cleaning the big building. A large pile of sand outside served as fresh flooring for the pens after she'd shoveled them out. At the end of the day, she was too tired to even check on Tikka, but she heard the chirping of more chicks as she went to sleep.

The next day, Saffron began herding chickens in earnest. She found that the heavy, fluffy hens were easier to catch than Curry had been, so she started with them. Her plan was to bathe them, dry them, and put them in the freshly cleaned egg house, filling one pen at a time.

Chapter Three

"Mano," the old man said, louder than necessary, "you ever seen anything like that?"
"Lotta hana," replied his friend. Saffron tried to ignore them. Just because she was kneeling in the grass

bathing a chicken didn't seem to be a good reason to hassle her.

She'd met Mano the day before at the local grocery. He was the one who'd asked her if she had bathed all the escaped chickens on the farm she'd inherited from her uncle.

The old men leaned on the fence, just over the sign that said, "Hau'oli ka Moa" and sported a picture of a chicken in a pineapple. It was an odd but fitting description of the strange place Saffron found herself.

The chicken, a docile brown hen, had finally settled down and lay lazily in the warm water. Occasionally, she reached down and pecked at the freckles on Saffron's hands.

"Ow!" Saffron splashed a little more water on the hen's back and decided she was done. Reaching for the beach towel beside her, she tried to lift the now-struggling hen and got a wet wing in the face for her efforts. The hen flapped and clawed her way down Saffron's arm, landing next to the towel. Saffron snatched it and dropped it over the ungrateful chicken, scooping her up and starting to rub the water off her wings.

At this, the old men began laughing in earnest.

Saffron straightened. She strode to the fence. She was used to dealing with taunts. She looked the old men straight in the eye, "How can I help you, gentlemen?"

This seemed to surprise them. Saffron peered out from under the huge brim of her hat. Its shadow fell across her arms and the disgruntled hen.

"We're just wondering how many chickens you've washed," one of them said.

Saffron tried not to sigh. It had been a long morning. "Half a dozen."

If old men could giggle, then the one with the beard did that. "How many more do you plan to wash?"

"All of them," Saffron waved an arm at the sprawling expanse of land that was now hers, realizing—not for the first time—that there were an awful lot of chickens out there in the undergrowth.

"And how many do you think that is?"

She shrugged. "A hundred or so."

"And you're gonna wash them all?"

Saffron lifted her chin a little higher. "Eventually."

"Okay," the one called Mano, with the trimmed white beard and laughing eyes, tossed her a shaka, the two-finger hand sign that she'd learned, in her short time on the island, meant anything from "I'm sorry" to "Thank you." This time it seemed to mean, "it's okay with me if you want to be insane."

"Look," Saffron said, trying not to let her annoyance show, "If you don't need anything, I hope you'll excuse me, because I've got a lot of chickens to wash."

This elicited another gale of laughter from the two men, but for the first time, Saffron didn't feel as if they were laughing at *her* so much as at life in general. She looked closer. Mano's eyes, sparkling brown, peered at her with affection and humor. She couldn't help but like him.

His friend's face was filled with the same playfulness, but he was much thinner. His cheekbones stood stark over the depressions of his cheeks. His smile flashed three gold teeth, and his bronze skin shone tight on his forehead and temples. Saffron felt sorry she'd been so harsh. The eleven-o'clock sun was hot on top of her hat, and they seemed to have walked out here—a good two miles from town. They must be tired and thirsty, too.

Saffron gestured with her head, rubbing the chicken in the towel as she did so. "I'm sorry. My name's Saffron. You're Mano and . . ."

"Bud," answered the thin old man.

"It's been a tough day. I didn't sleep well last night, and I'm still a little jetlagged. I'm sorry if I was harsh. Would you guys like something to drink? I've got cold soda."

If it was possible for their mood to get any better, it did.

The two old men followed her happily into the little blue bungalow. Inside she tried to guide them around the mishmash of belongings.

"I'm sorry about the mess. I haven't been here long and my uncle—" she paused, looking around, "he left a lot of stuff." It was at the mention of Uncle Beau that she saw why they were there. The men's merry eyes clouded, and Mano took off his hat.

"You were friends of his?" She asked, pausing in the doorway to the kitchen. "I've known him since we were keiki," he translated, "since we were kids. Your father, too," Mano said.

"And we spent a lot of time out here with Beau the last few years," Bud said.

"Three elemākule," Mano said, then smiled at Saffron's confusion, "three old men. Making trouble."

"Making tea," Bud corrected, and the way they laughed showed Saffron that this was an inside joke.

Still, she said, "I remember that he loved tea."

"Cup every morning and night and in between. Even when he visited your mother on the mainland?"

"Even then." Saffron said, "But his visits didn't happen often."

They nodded. "Still, Beau didn't want Abigail to be completely on her own. And he wanted you to have some family."

"He was certainly more family to me than my father ever was," Saffron had said it a million times, to a million people. She had spoken it as an apology, as an explanation, as a defense. But this time it was different. This time she said it to people who had known her father before he left her family. She wondered if they'd defend her father. Instead, they brought the conversation back to Uncle Beau.

"Beau, you old kolohe," Bud said with affection, holding up

a brightly printed shirt from the top of a pile. Saffron raised her eyebrows. He translated for her, "Old rascal."

The men sobered, "He was a good friend," Mano said. "So ono."

The little house filled for a moment with silence. Outside, a rooster crowed, then another. They had been at it all morning, and Saffron resented a little that they broke this reverent moment.

"There's your uncle Beau now. Crowing like usual," Bud said. "Sounds just like him. He never did know when to be quiet."

Entering the kitchen, the two men stopped and stared at the Tikka. When they started chuckling, Saffron tried to explain.

"I know it's weird to have that chicken there, but she's got babies hatching in that pot!"

This made them laugh harder.

"You just going to let her raise them there huh?" Mano asked.

"Well, not forever. But," Saffron didn't know how to tell them about her first night here, about the comfort she had taken knowing that there was some other living thing sharing this unfamiliar place with her. "I think I will keep them in here for a little while. Until they start getting out of their nest, anyway."

"Their mama will be out of the nest today. Not long after they're done hatching. And they'll follow her. They'll be all over this house then."

Saffron shivered at the thought.

The men laughed again. "Go get a box," Bud choked out, his eyes on Mano.

Mano left by the back door, his laughter following him into the bright Hawaiian morning.

"Where's he going?"

"We built some things around here. For one, we built a bunch of boxes to raise chicks in. They're called brooder boxes. They have heat lamps, feeders, waterers, and are easy to empty out when the chicks are big enough to go out to the coop. One of them will make a much better home for that little ohana than the pot on your stove."

Saffron turned just in time to see Mano maneuvering through the back door, keeping a big plywood box between Curry and the coveted kitchen.

"That one's determined, isn't he?" Mano said.

Saffron laughed. "He sure is." She watched as Mano nestled the big box into the corner of the kitchen next to the table. "You can keep 'em in here until you're ready for them to move out."

Saffron felt a surge of gratitude mingled with a strange wonder that the men would bother to help her with her problem.

Over ginger ale and a box of cookies Saffron had picked up in town, the two old men told her stories about her uncle

"He sure had a lot of stuff," she said waving a hand, "I don't know why anyone would keep all this."

They looked around. "Well," Bud said, "everybody should have a little nest egg, something for the future. Maybe Beau just kept these things as insurance that he'd always have something to sell if he needed to."

'Nest egg' made her think about all the time she'd spent scouring the long coop building, sweeping decades of dust and droppings out of it, chasing mice, and tearing vines off its faded siding. She told them about it, and they seemed impressed.

"It's really a brilliant design," she said. "Roosting areas and nest boxes inside, those nice little doors that lead to the foraging pens. It even has conveyor belts just behind the nest boxes where the eggs roll out, and you can turn a crank and bring them all to the work area."

"Don't talk too much about it. Mano already thinks he's our gift from the gods," Bud said.

"You designed it?"

"This guy can do anything with wood. He's a master craftsman and carver, makes ukuleles, carves beautiful things—beds, canoe paddles. You need a tiki?" Bud raised his eyebrows, "Mano can carve you a great tiki for your house. And he can build. Whoo! He builds." Bud closed his eyes and shook his head.

"But all three of us built that egg house together," Mano said, brushing the compliments off like sand, "Beau and his big dream. It was an improvement over the old barn his parents had, with walls of nests. He told me what problems he faced with chicken keeping, and I designed solutions for them. That's all. When it came time to swing the hammers, you helped as much as anybody, bruddah."

"Maybe, but I'm no artist. And that was a long time ago," Bud's eyes held a faraway look.

"When did Uncle Beau start the farm?" Saffron asked.

Bud was smiling his glinting smile, "When those two were just keiki." He gestured at Mano.

"You were already an old man then."

"You're older, then?" Saffron asked Bud.

"I've got twenty years on these youngsters," Bud said. "Seemed like a lot back then, but not so much now."

Saffron wouldn't have guessed twenty years. That put Bud in his late nineties.

He must have seen the surprise register on her face as she did the math. "That's right. I'll be a hundred next week."

"Oldest man in town," Mano slapped Bud's shoulder affectionately. "And still the most popular with the ladies."

Bud shooed him off. "Aw, now."

"That's what I hear. Lani. Mattie. And who else have you been out with this week? Oh, that's right. Sarah from the Senior Center. And you've probably got a date tonight!"

Saffron looked down at the chicken to hide her smile.

"Well, a man gets lonely."

"How can you be lonely?" Mano teased. "You've got a dozen people livin' in your house."

Bud took another drink of soda, "that's what makes me lonely."

A brief glance of understanding passed between the two men. Saffron's curiosity was piqued.

"A dozen people?"

"Not quite. You should learn that Mano exaggerates. My great-grandson-in-law," Bud said. "And sometimes some of his friends stay over. It's temporary."

"When will Naia be back from the mainland?" Mano asked.

Bud shrugged. "My great-granddaughter," he said to Saffron. His voice held both fear and sorrow. "About your age."

There was marked tension in the air. The mention of Naia had brought it. Saffron wondered why they both had grown so uncomfortable. The hen was beginning to wriggle in Saffron's arms. The chicken was dry now, and had been content, but either she felt the men's uneasiness, or she was just ready to get back outside and get dirty again.

"No you don't," Saffron chided her. "You're going right in the coop."

The men stood. "Let's see what you've done," Mano said.

THE COOP WAS A LONG, low building with dozens of nestboxes down the right side and high roosts down the left. The siding was a warm gray, with black steel hardware and white-framed screen windows that Saffron had taken great pride in uncovering. After the vines were stripped away and the shutters hooked back, the windows let in the light and a sweet breeze from the hibiscus that shaded the coop.

Saffron's arms were still sore from sweeping out the old dust and shoveling sand into the coop from the big pile outside near the stream, but stepping into the bright, clean coop, seeing the old men's faces beaming, made the ache worth it. She went to the first pen, where the other hens she'd managed to catch and bathe this morning were perching and preening their feathers. She thought she saw a little resentment in their glances as she came in and released the other hen. The chicken flapped off out the door and stood in the sunshine.

"Looks better than it has in years."

"As good as when we built it."

It did look good, and Saffron was proud of it. The chickens out in the run were still lovely and clean, which pleased Saffron. She watched one attack a patch of grass and come out slurping a long centipede down like a spaghetti noodle. She shivered.

"They love those things," Bud said. "And I'll tell you what, these feeders are okay, but we had just built some new ones right before Beau died. Meant to get them installed, but we didn't have the right bolts. I bought them before I heard he'd passed. If you want to come and get them, they fit nicely under the nest boxes there, and will keep the vermin out of your feed."

That did sound good. Saffron had been using a bag of chicken feed in the work area, and she had to weight it with a rock to keep the top closed so the scurrying rats didn't get into it. And the chickens obviously needed a better system, too. Already, the six hens in the coop had made a mess of the pan of feed Saffron had put down for them.

"Well, we'd better get going," Mano smiled.

"And I'd better get back to bathing. I get the feeling nobody has taken care of these birds for a long time."

Bud looked at her with the ghost of a smile around his mouth, "I guess we'd better tell you."

"Tell me what?"

"Chickens don't bathe in water. They bathe in dirt or sand. You don't need to wash them."

Saffron glared at him. "Are you kidding me? But you said to make sure they get their baths!"

Mano shrugged, "I meant to give them some fresh sand. I could have been more specific." The twinkle in his eye made her unsure whether he'd been teasing her or whether it was truly a misunderstanding.

Still, his kind eyes made it hard to stay mad at him, "This would have been useful information yesterday." She frowned.

They laughed again, and despite her damp clothes and the lost morning, Saffron smiled, too. As she watched the two old men start off down the road back toward town, Saffron promised to come by the next day and pick up the bolts. She should have plenty of time. Without chickens to bathe, her schedule had opened up considerably.

Chapter Four

A sharp tapping woke Saffron early the next morning. She stumbled to the front door, thinking someone was knocking, but there was nobody on the lanai. She heard it again, and this time, more awake, realized it was coming from the kitchen. She moved slowly, trying to decide if the intruder was back.

Picking her way through the crowded living room was difficult in the wan light of early morning. The tapping was sporadic but insistent. It was coming from the brooder box in the corner of the kitchen.

In just a day, Saffron had grown attached to Tikka's little family. She liked watching them while she worked. The brooder box Mano and Bud had helped her set up was just right for them. It had a proper nest, a small feeder and waterer, and plenty of sand for the little chooks to scratch in. She didn't have to worry about them venturing out of the pot and falling off the stove.

Saffron lifted off the pegboard lid and looked inside. Tikka was making the racket. The hen was peering with her right eye intently at the side of the wooden box, then pecking at a specific spot again and again. Saffron leaned down and squinted. What was it about that particular patch of the wall that had fascinated the hen? Saffron could see nothing. This was unusual. She was used to having the best eyes in the room. She wondered if this was how people felt when she saw colors they didn't seem to see. Saffron looked even closer. Still nothing, yet Tikka tapped on, intent.

The tapping was annoying, especially in the quiet of the kitchen and with Saffron's dawning realization that she was not going to be able to get back to sleep. She scooped up a handful of grains from the bucket she'd brought from the egg house and held it down to Tikka.

At the sight of the giant hand descending from the sky, the baby chicks went running for cover under their mama. Tikka swiveled her head to focus on the grains, then began to snatch her favorites. Her head moved in controlled jerks, and she cleared the corn from Saffron's hand first. The hen cocked her head sideways and looked up at Saffron with her left eye.

Tikka, covering eleven little chicks, seemed grateful for the treat.

The babies seemed to sense their mother's calmness and ventured back out. They were everywhere: in the feeder, on top of their mama, under her wings, running about the box.

Saffron's arm was getting tired. She poured the remaining grains off her hand into a little pile in front of Tikka and slid the top back on the box.

She washed her hands thoroughly, using the rough lava soap that Uncle Beau had left at every sink. It was cathartic, especially since she was still surrounded by piles of dusty junk. She found herself feeling a little claustrophobic.

She needed to get out. She had seen a cafe at one end of the main street yesterday, and the thought of a warm breakfast away from this mess was appealing. She showered and gathered her purse and keys.

Stepping out onto the lanai, Saffron stopped to take in the sweet Hawaiian morning. The sun was up now, casting a lazy glow over the rental car in the driveway. The lanai was speckled with early morning shade cast by the enormous monkeypod tree that grew beside it and stretched its tapestry of branches all the way over the house.

Saffron was still for a moment. She heard voices drifting toward her from the direction of the point. All beaches in Hawaii were public, the lawyer had told her, so even though her uncle's land stretched down to the shore and along the beach for about five miles, people could still freely come and go near the water.

She thought about pushing through the brush to say hello to whoever it was, but if they were out this early, it was likely they didn't want to be disturbed. Maybe they were out to watch the sunrise together.

She stopped first at the Oceanside Cafe, where a sign said she'd find "Maika'i's Best Breakfast!" After living on packaged snacks at the bungalow, the Oceanside's banana pancakes, coconut syrup, fresh pineapple, and spam convinced her that the sign was accurate.

The cafe was crowded, even this early. Of the dozen tables, only two were still empty as Saffron was finishing up her breakfast, and one of those wasn't actually empty, it was just that the woman who'd been sitting there was standing, talking over the high counter to the cook in the back. He was a small, neat man, and Saffron immediately appreciated his spotless white apron and the way all of his utensils were arranged smallest to largest on hooks above the grill. Saffron was so close that she couldn't help but hear their conversation.

"I could kill him!" the woman sputtered, "It shows me where I stand, that's for sure."

"Now, Lani, calm down. You don't know what Bud was up to."

Saffron's ears perked up. This had to do with her new friend.

The woman tapped her fingers on the high counter in agitation. "I know what he told me, Ed! And now, it's like everything has changed overnight."

"I've told you before. He's not worth the emotion."

"You would say that. I know you've never liked Bud." This must be one of the oldest man in town's lady friends. He was not, she could tell, very popular with her today.

"That's not true. I like him just fine. I've just never liked how he makes you feel." The cook scooped someone's scrambled eggs onto a plate with a precise flourish and set them on the high counter. He reached over and took Lani's hand.

"Can't you find another hobby?" He asked, "this one's wearing me out."

"Some brother you are!" Lani growled. "How could he have picked up a Beachy Breakfast Basket already this morning? Was he going on a date already? Even after what he told me last night?"

"Look, I don't know what he was doing, and I'm sorry I even told you he stopped by here. We'll talk about it after my shift," Ed patted her hand, "Go home and try to get some rest, please. After your late night, you shouldn't be up this early anyway."

Lani spun and wove through the tables, leaving the softly chemical scent of violet perfume in her wake.

Saffron opened the menu, trying to be nonchalant.

Beachy Breakfast Basket

Want to watch the sunrise over the ocean? Our Beachy Breakfast Basket is a pre-packed feast you can grab and go. All you have to do is enjoy your breakfast and return our basket, cutting board, containers, and utensils.

Your feast includes two Breakfast Musubis: Fried Spam and bacon topped with an egg cooked to order and sandwiched between two shaped rice blocks and wrapped with a strip of our premium Nori (roasted seaweed).

Also included are two servings of our tropical fruit medley, two taro bagels with coconut cream cheese, two ounces of hibiscus-smoked gouda, and your choice of drink.

WELL, that certainly sounded like something you'd buy for a nice date, Saffron thought. No wonder Lani was upset if Bud had headed out with one of those this morning. She wondered if he'd be back from his picnic by the time she dropped by his house to pick up the bolts.

She turned back to her pancakes. Lani had been furious. The phrase "hell hath no fury like a woman scorned" passed through her mind. She was just finishing when the server stopped by.

"Can I get my check, please?" she asked.

The server, a large, laughing woman whose nametag read *Bernadette*, shook her head, and waved a dismissive hand, "It's a gift."

"My breakfast is a gift?"

"Your uncle, he sent us a lotta extra eggs over the years. We paid for two dozen, he sent us five. We paid for five, he sent us seven. You come eat here whenever you want. Bring a friend," Bernadette waved a hand, "no charge."

Dumbfounded, Saffron stammered out her gratitude. She wanted to say more, but a commotion at the front of the cafe drew Bernadette's attention, and she headed for the door.

A man about Saffron's age was attempting to come in. He was dressed in baggy pants, muddy tennis shoes, and a blue tee shirt that made the ruddy patches on his drab ivory skin stand out starkly. He looked as if he'd been sunburned many times and had faded like old paper. He had been stopped at the door. It was blocked by the small middle-aged cook, Ed, who was holding a frying pan like a tennis racket.

"You're not coming back in here," he was saying.

The man gestured at Saffron. She noticed the uneven curve of his mouth. His lip was deeply scarred, and one side was drawn up in a sneer as he gestured toward her. "You'll let strangers in, but not locals?"

The little man glanced at Bernadette. A tangible tension filled the dining room. A line was beginning to form behind him, people waiting to come into the café. Some of them wandered off, apparently trying to avoid the conflict.

Bernadette was not small, but like Tikka, she was somehow able to fill even more space as she got angry. She moved forward and pushed her way close to the young man, jostling Ed out of the way. She held out a meaty palm.

"Derek, you'll pay for your breakfast," she said flexing her fingers in an expectant gesture. "It's forty-two fifty."

The sneering man said nothing.

"My cafe. My business." Bernadette said. Her voice had a hard edge. She flexed her fingers again, "You're getting enough freebies over at Bud's. You can buy your own meals."

The man tipped his head sideways, then righted it. "You have something to say about me?"

"I have a lot to say about you—that you're a freeloader and a cheat. You owe me for the last time you were in here when you skipped out on your check. That you're squatting at Bud's because you expect to get that old man's money. That you—"

"I'd be careful, big lady," he said in a growl.

Bernadette didn't even slow down. "We don't even know what you done with Naia. People are talking, Derek. We haven't seen her for months, and nobody can get ahold of her. The whole town knows what you are, Derek. The whole town." She shook her free hand at him, "Didn't you get enough attention as a child? Bruddah, it's like you want to be noticed for coming in here and making trouble. We see you, okay? We all," here Bernadette waved her hand in a gesture that took in the staring diners at their tables and the shifting line of customers lined up behind the scene, "see that you are here."

A strange glow of satisfaction lit Derek's eyes. He peeled his lips back from his dingy teeth. "I think you're the one that can't get enough attention," he said. "I hear your man left you cold." The blow made the solid Bernadette wince.

She straightened her shoulders then gestured to Ed, "Call Bradley," she said.

A look passed between them that showed Saffron they didn't expect the officer to come.

"You're gonna call the cops on me? I ain't even done nothing," Derek's voice still held a threat.

"Nothing?" Bernadette scoffed, some of her composure

restored, "that's about right. You ain't done nothing to help anybody, nothing to make things better, nothing to take care of your own wife," she leveled her gaze at Derek.

"You don't know what I've done," he said, and his voice was menacing, "if you did, you wouldn't mess with me."

Bernadette leaned close to him. When she spoke, every syllable was clearly enunciated, "Forty-two fifty."

They stared at each other. The only sound was the popping of the food Ed had left on the grill. Even the tourists had stilled.

Trembling with anger, Derek reached for his wallet. He took out the cash and laid it grudgingly in Bernadette's hand. She closed her fingers, and she and the little man with the skillet paced back to the grill behind the counter.

"I don't want to eat here anyway!" Derek said, turning back to the door. He pushed through, making the bell jingle as he left. Saffron started to speak, but Bernadette waved her away.

"Don't worry. Derek just goes around looking for trouble. Every couple of weeks somebody has to put him back in his place, and today it was my turn. Don't let him scare you. You come back whenever you like." Bernadette went back to her work.

Saffron thought about what she'd do next as she edged through the waiting crowd and crossed the street.

If Bud was out for a picnic, Saffron had a little time to kill. She wasn't ready to go back to the farm and face the mountains of stuff her uncle had left behind, so she walked down Holoholo street, the meandering main thoroughfare of Maika'i. Along it, in little old bungalows, shops beckoned. She meandered in and out of them, wondering if she could sell some of the stuff at Hau'oli ka Moa to these shops.

As she crossed an intersecting street, she looked up along it to see a beautiful flowered park and an old building with a sign that said *Tiki Thrift and Trade*. It wasn't on the main street. It was tucked back next to the park at the foot of the mountains.

A secondhand store. That would be useful. Saffron didn't walk up to it, though. Instead, she kept her exploration to the main street for today.

First, she wandered into Heluhelu Here, which looked like a bookstore. Inside, the overhead fans and an air conditioning unit on the wall made for a cool, dim shop. It was tidy and inviting, with sections on travel, mystery, kids, and dozens more. An old couple was sitting on a deep sofa behind the cash register, reading. They waved as Saffron came in, and she was relieved that they seemed so interested in their novels that they didn't make her stop and talk. She left a few minutes later, knowing that the last thing she needed at the farm was more books.

"Do you take donations?" She asked, standing at the door.

The old woman looked up from behind her owlish glasses. "Yes, and we pay cash or store credit."

That was good news. It would be easy to unload the boxes of books here, and Saffron might get a little money for them, too. There were a couple she might keep. She'd already set aside one on chicken-keeping that looked helpful.

Maybe, she thought as she left the little shop, there were more places to unload some of the stuff.

Down the broad boardwalk outside, just in front of the real estate office she'd been working with, Saffron walked right into another group of chickens. These were varying shades, from orange to black to white, and they all scratched and pecked at the fallen fruits of a group of bushes between Holoholo street and the boardwalk. The tips of the leaves brushed the boards, and beneath it, in and out of papery shells, were the crushed and whole orbs of some kind of fruit.

They looked like golden cherry tomatoes, but the color was wrong. Where tomatoes were a brassier marigold color, these were soft wheaten, with translucent skin. Saffron leaned down and picked one from the plant, listening to the chickens' disgruntled noises. They must not like her in their space.

"They like their poha berries," called a voice from the open door of the real estate office.

She turned to see her real estate agent, Rose, coming toward her.

"Poha?" Saffron tried out the word and liked it.

"Yeah. Some people call them groundcherries or gooseberries, but they're poha berries. They're good! You should try one!"

Saffron looked at the one in her hand. Bright orange, and wrapped in what was left of a dried-leaf jacket, it had a thin skin through which she could see many seeds, like a tomato. Saffron peeled the rest of the rest of the leaves away and popped it into her mouth.

It was sweet and a little sour, with a flavor all its own. The chickens protested loudly, and Saffron laughed.

"There are a lot of chickens in Hawaii," she said.

"Part of the rustic island charm that you'll come to love about paradise," Rose said, sounding exactly like an advertisement. She waved a hand at Saffron as she climbed into her silver Lexus. "Well, gotta go. I've got dreams to sell!" She leaned out of the car door, peering at Saffron. "How's the farm coming along?"

Saffron groaned. "I've got a long way to go."

"Well, stop loitering and get it done! We need to schedule an open house, and I've got some clients coming over from the mainland in a few weeks. We should coordinate," Rose tossed a shaka, then turned it into a phone by putting it by her cheek, "Call me and I'll let you know when we need to have it."

Saffron watched her go, stepped around the chickens, and continued down the street past a beach gear rental place. She walked on past a couple of restaurants, a home-décor store called Island Designs, and Coconuts and Bolts. A kitchen store tempted her in to buy a new pot that had never had a family of chickens living in it.

The petite woman behind the counter was watching a video on her computer. She had straight black hair and a somber expression, and she didn't look up as Saffron entered.

Saffron found her way to the pot aisle. As she was perusing the options, she heard the bell on the door jingle and looked up to see a fit woman in a tracksuit and walking shoes enter. The woman carried two beautiful woven shopping baskets full of what looked like boxes and cans and produce. A beautiful woman in her early seventies, she had blonde hair with steel-gray roots and was wearing more jewelry than Saffron even owned.

The shopkeeper looked up from her computer.

"Watching more infomercials, Fumi? I brought your order," the visitor said. Her words were rounded by the lilt of an Australian accent.

"Sumimasen," the shopkeeper replied with a slight bow. "Otsukaresama desu," Saffron recognized the sound of the Japanese language.

"No problem, I brought those cookies you like, and the pineapple. It's starting to smell sweet, so eat it soon,"

"I'm not worried. You always have the best produce on the island. But if you keep bringing me this stuff, the walking club's going to have to start going out twice a day. We missed you this morning. And why aren't you over at the market now? Are you taking a holiday?"

"Just running a few errands. I wanted to get these to you before lunch."

Fumi's voice was bright, "Thanks again. Now, to the important stuff. How was your night?" There was an unmistakable tone of teasing in her voice.

"Magical, as always," the grocer said, and Saffron heard the smile she couldn't see.

"That doesn't tell me anything, Sandy! Spill it all!"

Sandy looked pointedly in Saffron's direction, and Saffron busied herself with the pots.

Fumi must have understood, because there was a brief silence while, Saffron was sure, the two women communicated through gestures. Finally, Fumi spoke again, apparently deeming her question safe for prying ears, "Did you get a birthday present?"

"Several," Sandy replied, "a new pull cart for my books at the store, some jewelry . . ." here there was a delighted sound from Fumi, and Saffron wished she were closer to see what Sandy was showing her, "and a set of gorgeous woodblock prints for the front room."

"Sounds like a happy birthday."

Saffron approached the front and could see Fumi gazing at a beautiful jeweled necklace Sandy was wearing. She also sported a dazzling diamond tennis bracelet and a pair of enormous emerald earrings glinting against her silver hair. It did look like a happy birthday. Sandy stepped aside as Saffron approached, and the grocer beamed a smile at her.

"You must be Beau's niece," Sandy said, "such a shame about your uncle. Our condolences."

"Thank you," Saffron said, setting the pot on the counter and turning the handle in toward Fumi.

"I'm Sandy Vaughn," the Australian woman said. Her smile was bright and even. "And this is Fumi Masuda." Saffron tried to pretend she hadn't been listening in on their conversation. She could smell the pineapple. Glancing over, she saw its glossy leaves sticking out of the top of the bag. She could also see a bit of the nubbly skin. Thinking of the rich, sweet pineapple at the cafe made her mouth water again.

"Where's your market?" She asked Sandy, "I may stop by if you've got any more of those."

"Oh, the Paradise Market has pineapple!" Fumi said. She rushed around the side of the counter and snatched up a long device that looked like a steel tube with a handle.

"You'll probably need one of these, too," Fumi said, her eyes shining with excitement. "It's new. It's a pineapple slicer. You just cut the top off, then push this down and turn it. It makes perfect rings!"

Saffron was intrigued, but she shook her head. It didn't look like something they'd let her take on the airplane home.

"I'll probably just take the pot," she said, "but thanks."

Fumi looked disgruntled as she rehung the utensil.

Sandy seemed to be trying to restart the conversation. "The market's just a block down, before the bridge." Sandy headed for the door. "See you tomorrow at walking club," she said to Fumi.

"If you show up!" Fumi waved, and her friend went out into the street. Saffron said goodbye, too, and carried her pot back out onto Holoholo Street. She passed a quilting store, a pet store, and two churches before she reached the bright yellow building that was Paradise Market.

She didn't see Sandy inside, but a slouching teen tapped at his phone behind one of the three checkout stands. When Saffron asked him where the pineapple was, he raised a hand, but not his eyes, and pointed to a bright yellow and green display in the back corner of the store.

Saffron found her fresh pineapple quickly but stayed to peruse the remarkable display. She was astounded at how many pineapple products there were: canned pineapple, dried pineapple, pineapple juice, pineapple powder, pineapple candy, pineapple soda, pineapple jam. There was even a refrigerated section for pineapple almond milk and pineapple cheese. She supposed she shouldn't have been surprised. She was in Hawaii, after all.

She wandered around the rest of the charming little market and immersed herself in the smells of the tropical produce department. Mangos, guava, and papaya scented the air. Saffron took some of each and went on to gather more groceries. Milk and butter, sweet Hawaiian rolls, steak, and tuna. She supposed she'd have to do some cooking here, though she hadn't done it in a long time. With the ease and availability of takeout in DC and the mess that cooking seemed to always make, she'd given culinary pursuits up after her mother died.

She paid the disinterested teen and left the market with several sacks of groceries. Saffron peered up the street. She could see to the end of town. There was a full stream flowing out into the ocean. It was spanned by a bridge that kept Holoholo street and the sidewalk uninterrupted. On the other side of the bridge was the police station, the fire station, public library, and a gas station at the end of the street. Her arms full of groceries and her awkwardly balanced new pot, she decided she'd better go back to her car, parked at the cafe. It was already eleven o'clock—probably a good time to go visit the town's oldest man.

BUD'S HOUSE was a two-story square with a spacious lanai above a carport in front. The front door was up a set of steps, and she climbed it and knocked before she noticed the neighbor watching her. He was a tall man in his early forties. He had a tidy mustache and was sharply dressed in a tee and blue jeans. He was sitting on a desk in his outdoor office with a sheaf of papers in his hands.

She knocked on the door. The lanai next door was an arm's

length away, and the man with the mustache eyed her skeptically. "You live there, too?" he asked, his voice dripping disdain. She caught a hint of an accent.

"No," she said, "I'm here to see Bud."

"I have not seen him today," the man said. His words were clipped and precise. "Just that bunch of thugs he's got living there. But they left a while ago." From his light inflection at the end of each sentence, the 'd' sounds in 'there' and 'they,' and the warm, subtle roll on every 'r' sound, Saffron could tell that his native language was probably French.

She was relieved to know they hadn't come back yet.

"Are you visiting Maika'i?" He asked.

"No, just here cleaning up my uncle's farm so I can sell it."

At this, he stood. "Which farm?"

"The-" she paused, trying to remember how Mano had said it, "Hau'oli Ka Moa egg farm." Even she winced at her pronunciation, but the man either didn't know how to say it himself or was too polite to show how poorly she'd done. There was a spark of interest in his eyes.

"You're selling?"

"That's right. I've got a bit of tidying to do, but it's on the market."

He crossed to the railing and leaned over, offering her his hand. "I'm Sal," he said. "I'd like to come and see it."

She had to lean far out to give him an awkward half-handshake in midair. "You buying?"

"My wife and I own rental properties." He said. He waved a hand, "I've been trying to buy Bud's house for years, but he won't sell it to me."

Before Saffron could respond, the door opened behind her, and she turned to see a broad smile. Above it, dancing green eyes and tousled brown hair.

"Hey! You must be Uncle Beau's niece!" he said, "I'm Nik.

We all called him Uncle Beau, too. I guess that makes us cousins!" He threw his arms around her.

Saffron didn't know how to respond in the face of such familiarity. "I guess," she stammered.

"I'll come to see the place sometime this week," Sal called to her, "I could use a bigger property for groups."

"Leave her alone, Sal! You can't own the whole town!" The smile was gone from Nik's face, and Saffron felt a chill between the neighbors.

"Like I said," Sal tossed the words over his shoulder as he crossed the lanai back to his desk, "later this week."

A surge of hope overcame Saffron. Maybe she wouldn't have to clean it all up after all. She could sell it, then it would be Sal's problem.

"Grandpa told me he met you yesterday," Nik said.

Saffron peered at him. "Grandpa?"

"Bud's my grandpa." Nik corrected himself, "My great-grandpa, actually, though he acts so young, it's hard to believe."

The age wasn't what had surprised Saffron. It was Nik's translucent olive eyes and the shock of unruly brown hair.

"Isn't Bud Hawaiian?" She asked.

"Yeah," Nik affirmed, raising his eyebrows. He was incredibly responsive to her every facial expression, "You're confused?"

"Well, you don't—" she stopped herself. She didn't want to offend him.

"I don't look Hawaiian?" he said.

Saffron nodded.

"I'm hapa," he confirmed. At Saffron's puzzled look, he went on. "It means half. Although it's not really mathematically accurate for me. My Grandpa Bud married a haole—like you—that was my Great Grandma Annette," and they had three kids, one of them was my Grandpa Earl. He was the oldest. He married a haole, too—my grandma Faith. They had one son—my dad. And he married a Swedish girl he met at college."

"Also haole," Saffron said.

"Right. So Grandpa Bud is full Hawaiian, and I am an eighth Hawaiian."

"Now it makes sense," she said. Musing, she went on. "Hawaii is the most diverse place I've ever visited," she said.

"It really is," Nik confirmed, "More cultures are living side-by-side here than anywhere I've lived. They blend and mix and make an incredibly rich community. One day, you'll celebrate Chinese New Year, the next, you'll be eating the best Japanese noodles you've ever eaten, and the next you'll be at a luau. And everybody is just part of all of it, somehow. It's a very welcoming place, and I learned when I moved here that people make outsiders very welcome."

Saffron couldn't argue with that when she remembered Nik's spontaneous hug. She pulled her thoughts back to the task at hand. "Is Bud here?"

Nik shook his head, "No, sorry. He left really early this morning," Nik winked, "actually, I'm not sure he came home last night. When I saw him, it was still dark. He said he was heading out to your place with some bolts," Nik said, "and he said he'd get some feeders out for you, too. He told me to tell you he was out there if you came by."

She'd window-shopped too long. Saffron nodded, still shaken by Nik's friendliness. "Thanks for the info. I'll see if I can catch him there. I don't want him lifting things all by himself at his age."

Nik waved a hand, "Aww, Grandpa Bud's healthy as a horse."

When she got home, Saffron stopped in the kitchen to check on Tikka and the brood and found them happily scratching about in their box. The sand was fresh, and their food and water containers had been topped off, so Saffron assumed that Bud had been in to check on them. She glanced around and saw that the kettle was on the stove. Bud had made some tea, too. But he hadn't left his teacup in the sink. He must have it with him in the egg house.

Back home it would have bothered her if someone had come into her space like that, but Saffron didn't feel upset. Perhaps because she couldn't lock the bungalow, or because the little blue house wasn't really her home, or because Bud seemed to have such a long history here.

She went out to find him in the egg house. Inside, only the birds in the first pen greeted her. The wheelbarrow was gone from the work area, and the doors at the far end of the house were open, letting in the sunshine and the sweet island breeze. She could see immediately that Bud had been here a while already. In two of the pens, new feeders stood in sharp contrast to the worn nest boxes. She wondered if the girls had laid any eggs, and she took a moment to turn the hand crank on the conveyor that ran just behind the nest boxes. Sure enough, it carried three pretty brown eggs to her—one beige, one cocoa-colored, and one almost mahogany. A rainbow of browns.

She put them in the egg trays to carry in later. Walking down the center aisle, she admired the new feeders. Bud had installed a couple already, bolting them under the egg boxes. They fit perfectly.

Saffron called Bud's name as she walked out into the light. Blinded momentarily, she held a hand to her eyes and blinked several times.

Bud wasn't out here, either. Saffron walked around the sand pile and stopped. Here the foliage started. Dense trees and bushes grew behind the egg house, and if a free chicken hadn't caught her attention dashing into the leaves, she would never have looked closer at the jungle. She would never have seen the single muddy wheel print smudging the grass. But peering at it led her to spot a flat stone path nearly obscured by moss. She wasn't used to the verdant mosses and the head-high leaves that she had to push through to make her way through to the path. She was glad she'd worn old clothes as she made her way through the dense foliage.

The path stretched into the dappled woods. It was pleasant and private. Two more rectangular feeders were lined up on the stones, and she saw fresh screws holding down the metal tops. Bud must have been doing some repair work. But why here? Where did this path go? There was still no sight of him. The encircling bushes and trees made the path feel entirely isolated from the rest of the farm.

It was even damper in the trees, and she stayed on the stones to avoid the mud on either side. Deep ruts showed where the wheelbarrow's single wheel had slid off the path here and there. A distinct footprint or two, pressed into the mire, showed where Bud had angled it back on. Saffron had no doubt that she would sink, too, if she stepped there. The line of the tree trunks ahead was soon broken by the horizontal plane of a small rooftop. It was a little green building—just a shed, really. She made a mental note to put that in the property description as another structure.

She saw the outline of the shed, with two more feeders lined up outside. Bud must be working inside. She called his name so she wouldn't surprise him. The moss on the path was wet and spongy as Saffron walked toward the open door. Bud didn't answer, so she called again as she stepped into the dimly lit shed.

It was tidy, which made her sure that Uncle Beau hadn't used it much. To the right was a waist-high workbench that held a few tools and the missing cup of tea. Bud must be nearby. To the left, assorted lawn maintenance equipment, another feeder, hoses and old beach toys. There were some big barrels marked with the word "FEED," and behind them some shelves. There was no sign of the wheelbarrow that had made the tracks by the path.

Saffron called Bud's name again. Out the grimy little window high in the back wall of the shed, she could see the trunks of more trees, but no sign of the town's oldest man.

She stepped out and looked around. Perpendicular to the path was another deep rut, which ran in a broken line along the side of the shed and disappeared around the corner. She followed. It appeared Bud had gotten a little bogged down himself as he tried to turn the corner. Deep tracks were smeared in the mud.

The ground on the side of the shed was more firm, and the rut disappeared. Saffron kept walking and turned to look behind the little building, just to be sure.

A jolt went through Saffron. Bud was sprawled across the wheelbarrow, his skin the color of ash.

Chapter Five

Dead. Just a day after she'd met him. The cheerful old man.

After the necessary emergency call and the ambulance, after leading the paramedics and the police and Nik through the egg house and down the path, after watching them take him away, after all the paperwork, after leaving the now-somber Nik to make his way home, Saffron had found her way back to the cafe. She sat at the only empty table, a little two-top in the far corner, and stared out the window at the ocean. The buzz of the crowded cafe faded as she thought about Bud.

She hadn't cried. Why would she? She'd only met Bud once. Still, she felt an emptiness at his passing. She wondered what Mano would do, who would tell him. She wondered if Lani would be sorry she'd been so mad at Bud. She wondered if Derek, the crude great-grandson-in-law, would get the house. She wondered how she could have lived this long without ever seeing a dead body before.

She saw Bud's open eyes whenever she closed her own.

And his clenched fists. She held her cold soda can up to her forehead.

"Can I take this seat?" A deep voice drew her attention. She opened her mouth to answer, but when she looked up at the speaker, she lost her words.

He had the kindest eyes she had ever seen. She placed them in her mental color catalog immediately: They were the same rich amber color of the koa wood she'd seen on the bedframe. His warm skin was a shade lighter. It was the color of the sand just at the edge of the wide Hawaiian beaches, where the retreating surf left curves of tawny topaz next to the brighter gold of the dry sand. He had close-cropped black hair. Saffron nodded numbly.

He was big. A powerful man who sat down carefully and picked up his menu with a surprising amount of delicacy. It was as if he was used to careful work with his hands. A fleeting thought went through Saffron's pounding head—maybe he was an artisan of some sort?

"Are you feeling okay?" he asked.

She shook her head.

"Can I help?"

She shook her head again. Bernadette approached the table, wedging herself between their chairs.

"Keahi! You haven't been in for a while."

He ducked his head, "Sorry Bernie. Working a lot."

Bernadette made a sound that clearly meant she didn't think that was a good excuse, "okay, if showing off for the tourists is more important than visiting your aunty . . ."

He pointed to his menu and waved her off, and she slapped his shoulder as she left with his order.

"I'm Keahi Kekoa," he said, giving Saffron an understanding smile. "I've had enough bad days to know what one looks like."

Saffron nodded. She didn't want to talk about it, but it was nice having him there. He seemed solid, and she felt just the opposite.

"You on vacation?" he asked.

"Not exactly. My uncle used to live here. I'm fixing up his farm to sell it."

Keahi raised his eyebrows, "The egg farm?"

She nodded.

"Things aren't going well out there?"

Saffron shook her head. "They're fine. It's just today I—" she didn't have words for what had happened. Anything she could think to say sounded too coarse, too final.

Keahi's expression was sympathetic, but a cheerful burst of ukulele music from his pocket cut their conversation short.

Saffron tried not to listen, but it was apparently bad news, and she was riveted.

"When?" he asked, "Yes. I'll be right there."

He stood, running a hand through his thick, curly hair. "I'm sorry, I have to go. Will you give this to Bernadette?" He handed her a twenty-dollar bill. "You eat my burger. You'd be surprised at what a good ono burger can do," he smiled through the worry in his eyes. "I hope your day gets better."

When the burger came, Saffron gave Bernadette the money and peered at the plate. "Excuse me," she said, "what kind of burger *is* this?"

"It's an ono burger," Bernadette said as she rushed off to help a table full of tourists that were waving frantically at her.

Saffron picked up the menu. Nestled between the "Island Surprise" and the "Aloha Chicken" she read:

Ono Burger
Oceanside Cafe Specialty

1/3 lb grass-fed beef patty topped with a seared ono fillet, honey-garlic mayo, and mango avocado butter on a toasted taro bun.

THE MOST STARTLING thing about the burger was the bright purple bread. The second most startling thing was the slab of white fish atop the beef patty. Saffron suddenly realized that she was hungry. She hadn't eaten since breakfast, and as she gathered the gargantuan burger and took a bite, she was acutely aware of the flurry of flavors and textures. The smooth, firm fish complemented perfectly the coarse beef, the creamy avocado contrasted with the bright mango flavor and the sweetness of the honey. She took two more bites before stopping to sip her soda.

Saffron felt renewed when she left the cafe. She tried to think of Bud's smile, of his cheer. She tried to forget the scene behind the shed and remember him as she'd seen him yesterday, laughing and teasing in the sunshine.

SAFFRON DIDN'T ATTEND the funeral. She stayed home and cleaned the living room. The funeral would be too crowded, she thought—she saw the streams of cars passing on the road to town, and she heard later that they had had to use both churches, with a video link to one, to hold all the mourners. Bud sure had gotten around. And she hadn't known him, not really. And she didn't feel like she ought to go since he'd been helping her when he died.

It had been days since the funeral and more than a week since she'd found him, and Saffron still carried the weight of her guilt and regret as she sat staring at a beautiful bowl in the middle of the kitchen table. It was carved in the shape of a hibiscus flower, and Saffron hadn't put anything in it because she couldn't stand to cover it up. Tikka was making a soft, contented purr from the box in the corner of the kitchen. It was calming, and Saffron appreciated it as she ate her breakfast cereal and perused one of Uncle Beau's more interesting books.

She was less shaken than she'd been the days after she'd found him, but Bud's death still hung over her like the lowering island clouds that were sprinkling the roof of the farmhouse. She'd spent the last several nights waking with inescapable guilt. He had been helping her. How long he'd been at the farm, she didn't know, but it had, apparently, been most of the morning. Nik had said he'd left very early, and he'd only stopped to pick up the Beachy Breakfast Basket at the café. Saffron wondered where he'd gone with that after he'd picked it up.

She watched Tikka with her babies. The hen was tucked into a corner of the box, her wings slightly spread, and the growing wisps were mostly nestled under and atop her, their little heads drooping with sleep. They were only a week and two days old, and their fluffy little wings were already jutting out with awkward baby feathers. Their mama was having trouble keeping them all underneath her, but Hawaii was plenty warm, and she was safe in the house, so the hen was growing more casual about keeping them close.

Saffron was surprised at the array of colors they came in. Black with gold stripes, black with gold speckles, black with a white spot on the head, brown with black stripes, and one little fuzzy one that was the color of sunshine. She turned back to the book—*The Rewarding Art of Chicken Keeping*. Published in 1972, it was well-worn and dog-eared. Notes in several different types of handwriting told her that it had been used by many. She turned to the section labeled *Brooding*. There, she read that a hen will raise any chick she hatches, more or less. She doesn't care if they are from her own eggs or not. It was likely, according to the book, that several chickens had found Tikka's nesting spot and deposited their eggs there as well. When she "went broody" or decided to stay on the nest and hatch her eggs, the other eggs developed, too, which explained the colorful family.

She couldn't help but think of Hawaii. It seemed that people came here and were nurtured regardless of where they had originally started out. The people here took care to include others, to make the island feel like one big family. To be in Hawaii was to be local.

A brisk crowing came from outside the door. Saffron had spent stray hours over the last few days rounding up more chickens and putting them in the pretty pens in the egg house. She'd only caught a couple of roosters, and they were in pens by themselves at the far end of the egg house, which helped with the noise levels. But the racket from the lanai had stayed constant. Curry had never allowed her to catch him, and he kept vigilant watch just outside, day and night. He tried to rush in whenever she opened the door.

"You've got a pretty devoted man there, Tikka," she said, and the chicken tipped her head to fix an eye on Saffron. "Hang on to him. They're hard to come by."

"Brrrrrk," Tikka replied, reaching out and directing one of her babies back toward the warmth of her wing.

It was then that Saffron heard it, over the sounds of the happy hen: "Hey, hey, he-he-hey!" Curry's crow had changed to an insistent alarm. Instantly, Saffron was on her feet. She glanced at the back door to be sure the deadbolt was vertical—which meant it was locked. She strode into the living room to check the front door and caught a glimpse out the front window, where she saw a small SUV in the driveway. The man from the diner—Keahi, she thought—was helping Mano out of the front seat. The two men approached, and Saffron pulled the door open, her heart pounding. She didn't know what to say, didn't know how to tell Mano that she was so sorry.

Mano didn't have the same flippancy she'd seen in him before, but neither did he seem angry or depressed. He smiled as he climbed the stairs.

"Didn't quite have the energy to walk out here today. Had to bring my chauffeur," he gestured at Keahi, who smiled too.

The words came pouring out before she could stop them. "I'm so sorry. I didn't know Bud was going to bring them out here by himself, and by the time I found out . . ." She stopped, blinking back the first tears since that awful day. Saffron couldn't look at him. She felt like she had taken something from him that she could never restore.

Mano crossed the lanai. He laid two strong hands on Saffron's shoulders and drew his face close to hers. Eyes closed, he touched his nose to hers and was still for a long moment, inhaling. Saffron found herself calmed. She breathed in, too, and when he pulled back, and they opened their eyes, she found her tears had gone.

THEY SPENT the afternoon talking in the living room. Mano was in a reminiscing mood, and Saffron gave him some framed photos of himself, Bud, and Uncle Beau that she had found in one of the bedroom boxes. One picture showed them as young men on the beach, a small grill between them and pretty young girls at their sides.

"There they are. Our other halves," Mano stared at the photo. "This was the last time we were all together. Bud's first wife, Annette, left less than a year later. Your Aunt Ila died not too long after that. "He handed the photo to Keahi. "See that girl? Recognize her?"

Keahi laughed a warm, sincere chuckle. He'd been so quiet

that Saffron had almost forgotten he was there. Almost. "Grandma?" He looked at Mano, "Wow! Look at that hair! Some beehive!"

"That's right. Glenda was always beautiful," Mano's eyes were sad for a moment. "Hard to believe they've all gone now. Just me left."

Neither of the young people knew what to say in the face of this realization. They allowed him a long silence.

"Just too mean to die, I guess," Mano said, then cleared his throat. "You've made a difference in here," Mano said, looking around. "I didn't even know this room had a floor."

Saffron was pleased. It did look sensational. Over the last few days, she'd hauled six boxes of books to Heluhelu Here and two seventies-style side tables to the furniture store. She'd burned every scrap of fabric in the room after finding cockroaches and mouse droppings on them. She'd scrubbed every inch, even the ceiling, with bleach and two kinds of cleaner. The broad beams that made a grid on the ceiling shone their original white, and the ceiling fan, free of grime, now gleamed with rich wood hues.

The day was humid, and Keahi's forehead shone with sweat. He reached for the switch on the wall over his head to turn the fan on, but nothing happened.

"Fan broke?" he asked.

Saffron nodded.

"Keahi can fix that!" Mano seemed relieved to have something else to talk about.

Saffron was going to protest, but Keahi was already on his feet.

"Tools?" he asked.

Saffron looked around and held her hands up. "Honestly? They could be anywhere." She knew where a few were, but she was not ready to go back there just yet.

"That's okay. I've got some in the car."

For the next hour, Keahi stood on a stepladder and worked on the fan. Something in the motor needed adjustment, and when he had finished, it ran smooth and quiet, pushing the air down and cooling the room considerably.

While they worked, Saffron made tea. There was a conspicuous space in the cupboard where Bud's teacup had been, and she realized it was probably still down in the shed. She tried not to think of it while they drank and finished their chat in the front room.

"You are doing well," Mano said. "Listen, could I ask a favor?"

"Anything," Saffron said and meant it.

"If you find a box—wooden, about this big . . ." he indicated with his hands framing a space the size of a toaster, "carved with a shark, do you mind letting me know? I'll buy it from you."

Saffron waved him off. "If I find it, you can just have it."

He nodded, smiling, and thanked her. She saw weariness in his eyes.

"Well, we should be going. I'll be back to help finish putting in the feeders tomorrow."

Saffron held up her hands, "Oh, no, no. I'll be fine."

The pleading tone in Mano's voice stopped her protests, "Please. I need something useful to do."

She glanced at Keahi, who nodded, before she consented. To tell the truth, she'd enjoy the company.

"You come with me," Mano said to Keahi.

"I can't. I have to work all day tomorrow."

Mano shook his head, "you should be doing your real work."

"Tutu, I like working the luau. And it's good pay."

"Good pay! Nothing like you were making before. And more than that, you're not using your talents! You're—"

Keahi interrupted, addressing Saffron, "I'm sorry, I won't be able to come."

"Oh, no worries! I'm doing just fine. Thanks for fixing the fan." The early Hawaiian evening was coming on, and Saffron hoped the dimming light was enough to hide her disappointment.

Chapter Six

Early the next morning, Saffron made her way down to the egg house. She could get started by hauling the feeders up from the shed.

The first few, the ones along the path, were easy. The paramedics had cut the foliage back so they could get the gurney in to bring Bud out, and the path now led easily to the little grassy area and to the back doors of the egg house. The wheelbarrow would have made moving the feeders easier, but she couldn't bring herself to go get it. Once she'd carried the few feeders from the path into the building, the last ones were out at the shed.

"You have to go there sometime," she told herself, walking carefully down the mossy path. Her eyes ran over the neat footprints, and she imagined the comfy slip-ons that Bud had been wearing. She remembered seeing them sticking out from the sheet on the gurney. She turned her eyes back to the path.

As she approached the shed, she saw the door still open, the other feeders lined up. Saffron felt a desire to flee, to run back to the house, back to the airport, to go *home*. She didn't want to spend any more time here than she had to.

"If I use the wheelbarrow, this will go faster," she said out loud. "I won't have to come down here so many times." She felt herself stepping off the path, pulling against the stiff mud, approaching, as she had last week, the corner of the shed.

Saffron stopped to breathe. This was ridiculous. Bud wasn't there anymore. All that was behind the shed now was an empty wheelbarrow. She leaned against the shed and looked at the ruts in the ground. An old question pushed its way back into her mind. *What had Bud been doing around the back of the shed?* From the looks of the tracks, it had taken a lot of effort to move the wheelbarrow back there, and there was no feeder back there that she could see.

The question had been nagging at her for days. It was like a stray centerpiece at a wedding: out of place, and her mind just couldn't let it go.

She walked around to the back. There was the wheelbarrow, mired in the mud. She put her hands on the handles, suppressing a shudder, and wrenched it free of the muck.

Once cleared, the wheelbarrow felt light and bouncy as she drove it in a circle and turned back toward the shed. Expecting to fight the mud, Saffron got a little run at the corner and went around it. To her surprise, the wheelbarrow skimmed over the ruts, careening effortlessly around the corner. Even Saffron's feet didn't sink as deep as she thought they would.

This was wrong, too. It should have been harder to push the wheelbarrow. The ground hadn't dried out over the intervening days. Saffron left the wheelbarrow on the path and went back to the ruts that went around the corner.

They still showed as deep gashes, and the fact that there was more than one indicated that the wheelbarrow had been mired, backed up, and run at the corner again. They looked like finger tracks in icing.

That happened once, Saffron remembered, at a wedding she'd organized. One of the bride's little nephews had attacked the two-thousand-dollar wedding cake, his chubby fingers leaving paths in the buttercream sides.

These they had smoothed over, though. It was when the little boy climbed onto a chair and, using his whole weight, dug a hand into the top of the layer that the real damage had been done. He'd gotten several handfuls, making it to the raspberry ganache filling between the layers before anyone had seen him.

Weight.

That was the difference. The empty wheelbarrow had skimmed over the mud, but if there had been more weight, then it would have sunk deep, just like that little boy's grubby fists. The wheelbarrow must have been weighed down when Bud rounded that corner.

But what could he have been hauling? The feeders were all here, and there was nothing in the wheelbarrow when they found Bud.

Actually, that wasn't entirely true. Saffron wrapped her arms around herself as sudden chill ran through her, despite the balmy Hawaiian morning. The wheelbarrow wasn't empty when they found it. It had been underneath Bud.

A horrible realization began to dawn. Saffron looked at the tracks again. For the first time, she saw the clefts at the edge of the footprint: heavy traction on the shoes. Those were not the tracks from Bud's loafers.

Someone else had been here, and they'd been pushing Bud's body in the wheelbarrow.

SAFFRON WAS STILL SITTING on the feeder when Mano came down the path, looking for her.

"There you are!" he said. Saffron noticed that he kept his gaze on her eyes, not letting it rest on the wheelbarrow or the shed. "Good news! Keahi is off today. We could call him to help us out here!"

Saffron shook her head. She wasn't sure how long she'd been sitting there, trying to talk herself out of this crazy idea. She was alone in a new place, it was natural that she would be a little jumpy. She had just found a person dead. It was natural that she might think of ominous events.

"No, it's okay," she said, knowing that if Keahi were here she would have to act completely normal all day, "I think we can get it."

"Come on, he'd love to. He talked a lot about you on the way home yesterday," this made Saffron's cheeks burn, "I think he'd like to get to know you a little better."

She shook her head, unable to concentrate on this new information. Her mind was still crowded with shock. She looked up at Mano. "Was there an autopsy?" she blurted, too worked up to remember that this was a sensitive subject for him.

Mano stopped as suddenly as if she'd slapped him. His light tone had gone flat, "What?"

"Bud. Did they do an autopsy?"

Mano's expression was unreadable, but his voice was kind, "Ipo, when the oldest man in town dies hauling heavy feeders, there's not much mystery about what caused it." Mano stepped closer to her and laid a hand on her shoulder.

"But how do they *know*?" she said, "How do they know how he died?"

"It doesn't matter. He is dead."

"But it *could* matter," Saffron began, but Mano cut her off with a gently raised hand.

"Bud was my friend—my last *good* friend, and I would have kept him here if I could, but he has gone on, and I have to let him go. We say, 'Hoʻokuʻu.' We let them go, set them free, and in turn, we are set free, and we can go on. You must let him go and go on, too. You couldn't have stopped him from working, and you couldn't have stopped him from dying."

The last word, Saffron could see, cost Mano something to say. This whole conversation, she realized, must be hard for him. But she had to tell him what she thought, what she'd noticed. She pulled her gaze from his face and looked down, trying to formulate the right words.

Her gaze fell on Mano's feet, and Saffron felt a rush of fear. Mano was wearing sneakers. Their toothy soles jutted out on the sides, providing ample traction. What was more, they were not new, but they gleamed white. They'd been recently cleaned, and, judging by the gray smudges on the black laces, polished with white shoe polish. She didn't speak.

"Come on, come on," Mano said, rousing her, "If we're not calling Keahi, we're going to have to get to work. We've got lots of feeders to install." He lifted the feeder beside her into the wheelbarrow and navigated it expertly down the path toward the egg house. Saffron tried not to notice how skilled he was with the wheelbarrow or how his corded arms maneuvered it with ease. Was there a reason Mano didn't want her looking into Bud's death? Numbly, she stood and followed him, pushing her own circling thoughts into the corner of her mind.

Saffron willed herself calm as she followed him. She thought of Bradley's chiding when she'd called about the person in the house. Was this more of her own habitual paranoia?

Working with him made her uneasy. If he had killed Bud, who was to say he wouldn't kill her? But he was lifting and hauling, and there was no easy way to get rid of him, so she just stayed extra vigilant.

The hard day's work was therapeutic for her anxiety. She let herself get lost in the routine of crouching in the pens, lifting the feeders into place, holding the screws while Mano tightened them from the walkway side of each pen wall, and going back for another feeder.

When she pulled the last feeder from the shed and hefted it into the wheelbarrow outside on the path, Saffron turned and put a hand on the shed door. She was alone here, as she had been in the moments before Mano came. Right now he was back at the egg house, adjusting the flow of feed that would come out of each feeder, and she stopped to think how absurd her suspicion was. She'd worked with him all day, and he had only been kind and helpful and calm. Why would she think he even *could* do what she was imagining?

Her mother had always said that she had an active imagination, and it had been a boon to her in her work. When she began planning an event, she could see it in her mind in perfect detail: the flowers, the buffet table. She could hear the music and taste the food. Making those mental images a reality was her specialty.

But now, in the warm, wet quiet of the island, her mental

image of foul play seemed silly. As the door closed, she saw, through the crack, the lone teacup on the bench. It sat in calm silence, a testament to the last quiet moments of Bud's life. She would come back for it sometime.

Mano was right, she thought, wheeling the last feeder back to the egg house, she had to put Bud's death behind her. As she swung the shed door closed, she told herself that she was closing the door on the awful event of Bud's death. It wasn't her business either way. She needed only to get this place salable, find a buyer, and get back to her life. Playing detective in a tropical island paradise was not in her future plans.

As she approached the egg house, she heard voices. Mano's, of course, and another that wasn't familiar to her. Her heart began to pound again. Despite the pep talk she'd just given herself, she walked into the egg house feeling apprehensive.

The short, square Mano stood up by the first pen on the right near the work area, talking to a tall, neat man in jeans and a tee. Sal, the real estate investor that she'd met at Bud's house.

Sal smiled as she approached, but Mano did not.

"Hello again," Sal said, extending a hand, "I hope you don't mind, but I've been prowling about the place a little, and I like what I see."

Saffron found that she did mind. Especially since her recent suspicions, it made her jumpy to think of him wandering around out here without her permission.

"I would like to see inside the house. It was locked up."

"Of course it was locked," Saffron started, but Sal didn't stop talking.

"I'm definitely interested. It has so many cottages, and even this," Sal waved a hand at the egg house, "could be converted to hold more guests."

Saffron looked around doubtfully. That would take a lot of renovation, she thought.

Mano grunted, and Saffron looked at him.

"You'll be paying top dollar, I'm sure," he growled.

At this, Sal's mustache twitched, "The place is in rough shape, and I'd have to take that into consideration in any offer, of course."

"Mmm-hmm," Mano said, giving Saffron a warning look.

"Well, you are busy," Sal said. He handed her a card. "I will be in touch with your Realtor." He turned and glided out of the egg house, leaving her and Mano to install the last feeder in silence.

Finally, when it had been tightened and three scoops of feed had been poured in to test it, Mano spoke.

"I feel like I should warn you that Sal has a history around here of snatching up property and paying a fraction of what it's worth, then making a mint off of it."

"Isn't that what you're supposed to do in real estate?" Saffron asked.

"I suppose," Mano looked her in the eye. "Just don't let him take advantage of you. Your uncle put a lot into this place, and it's sort of a landmark in this area. I'd hate to see it become a party destination for groups of spring-break coeds just out to get drunk in Hawaii."

That did sound distasteful. "I'll be careful." She said, "But I do want to sell it, and I'll consider his offer."

"Fair enough. Just get what it's really worth, at least."

Mano had walked to the work area, where he was attempting to work the feed lift. It was stuck. Saffron stepped up to help. Together, they tugged at the crank until they were both red in the face.

Mano reached into a cupboard under the sink nearby and extracted a can. He sprayed its contents onto the crank, then they tried again.

The two struggled side-by-side for several minutes, but the crank barely budged. Together, they strained until it was apparent they weren't going to move it.

Mano straightened and ran a bandanna across his shining forehead, "It's not goin' anywhere."

She nodded, catching her breath.

"You know who you oughta call?" He said, drawing each word out as if it were just dawning on him.

Saffron knew better, "Don't say it."

"Keahi could move this in a minute."

"I'm not calling Keahi."

"Why not?" Mano leaned heavily against the house, and Saffron realized how hard they'd been working. He needed a break. She gestured him toward the farmhouse and tried to explain on the way.

"I don't want to call him, because I don't want him to get the wrong idea."

"What idea?"

Curry flapped out of the way as they climbed onto the lanai, then rushed the door as Saffron snapped it closed behind them. She got two ginger ales from the ancient fridge and sat across from Mano at the table.

"I don't want him to get confused about me needing help and think I'm . . ." She searched for the right word, "chasing him."

The kitchen fan ruffled his silver hair as Mano leveled his gaze at her, "Ipo, Keahi knows when a girl is chasing him. He has had . . . A lot of experience with such situations."

Saffron felt her cheeks flush again, "I'm sure he has," she said. She used her flattest tone in an attempt to end the conversation.

But Mano went on anyway, "Every girl on the island has chased that boy."

Saffron didn't like the way that made her feel. She opened

her mouth to change the subject, but Mano kept talking. "None of 'em's caught him yet, though." He held her eye just long enough to be sure she recognized that he was making a point, then downed his ginger ale.

Chapter Seven

The house was quiet after Mano left. The stillness of her metropolitan apartment hadn't bothered her back in DC, but she supposed that was because the city was never tranquil. There was always a siren or traffic, or neighboring apartment noises. Here, the sounds that kept her company were not man-made. There were birdsongs and cries from the trees outside, the creaking of the monkeypod tree over the lanai, and underneath it all, the constant shush of the waves on the shore. Saffron listened to them for a long time after Mano disappeared down the beach.

She'd asked him if he wanted a ride home, and he'd declined, saying that his walking time was his thinking time.

Saffron decided on steak and grilled pineapple for dinner. Idly, she tried to think how much this meal would cost her back in DC. Tikka was scratching happily, and every once in a while the kitchen rang with the sound of the incessant tapping as she accosted her favorite invisible spot on the side of the brooder box.

Saffron put the steak seasoning back in the cupboard and turned it so that its label faced forward, easily readable. She shifted a couple other spices and closed the cabinet, satisfied that they were tidy.

A jaunty trill of classical music drew her attention to her phone on the counter. She picked it up to talk to Trish.

"Saffron," her assistant's light voice cut through the miles between them, "When will you be back?"

"Still working on things down here," Saffron said, going out on the lanai to take her steak off the grill. Curry announced her presence with what she had come to know as his hello crow.

"Is that a chicken? What are you, on a farm or something?"

"Exactly that," Saffron said, "a chicken farm."

"What are you doing on a chicken farm?"

"That's the house my uncle left me," Saffron tried to explain, "it used to be an egg farm. I'm trying to clean it up to sell it."

There was a long silence. Saffron wondered if Trish, who had grown up in central Miami, had ever even seen a real chicken. The steak was perfect, and Saffron tried to chew quietly as Trish went on, "Okay, well, we've got the Granden wedding coming up."

The words brought a flood of images to Saffron's mind. Miko Granden, her handsome young fiancé, and the wedding Saffron had planned for them at the National Aquarium in Baltimore. It was going to be a fun and elegant affair, with accents in deep blue and the brilliant colors of tropical fish, a towering draped cake with edible starfish and pearls, and a ceremony in front of the dolphin tank, with the dolphins looking on as witnesses.

"I know the one," Saffron calculated, "twelve weeks out, right?"

"Right," Trish said, "only Miko called today to cancel."

This jolted Saffron. She put down her fork. "What? Cancel what?"

"The whole thing. I told her there were no refunds of the downpayment, but she didn't care. Just said they were calling it off."

Not only was the rest of the Granden payment necessary capital for the next six months of business, but Saffron also really liked the young couple, and they seemed nicely matched. The last time they had talked—three weeks ago before Saffron had come to Hawaii—Miko had confided that this was the first time in her life she felt entirely sure of something. Saffron felt a little guilty remembering that she'd had to bite back a cynical response about how that usually meant the end was coming.

She assured Trish that she would handle it. Ten minutes later, she was on the phone with a sobbing Miko Granden.

"I just think he deserves someone better!" Miko's voice was weak and weepy.

Saffron had heard this before. In fact, she'd listened to this and a thousand other excuses for cold feet. Some of them were valid, and when she recognized those, Saffron was as good at canceling a wedding as she was at planning one. But this one, coming from the kind, intelligent, talented Miko, was not.

"Now why would you say that?" Perhaps an old flame had shown up? This made Saffron think of Reggie, her old flame, who was somewhere in Honolulu right now, as far as Saffron knew.

Miko was talking. Saffron returned her focus to the bride. "And I didn't know what to tell him, so I—I."

Saffron tried to fill in what she'd missed. Maybe Miko didn't really want to go live in Philadelphia with her fiancé after the wedding?

But it was neither of the reasons she'd imagined. Miko had stopped to sniffle. "Because we——"

Saffron waited.

"We had a fight!"

Saffron breathed out and took another bite of steak. She

chewed while she gave Miko time to explain. By the end, Saffron was sure that this was nothing serious. She let Miko know that of course, she would help her cancel if that was her final decision, but that Miko should have one more conversation with Cole and that Saffron would call her tomorrow for a final decision.

She hung up and texted Trish to put a hold on canceling, she'd let her know. Trish texted back an icon of a crowing rooster.

The air hung warm and heavy around the lanai as Saffron watched the sun sinking into the sea. The palm trees on the beach made stark silhouettes against the golden sky, and she ate the last of her pineapple, savoring its sweetness.

Curry was chasing a gecko across the painted floorboards and cackled in annoyance as the little lizard slipped up the wall and positioned itself near the porchlight.

Saffron froze. The gecko was positioned directly over a strange mark. She had never noticed it, and if she had seen it from another angle, it might have just appeared to be a smudge on the worn siding. But now, from the center of the lanai, she could see it clearly for what it was: a handprint.

Don't get carried away, Saffron thought as she stood and walked over to it, *it could have come from anyone, anytime.* But all she could think of were the break-in, the strange tracks and the dead man she'd found in her backyard.

She looked around the lanai. The railing was covered with fine black algae, and as she looked at it, she saw places where it had been disturbed. That made her feel better. Someone must have been using the railing as they walked up and gotten the algae on their hands.

The gecko scurried away, and Saffron tried to think why a person would have their hand there. She reached up and held her hand over it, not touching the siding, just hovering a few inches from the print. The fingers were spread wide and were longer than hers, and the placement was higher than was comfortable for her, leading her to believe that it was a man's handprint. She stretched up to her tiptoes, and her blood froze. Standing in just that position, she could see directly through the little windows high in the door, to the futon in the living room and on into the kitchen table where she ate breakfast.

Saffron eased back to the soles of her feet. She pulled her phone from her pocket and dialed the sheriff's number from the card he had given her.

"Bradley," he answered.

"Hi, Officer," she said, introducing herself while trying to think through her fear, "I wondered, well, if you had any concerns about the death of Bud Samson?"

There was a long pause, "No, ma'am. Do you?"

"Well, it's just that there were tracks down there by the shed, and, and now I found—" she hesitated. Did she really want to show off her paranoia in full? But she was leaving as soon as she got this place sold. Why should she care what he or anyone else thought of her? "Now I found a handprint by my back door."

"A handprint?"

"Yes, sort of smudgy. I think it's from the algae on the railing."

"Oh," Bradley's voice was more relaxed, "that happens a lot here. That stuff smudges everywhere. Clorox usually takes care of it pretty well."

This wasn't a housekeeping call. "Yes, but, well, I was a little worried that maybe someone had been here again, or maybe someone had . . ." It sounded so harsh, "had *hurt* Bud on purpose?"

Someone was talking to Bradley in the background. She heard him reply in a muffled voice, as if his hand were over the receiver, "Again? I'm going to have to cite them. But I'll go easy on Derek, his grandpa-in-law just died."

Saffron strained to hear. She hadn't thought of Derek since the day she'd met him. But the thought of his lopsided sneer and cold violet eyes did nothing to help her pounding heart.

"Listen, I'm dealing with some local thugs, it'll be a while before I get out there."

It seemed more foolish by the moment. Saffron imagined Bradley swarming out here with his gun drawn just to be shown some muddy tracks and a smeared handprint.

"No, no that's fine. Don't worry about it."

Saffron went back into the house. She'd finished both bathrooms and was starting on the bedroom across the hall from the master.

Going in, she knew immediately what purpose the room had served. A framed print of a sailboat hung on the pale blue wall, and the white frame of an old-fashioned lathed baby crib stood under the window against the far wall. This would have been the nursery.

And here was where, she soon saw, Uncle Beau had stored all of Aunt Ila's things. Dresses, knickknacks, jewelry. All of it piled high and deep on the crib and a changing table, on a beautiful koa wood rocking chair, on the floor.

She found herself saddened by it. The baby's toys and furniture were tossed in on the piles as well: a teddy bear, a high chair, bottles, and cloth diapers.

Saffron imagined the young man that Uncle Beau had been then, scouring the house for reminders of them, stuffing them in this room as tangible symbols of the grief he was locking inside. He had never dealt with it, from what Mom had told her, and had carried it with him to his grave.

She started sorting through a pile of loose dresses. She recognized them as muumuus. Their bright colors were still bold. She could see how they would have complemented her aunt's stunning amber skin and long black hair. She held some up and looked at the dusty mirror across the room. They even looked good against her own coral-pink cheeks and topaz freckles. She laid them aside.

The mirror was covered with streaks of dust. The sight of them superimposed over Saffron's reflection reminded her of the tracks and the handprint. There was something heavy and ominous in those thoughts, for all she tried to explain them away.

Saffron pushed open the closet and hung the muumuus on some empty hangers. She dove back into the pile and found more clothes. The mice had apparently not found this room, and she was grateful. She uncovered jeans and sweaters, classic pedal pushers and saddle shoes, and put them all out in the hall to be taken to the secondhand store she'd seen in town.

Underneath Aunt Ila's clothes was a suitcase. She set it on the floor and opened it to find it full of papers. Atop the stack was Uncle Beau and Aunt Ila's marriage certificate. She set that aside, then sifted through birth certificates, photos, and ticket stubs. Every one of them, she was sure, was significant in some way to her uncle, but now they just looked like the detritus of a life, flotsam washed up on the now-vacant shore.

There was another picture of Uncle Beau and Bud and their sweethearts. Mano wasn't in this one. But Bud had his arm around a girl. She was kissing him on the cheek. Saffron studied the photo and raised her eyebrows. The girl's beehive hairdo was very distinctive. This was Mano's wife, Keahi's grandma. The past was just full of surprises. Saffron tried not to read too much into it, but her mind was still churning with possibilities, and she couldn't deny that the photo was . . . strange.

Checking the time, she put the photo back down and left the suitcase there. She needed to get some things ready to take to the second-hand store tomorrow.

She started going through the baby's clothes. That baby, she realized, had been her cousin. Little blue jumpers and corduroy overalls. Tiny shoes. She saved some of the most attractive, keeping in mind a vintage baby shower theme she'd been thinking of for a client back home. The rest she arranged in boxes in the hall. When she had cleared out all the clothes she could find, she loaded the boxes into the car.

THE NEXT MORNING she drove down to Tiki Thrift and Trade.

She paused to take a call from Miko Granden, whose voice was warm with relief. The wedding was back on. Saffron texted Trish to tell her not to cancel, and Trish texted back with a happy face.

The woman inside Tiki Thrift and Trade introduced herself as Consuela Limon.

She gestured at Saffron's sunglasses. "You can see in here behind those?"

Saffron felt her cheeks warm. She was so used to wearing them that she sometimes forgot them. She pulled them off and saw Consuela more clearly. The woman was in her late seventies, with a short salt-and-pepper pixie cut. Her eyes were the rich brown of cowrie shells, and her skin was acorn with warm magenta undertones. She had kindly wrinkles around her mouth, and a reserved smile.

"That's better. Now I can see your lovely green eyes." Consuela focused on the boxes. She picked up the little overalls with tenderness. The look she gave Saffron was long and meaningful. Saffron left feeling that the loss of her aunt and cousin had been felt deeply by the whole community.

This was new to her. She had always lived in massive cities, and her mother had kept mostly to herself. So, though Saffron had plenty of friends at school, she had never been deeply integrated into a neighborhood or community. To think that this woman remembered people who had died over thirty years ago gave Saffron a sense of the very deep roots that her family had here.

Consuela's voice was as soft as her gaze, and Saffron leaned forward to hear her. "That niño, your cousin, was so sweet."

Saffron didn't know what to say. She had never known Warren Wayne. She just watched as Consuela carefully evaluated every item, then wrote out a receipt for store credit.

"Oh, no," Saffron said, holding up a hand, "you just take them. It's a donation."

But Consuela wouldn't hear of it. Her voice was firm when she said, "No. You never know when you'll need this." She handed Saffron the little slip, and Saffron thanked her. She slipped it into the receipt pocket in her purse.

Consuela walked with her to the door. "You are in a hurry to go." She said. The rounded vowels of Spanish warmed the syllables of the English words.

Saffron jerked to a halt on the boardwalk outside the shop and turned back to Consuela, trying to appear nonchalant.

"No, no," she said, "I've just got lots to do, is all."

Consuela pressed her lips together and fixed Saffron with a steady gaze. "You are too young to be in such a hurry," she said.

Saffron considered this.

"You have lots of time," Consuela said, "If anyone should hurry to do things, it's old people like me. You should be surfing, or gathering shells on the beach, or napping. You have all the time in the world."

Saffron didn't feel like she had all the time in the world. She didn't even have time to stand here and philosophize about how much time she had. There was so much to do back at the bungalow, and her business in DC to run, and the chickens to feed. Saffron felt like a guitar string, pulled tight between today and tomorrow, between the past and the future. In the midst of these swirling thoughts, she stammered out a response, "I don't feel like I have all the time in the world."

Consuela clucked in empathy, "I know. But it is there. You just have to stop hurrying away from happiness."

This struck Saffron. Was that what she'd been doing? Before she could respond, she heard someone calling from across the parking lot.

"Consuela!"

"Ah! It's my walking club," Consuela smiled. She pulled a key from her pocket and locked her shop. Saffron noticed, for the first time, that the old woman was wearing tennis shoes.

A group of women was approaching briskly. She recognized Fumi and Sandy, but the other three were new to her.

Sandy patted Saffron on the arm, "How is our resident chook chaser?" Sandy's Australian accent and strong voice rang in the morning air, "How's the clean-up project? Pretty big job, isn't it?"

Saffron nodded.

"How are you even surviving out there? That kitchen isn't fit for cooking in."

"I've been working on it. It's pretty livable now. Just clearing out the bedrooms."

One of the other women, whose cheerful face and short stature made her look a little like Mrs. Claus, spoke up. Saffron tried not to look surprised when she said her name. "I'm Betty Claus. We're glad to finally run into you! Do you want to join us for our walk, dear? You can join the Maika'i Walking Wonders! We're the best walking club in town." The little woman had rose-tinged skin and a button nose. Looking at her, Saffron finally knew the meaning of the phrase, "a twinkle in her eye."

"We're the only walking club in town," another woman put in. She was very thin. Saffron tried not to stare at the sticklike arms that made the knobs of her elbows look enormous. The woman's skin was pale and gray, and she had a sour expression permanently etched into her tight face. "And you can't walk with us today, because we're done. Half of us have already left, and I'm leaving too, before this pack of lunatics makes me go another step." The thin woman broke away from the group and stalked off toward a luxury sedan in the center of the parking lot. There was a stark silence as they watched her go.

"Oh, never mind Miss Vinny Dingley," Betty Claus waved a plump hand. "She's always cranky at the end of a walk. I think her blood sugar gets low."

The women concurred in a low murmur, not unlike one of the sounds Saffron's hens made when they were together.

"Thank you for the offer. I've actually got a lot to do out at the farm." Saffron said, glad to have a reasonable excuse not to join them in the future.

"Well, all right, if you don't want to be fit and sassy," Mrs. Claus stuck out a hip.

"You call on us if you need anything," Sandy offered as the group started to move away. "We'd love to help."

"And you remember what I told you," Consuela said, patting Saffron's arm, "don't hurry away from happiness."

Saffron appreciated that, and she said so. She found that Mano's help had softened her assessment of do-gooders over the last few weeks. She was discovering that people were warmer and more welcoming than she had thought. She found herself not only trusting them more, almost enjoying them.

As the women paced off around the park, Saffron felt again the sense of community that was so strange to her.

Saffron paused before she climbed into her car. She thought about what Consuela had said. Was she hurrying away from happiness? It had the ring of truth to it. She felt, on a deep level, that the woman was right.

Saffron reached into the console and extracted a bottle of sunscreen. She put some on her arms and cheeks, then pulled her wide-brimmed hat from the passenger's seat. The steep mountainside that nudged the little village toward the ocean rose up behind the park next to the thrift store. There was a trailhead with a sign that said, "View Area Ahead." What better way to slow down than to take in an island view?

The trail was steep and rocky, and Saffron had to stop for breath a few times. The foliage surrounding her blocked out any view of the town below or the ocean beyond, so she kept climbing through the emerald trees bejeweled with their bright flowers until she reached a flat place in the trail.

Like a picture window, it opened onto a vast panorama of color. Saffron pulled off her sunglasses and felt the scene like an explosion in her mind: fuchsia, magenta, tangerine, aqua, vermillion, she couldn't name the colors as fast as her mind registered them. Leaves and flowers, the vast sky, the multicolored ocean, the beach, the sea foam. Saffron drank it in.

And for the first time, she realized that she was hungry for color. She'd been trying so hard to control it in her life, to avoid being overwhelmed by it, that she had forgotten how it filled her. She had hidden from it, and from other things, for too long.

SAFFRON STOPPED in at the Oceanside diner to grab some lunch. She'd resigned herself to the fact that Bernadette wouldn't let her pay, but she was craving an ono burger, and she didn't know any other place to get one.

The first person she saw was Lani, leaning heavily on the counter, talking to her brother. She was dressed casually, in jeans and tennis shoes. Saffron assumed that she had just come from the Walking Wonders. Saffron didn't take up a table this time, just stepped up beside Lani and gave the cook her order over the counter. She watched as he slapped the meat on the grill. The older woman glanced at Saffron. Trying to be friendly, Saffron smiled and said, "Did you enjoy your walk with the club?"

Lani's face tightened. "Don't fool yourself. Just because I'm old, too, doesn't mean I would spend a single minute with those hypocritical old bats."

Saffron tried not to let her surprise show on her face.

Lani went on, "They're all a bunch of scheming, sneaky liars. You can't trust them."

Saffron thought of the warm little women. Right now Lani, whose face was folded in anger, seemed just the opposite of Mrs. Claus, sour and gray.

Lani seemed to sense Saffron's discomfort. She looked away, then seemed to make a conscious effort to brighten her expression. When she turned back to Saffron, she shifted the conversation with a little small talk about the farm and her uncle, as everyone did.

"We all had some good days, back in high school," she said warmly, "Mano, Ila, your uncle, your father."

As always, Saffron's mind swarmed with questions about her father. She wondered if Lani had seen him since he left DC, if she knew why he'd left his family and never come back. But she was too afraid of the answer to ask. Instead, she focused on someone else. "And Bud?" Saffron asked.

It was as if Lani had suddenly tasted something awful. Her attempt at cheer washed away with the words. "Not Bud," she shook her head forcefully. "He was older than us. The good times were before Bud came in causing trouble."

Saffron was uncomfortable speaking ill of the dead, but she was also curious. "He wasn't in town then?"

"He was here, but he was much older than we were. Just a man in town until—" the cook made a loud noise, like a cough, and Lani's gaze snapped back to him. Saffron caught a swift shake of the man's head. Lani seemed to reconsider. "Bud was always a troublemaker, let's leave it at that."

Saffron couldn't stop herself from glancing down at the traction on Lani's shoes. The edge of the sole was as rugged as the tracks she'd seen. She tried to stop thinking what she was thinking.

The cook seemed to want rid of Saffron. He put her burger together before the other orders and scooped her fries off a plate waiting to be delivered to the dining room. He set the bag down on the counter with finality. Saffron thanked him, said goodbye to Lani, and left.

SAFFRON WAS FINISHED with lunch and halfway through organizing the nursery when the day turned drizzly. Soft rain fell outside the windows, and she stopped sorting baby toys and went into the kitchen for a cup of tea and some cookies.

Saffron took the cover off the brooder box and watched the little family.

They were growing. The little gold one was perched on top of the water container, peering up at Saffron. Tikka glanced at her, then went back to staring excitedly at a grain on the ground. She picked it up with a new kind of sound. It was a deep, throaty chirp. Instead of eating it, Tikka put it back on the ground as the babies came running from all the corners of the box. Again, Tikka picked it up and chirped, then put it down. The babies stabbed the ground repeatedly, getting beakfuls of sand. Tikka's chirp grew more insistent. She picked up the grain and put it down for the third time.

Suddenly, the little chick flapped her unwieldy wings and flopped down from the top of the water container. She landed next to her mother, righted herself, and snatched the grain. Instantly, Tikka's sounds changed to bright, happy clucks.

Saffron saw now. "You're teaching them what to eat!" she said, marveling at the wonder of nature, "and when he found what you were trying to show him, you praised him!"

Tikka wasn't interested in commentary. She found another grain and repeated the process.

Saffron took a handful of grains from the bucket next to the box and sprinkled them in. Tikka looked up, seeming grateful to have more to work with, and went on until every chick had found a grain and been praised.

The grains disappeared more quickly then, and Saffron gave the little family two more handfuls before making sure the feeder was full and closing up the top. By then, her feed bucket was empty.

One thing she liked about the egg farm was that there was always something useful to do. She slipped on a jacket and headed down through the rain to the egg house with her bucket.

She stopped to convey the eggs from the first few pens to the work area and stack them in the egg holders, then took a few scoops of feed and put them in the feeders, smiling at how neatly the feeders contained the grains.

A few of the hens came to investigate and happily started pecking at their feed. They were beautiful. The rest didn't bother with the feed. They were standing near their doorways, looking out at the falling rain, and their drawn-out *bawks* sounded distinctly annoyed. The hens came in so many colors. Golden ones, black ones, bright red and brown. The black feathers reflected the light around them with violet and emerald sheens. Saffron saw complexity even in the brown feathers—some were pale with dusty hues, some earthy and rich. Some of the poultry had solid-colored feathers, and others, like Tikka, had patterned feathers. The patterns ranged from prominent, bold edging like Tikka's to fine lines of contrasting colors penciled on to each tapered feather.

The rain tapped on the roof, and Saffron felt warm and cozy inside with them for company. She pushed away the thought that she was beginning to like it here.

"It will clear up soon," Saffron assured them. "Don't worry."

The frenzied tapping sound of the hens pecking at their feed trailed off into a few scattered rattles, and she realized with dismay that the feeders were nearly empty again. She went back to the bag and found it empty. She had used all the feed in the Egg House. She knew there was more in the big feed barrels, and as much as she hated to go there, she knew she'd have to sooner or later. She set her bucket down and headed for the shed.

The path was slick, and she noted that the tracks beside the shed had become smooth with the rain. Even if Bradley did show up, now there wouldn't be much to show him.

The little shed smelled warm and damp. There was more room to move now that the last feeder had been installed in the egg house. She pulled the top off the first barrel and saw several bags of feed crammed into it. Mano had said that even though the feed was old, it was still good as long as it wasn't moldy. The bags seemed intact and full as if they'd never been opened. It took all of Saffron's strength to heave one out of the barrel. As she did so, she caught sight of something.

She set the sack down and peered behind the feed barrels. There, on one of the low shelves at the back of the shed, between two dusty boogie boards, was a neat little nest. Inside, scores of white eggs gleamed like pearls.

A wild nest. Just like the one Saffron had seen the first day in the bushes, except that these eggs were white. But the shed had been closed up since they'd found Bud. Whatever chickens were using it had probably moved on to laying somewhere else.

Saffron put the top back on the barrel and hefted the sack of feed onto her shoulder. She'd have to clear out the nest sometime, but she couldn't carry the eggs as well as the feed. They'd been here a while, and they were probably rotten. She didn't look forward to extracting rotten eggs, and she couldn't risk dropping any. She decided to come back later.

WALKING into the kitchen with the newly-filled bucket of feed, Saffron realized she'd made a mistake. She'd forgotten to put the cover back on the brooder box, and Tikka was strutting about the kitchen, enjoying some relief from her eager offspring. They were still in the box, peeping in panic.

Tikka tipped an eye toward Saffron and bobbed her head. She flapped up onto the counter by the toaster.

"Oh, no!" Saffron cried, "You can't go up there." She dreaded trying to catch the bird.

Tikka peered at the Formica countertop and made her deep, throaty chirp. The chicks in the box went crazy, crying out and scrambling toward that side of the brooder.

"They can't come," Saffron said, "And anyway, there's nothing on the counter. There's nothing there to feed them." She took a few steps forward. Tikka's chirp became more insistent. She twitched her head to the side, scratched, and made a louder chirp.

"Settle down," Saffron said, but the hen simply looked at her and made the sound again.

Saffron walked slowly and raised her arms carefully. "Easy now," she said, "easy." She reached toward Tikka, expecting another wing in the face.

Instead, Tikka crouched, arching her back down and her folded wings upward. She dropped her head and stood perfectly still. Saffron tried not to get too nervous as she decided to try the technique she'd seen in the book. She placed a hand firmly over each wing, holding them down as she lifted the heavy hen from the counter and brought Tikka to her chest. Tikka seemed at ease, her feet dangling, her head raised inquisitively. Saffron shifted her so that she had one hand free, tucking Tikka in her arm like a football, and moved carefully across the kitchen. Tikka didn't protest.

She also seemed happy to see her babies again, and as Saffron slid the cover back on the brooder, she felt a sense of accomplishment.

A knock on the door made Saffron jump. She glanced up to see Keahi standing out the back door on the lanai, eying the rooster. He smiled when she opened the door. In his hands was a white paper box.

"Tutu—my grandpa—sent these over," Keahi said, opening the box. Inside were what looked like lumpy little donuts. Dark brown and studded with crystalline sugar, they made Saffron's mouth water. "Poi malasada from Juno's Bakery. Local favorite. Try one." Saffron picked one and took a bite. Bright purple on the inside, it was, easily, the best donut she'd ever tasted. Rich and sweet, filled with coconut custard, she didn't stop herself from snatching another.

"These are amazing!"

"Well, Tutu was insistent that you needed some right now, this morning." Keahi grinned, looking her directly in the eyes. They both saw through Mano's thinly veiled matchmaking.

Saffron couldn't deny that there was a spark. She liked how Keahi could fix things, how he looked after his grandpa, how his grin lit his warm brown eyes.

"Thanks! Come in," she said, waving a hand through the door.

Keahi walked past her, moving to the counter by the toaster to put down the plate. He hesitated, and Saffron noticed, for the first time, that where she had just taken Tikka from was covered with a fine dusting of white grit.

"Oh! Sorry! That's just chicken sand!" She grabbed a sponge and washed it off. "I'm so sorry. I'm usually pretty tidy."

He glanced around, "I can see that. It's pretty impressive, what you've done here."

Saffron beamed. She hadn't had much praise for her efforts while she'd been here. Running *Every Detail Events*, she was used to people exclaiming and gushing over her work. It felt good to have someone take notice.

"So," Keahi said, "I gathered from our conversation the other day that this was your first visit to Hawaii?"

She nodded. "My first."

"Well, even though you've done some great work here, it seems a shame for you to spend your whole visit inside cleaning."

Saffron sensed, for the first time in a long time, an invitation coming.

"I was wondering if you'd like to go to the luau with me tomorrow? We could look around, then have dinner there?" He raised his eyebrows, "I get an employee discount."

She laughed, then remembered something that Mano had said, and before she could stop herself, she teased, "Not a frequent flyer card?"

He looked at her strangely for a moment.

"You take a lot of dates there?" As soon as the word *date* was out of her mouth, she regretted saying it. Now there was a new tension in the air that hadn't been there before.

Keahi looked thoughtful, "Not *a lot*," he said, "I don't think. I've kinda lost count."

He was teasing her, and she liked how he didn't make a big deal of her faux pas.

"It sounds like fun," she said.

"Does tomorrow work? I'm off so I can come to get you about six, and we'll go on a little backstage tour."

Saffron's voice was brighter than it had been in a while when she said, "Wow, the VIP package."

"Well, I wouldn't want you to be disappointed, coming out here from such a metropolitan area. I know girls like you are hard to impress."

Saffron wondered briefly if that was true, "well, you've got a big job ahead, then," she said. "I'm pretty metro."

"I can see that," he gestured at the box of chickens in her kitchen, and she couldn't help but smile. Keahi shifted a little, seeming reluctant. "Well, I guess I'd better go. I work tonight, and if I'm not there for the fire knife dance, I won't have an employee discount to use tomorrow."

"Well, we wouldn't want you paying full price," she said.

"Full price for *two*," he responded.

"Plus the cost of malasadas," she said, "I'll be expecting more of those."

"Oh, I'll be sure to have all the malasadas you can eat," he agreed.

"This is going to make your tutu so happy," Saffron patted his arm, and a little thrill went up her fingers.

"You'd better believe it," Keahi said.

Chapter Eight

Saffron was ready an hour early the next night, dressed in dark leggings, a tailored top, and her best boots. As she was clipping a heavy triple-strand necklace around her throat, she realized she had forgotten to gather the eggs from the three pens of hens she'd finished catching today.

She glanced at the clock. She should have time. Slipping on her sunglasses, she went to do the chores.

Saffron was beginning to understand why people liked living on farms. There was a comforting rhythm to life here—the chores needed to be done at the same intervals every day, the chickens lived lives of contented routine, oblivious of the turmoil around them. She was in the egg house when Keahi came to find her.

Proudly, she showed him the two dozen eggs she'd just put in cartons. "Aren't they remarkable? I love the colors."

Eggs in DC had all come from a carton.

"I never saw eggs like this until I came here," she said. "They were all eburnean back home."

Keahi peered at her quizzically, and it took a moment for her to recognize that she'd used a color word unfamiliar to him. This happened sometimes. Because of her color sensitivity, Saffron rarely called anything "white" or "off-white" or any other basic color name. They just weren't specific enough. In her mind, white was thousands of different shades, and snowflake was as different from marshmallow as it was from ebony. She thought back to her sentence and pinpointed the word.

"Eburnean. It's ivory. Like a bright, warm white?"

The puzzlement faded from his eyes as he tried out the word, "Eburnean, huh?"

"Right. The eggs were all that same white from the store back home. But look at these!" Saffron slid her sunglasses up onto her hair and plucked a brown egg from one carton. She held it up. "See the variation? This one's hazelnut colored, and this one's cocoa." She put them back and grasped a pale green egg, "this one's artichoke green, and this one's got some blue tones that make it look minty! This one's camel colored, but see the copper speckles all over it?"

Keahi was smiling and nodding. "You know," he said, "I never knew how beautiful and interesting an egg could be."

"Neither did I!" Saffron admitted. She liked that he appreciated their uniqueness.

"And I never knew anyone who could describe color like you can. That's amazing."

She dropped her gaze back to the eggs and pulled her sunglasses back over her eyes. From behind them, the colors were more dull, closer to each other, less remarkable. She closed the cartons. Even when she didn't bring it up, her rare color perception always became obvious. And ghosting behind Keahi's praise were the words of kids at school who had teased her. She remembered one comment in particular, when she was in kindergarten, and the class was supposed to be sorting colored wooden animals into different groups. She couldn't place the liver-colored elephant in the "gray" pile, because it was, to her, obviously much closer to purple. *Don't your eyes work?* One of the girls had sneered, and she'd wondered that ever since.

Saffron pushed the echoes of the past away and switched the subject. "I want to drop these eggs off as a little gift to the Oceanside Cafe as we go into town," she said, "if you don't mind."

"Sounds great," He said. There was still a sparkle of admiration in his gaze, and Saffron found that she liked seeing it.

She set the eggs on the counter and walked to the bag of pellets sitting on the inert feed lift. "Just let me throw a couple of scoops of this feed in for the left-hand pens, too," she said.

Keahi looked confused. "I thought Tutu's feeding system took care of that in a snap."

Saffron shrugged, "The other side works great, but this side's stuck." She patted the bag of feed on the lift.

Keahi stepped close to her, reaching around for the crank. She smelled a hint of orange as he drew near. He took the crank and set his strength against it.

The crank held firm for two breaths then gave under what Saffron could tell was enormous pressure and spun free. The crank turned, the belts rotated, and the lift rose, raising the lid on the feed bin as the bag tipped and poured into it. The lid closed as the empty bag rode back down the other side of the lift and ended up where it had begun.

Keahi gestured to the pipe. "Give it a try," he said.

Saffron stepped to the crank on the bottom corner of the feed bin and turned it. Pellets rattled into the pipes and poured into the feeders. She smiled her thanks to him, trying not to look too long at his strong hands.

"That is going to save me so much time!" Saffron smiled at him.

Keahi retrieved the eggs from the counter, and together they walked back to the house, chatting about Mano's designs.

She locked up, then climbed in as he opened the door to his steel-gray SUV.

BERNADETTE WAS DELIGHTED to receive the eggs. "If you have enough, I'd buy five dozen a day."

Five dozen? Saffron couldn't imagine that many egg recipes, but she promised she'd bring some more by as she got them. Truth be told, she'd figured out what the avocado-colored fridge was for, and why Uncle Beau had stockpiled egg cartons like some people hoard gold bars. She was already up to her eyeballs in eggs. The spare fridge was already full, and her own egg consumption was not particularly impressive. She was glad to be giving a little back to the cafe where they'd made her so welcome.

They drove back through town, down Holoholo Street, and across the bridge. The palms cast stripes of shadow on the car as they drove out of Maika'i a few miles, then joined a line of cars turning onto a small road that headed toward the mountains.

"Popular place," Saffron said.

"The best luau on the island. People come up from Honolulu, down from the North Shore, we're full every night."

It took a few minutes to park and weave through the sea of cars. Walking under the big arch that held the "Laki Luau" sign. Saffron wondered what that meant.

Keahi seemed to know what she was thinking. "Laki means lucky," he said. "Lucky Luau."

Saffron was feeling pretty lucky to be there. The arch was supported by two enormous tikis, and torches lighted their way in. The grounds were covered with blossoms, and the air had the sweet smell of ginger and jasmine.

Saffron stopped to watch a Fijian man with a quick wit and

bright smile husk and shred a coconut in twenty seconds. She eyed a little shop with flowing island fashions. She tasted hand-pounded poi and took three samples before Keahi scooped her a banana leaf full to eat as they walked along the paths between the traditional huts and stone buildings representing different Polynesian cultures.

Everyone waved or called out to Keahi as they explored. One woman, in particular, drew their attention.

Keahi's smile widened as he walked over to her. The most remarkable thing about her was the glow of gentle humor on her face. The next most remarkable thing was her size. The woman filled as much space as two of Keahi, and she sat in a wheelchair flanked by two big men. She had a presence to match her size, and the word that came to Saffron was *regal*. Her hand moved, rhythmically petting a fluffy little creature on her lap.

As they approached Saffron saw with surprise that the creature was a chicken.

White and fluffy, the chicken was covered in what looked more like fur than feathers. It had a full poof on its head that made it appear to be wearing an extravagant hat. It sat perfectly still, purring at its owner's attention.

"You like chickens." The woman said, and Saffron could tell it was a command, not a question.

"I do." She said.

Keahi smiled. "Saffron has a pet chicken in her kitchen right now," he said.

The Empress' face drew upwards in delight. She reached forward and took Saffron's hand in both of hers. "We are friends." It was another command.

The bird on her lap was obviously perturbed that she had stopped petting it. It gave a shrill honk of disapproval.

Immediately, the Empress released Saffron's hand and

resumed petting, murmuring, "it's okay, manamea." The chicken lay down again.

"She's very needy," the Empress apologized.

"I understand. My chicken, Tikka, has strong feelings, too," Saffron said.

"Chickens see the world differently. They can focus on the important," the Empress said.

"You know, I was reading about that," Saffron said, "and they really do. Their eyes are different than ours, and they can move them independently."

"Yes," the Empress said, "they have different cones in their eyes some are UV cones that allow them to see many more colors than we can, and better tell between shades and reflectivity."

The last word was said with great care, as if the Empress had practiced it. Something had sparked in Saffron. She had felt a kinship with the hens, a connection, and now the feeling was stronger. They saw color differently, and so did she. Although she was sure that her eyes didn't necessarily show her things in the UV spectrum, she and the chickens both saw more than other people did.

The Empress went on, "and did you know that one of their eyes is used for focusing on things that are nearby and the other for focusing on things that are far away? They have different vision in each."

"I didn't know that," Saffron hadn't read the whole chapter yet.

"That's why they look at you with one eye and cock their heads like that," the Empress said.

"What's her name?" Saffron asked.

"Her name is Princess." As soon as Saffron heard it, she realized that it couldn't have been anything else.

Princess was a striking white against the Empress' bold purple outfit.

"Your dress is beautiful," Saffron said.

The Empress smiled graciously but held up a hand. "Thank you. Not a dress, though. A puletasi. And if you see people wearing just this part," she patted the skirt, "it is an ie lavalava, or an ie."

"EEE-eh," Saffron tried out the word, and the Empress and Keahi both smiled their approval.

The Empress looked so comfortable. Saffron realized that her own clothes were less than ideal for the island climate. The tailored top clung to her, and the leggings captured the heat. On a DC evening that was often a benefit, but here it was beginning to be a real detriment. She ran a hand across her forehead, where beads of sweat had appeared. Even her favorite boots felt bulky and confining.

Looking around, she saw that most people were wearing tees and shorts with flip-flops. Many of them wore bright, breezy aloha shirts, and even from behind her sunglasses, Saffron could see that their shirts were in vibrant tones of red, blue, purple, and orange. Her own outfit was perfectly coordinated shades of gray. She was overdressed and under-hued.

She envied the Empress' puletasi. It was flowing and royal purple, with a deeper purple banana leaf design across the blouse-like top and along the bottom of the ie. It set off the Empress' silver hair, piled atop her head like a crown. The little chicken was purring happily now, its thrumming rhythm keeping time with its owner's large and graceful hand.

"It is beautiful," she said again.

The Empress leaned her great bulk close to Saffron, "and it's comfortable." She winked. It was as if she'd read Saffron's mind. "Maybe you could use something a little more comfortable?" The woman nodded toward Saffron's shoes.

Saffron liked the Empress.

"Beautiful girl like you could wear anything and be lovely," the Empress smiled at her. "Your hair is like an island sunset, and your smile is radiant. And such graceful softness."

The praise made Saffron smile even more. Too often, she worried about the fact that she was not a dainty, willowy person. She had always been strong and curvy, and it was sometimes difficult to see her own beauty when Trish and the rest of DC belonged to the cult of thinness and worshipped jutting collarbones and small frames.

That was not the case here. The admiration in the Empress' eyes was unmistakable. As Saffron glanced at Keahi, her cheeks flushed. He had the same look in his eyes. She felt beautiful reflected in their eyes.

"Are you in the show?" she asked the Empress.

Keahi interrupted, "the Empress *is* the show," he said with a broad grin. "She sings the closing number, and it is so ono. You're going to love it."

The Empress just smiled, obviously pleased by the praise.

"You'd better get some good seats, or you won't be able to hear me," the Empress said, her eyes wide. The look that passed between her and Keahi told Saffron that she was teasing.

"We'll be right up front," Keahi promised as they walked away.

They stopped to look over the tiered luau area, with the stage in front and the buffet tables in the back. Between them, scores of wicker chairs and long tables decorated with orchids, torches, and tiki. Behind the stage, tall palms swayed in front of a pink and orange sunset.

"That's the prettiest thing I have ever seen," she said.

"I know what you mean," Keahi said. Saffron blushed when she realized that he was looking at her. "Come on, I'll show you backstage."

She liked how he walked confidently through the "Employees Only" door, and she felt a little rush of importance, too, as they entered. Backstage, people were in all sorts of states of readiness, from a striking girl in full hula dress to a lost-looking teen wearing leaves around one calf and carrying an armful of costume pieces.

"Sione! Don't be late onstage again!" Keahi was obviously ribbing the kid.

"I can't find my mom! She's supposed to have the rest of my stuff!" Sione wove his way off through the performers.

The energy backstage was exciting. Beautiful women, the age Saffron's mother would be now, were helping each other with elaborate headpieces and chattering.

One of them looked up and called out to Keahi in Hawaiian. The way he ducked his head told Saffron that she'd said something about his date. The woman came over and kissed him on the cheek, then she slipped beautiful ginger lei from her neck and slipped it around Saffron's neck, kissing her on the cheek, as well.

"Aloha," she said, "We are glad you're here. Keahi hasn't brought a girl around here in a long time."

Saffron laughed nervously and caught an apologetic gaze from Keahi.

"Your uncle came nearly every night there at the end," the woman said. "Such a good man."

Saffron was about to respond when a howl broke the silence. Several good-looking young men, who were inking complex designs on each other's backs, were calling out to Keahi. From their raucous laughter, Saffron knew they were commenting on her.

The woman scolded them as she went back to the other ladies, and they quieted down a bit. A little girl, sitting like a princess in a stunning yellow lavalava, grinned up at Saffron as Keahi took her hand and led her through the sea of color and voices. It was an event grander than Saffron had ever planned, and she was dazzled by it all.

"I can't believe you all do this every night," she said. "There are so many performers!"

Keahi smiled, "It's a lot of fun, most nights."

One of the young men called to them. "Keahi! Come finish this! We need your surgeon's steady hand, and I've got to do the preshow." He held out the pencil he was using to draw the design on his friend. Keahi looked at Saffron.

She waved him away, curious about the surgeon remark. "Go! Absolutely. I can entertain myself for a few minutes." He smiled gratefully and went over to them. Saffron watched a moment as he took the pencil and began to move his hand in a circle. An intricate pattern appeared below his pencil, bold lines that made Saffron ache to know their meaning.

Finally, she left him to finish and wandered through the performers. Several yards into the staging area, she smelled the enticing aroma of kalua pork.

She couldn't help but follow her nose. The scent hung thick and rich in the air. Just past racks of costumes, Saffron saw a doorway. Bamboo fences stretched a few yards from the doorway to a wide field of cooking pits. Employees were shuttling whole pigs back and forth from the leaf-lined depressions.

Saffron stood in the shadow of the doorway and watched for a moment. The heat from the pits wafted over along with the delectable scent. She was melting. Her outfit may have looked good, but it was, she saw, completely impractical here.

The men and women moving the pigs from the pits were laughing, talking. They seemed more than comfortable, though they were working hard. Saffron envied their roomy shirts, their flowy dresses. Everyone was so efficient, so cheerful, as they went about the heavy work, that when she heard the sour voice from the other side of the bamboo fence, Saffron was momentarily jarred.

"I guess it's regret," the voice said. Saffron recognized the timbre of it. She peered through the fence and froze when she saw Lani. Saffron didn't mean to listen, but she didn't move away, either. Lani was on the phone, tucked in the corner of the fence where she apparently thought no one could hear her.

"I didn't mean to. I was really just angry," Lani paused, "*hurt*. Yes. Hurt is the word. It was only the night before that he told me he loved me and even though we didn't have much time left, we'd spend it together."

Saffron's heart was pounding. *Regret*. What was it that Lani regretted? Saffron knew what she'd hear before Lani spoke again.

"I just miss him. I hate knowing that he'll never come knocking on my door again. I hate that we can't walk on the beach together," Lani was crying, and Saffron took a step back, feeling intrusive. But Lani's next words froze her blood.

"No, I don't think I left any evidence." A pause. "Of course I haven't told anyone. I'm not stupid." There was a pause while the other person on the line spoke, "Yes, I'm sad. But Bud was who he was. We both know I only gave him what he deserved. I loved him, but I'm not pretending that he wasn't a cheat and a liar. He had it coming. Someone had to do it." Another pause, "that's right. If I hadn't done it, someone else would have. He's been asking for it for a long, long time."

Saffron wanted to hear more, but at the same time, she didn't want to listen to anymore. She felt sick and weak. Had Lani killed Bud?

"Jail?" Lani was saying, "I don't even know if I would live through a trial." And then she was pleading, "Please, promise me you won't say anything. Not to anybody. Please."

The insistent beat of drums started up somewhere behind Saffron. The show would be starting soon. She had to go find Keahi and pretend that nothing was wrong. But now, at least, she had reason to believe that Bud's death had not actually been her fault. She knew, too, that she was going to have to prove it.

. . .

Keahi was waiting for her when she found her way back.

"Getting a jump on the crowds for dinner?" he asked, waving toward the pits.

"That's right. Just smelling it is making me hungry."

They walked together to the dining area, and he seated them at a table for two in the center of the second tier from the stage.

"You can see better from here," he said. The scent of pork and pineapple wafted down to them, and he was on his feet again.

"Let's go," he took her hand and pulled her behind him to the buffet tables at the back. When they got there, she saw why he was rushing. Hundreds of tourists had just entered the dining area. They were all being graced with leis and alohas before wandering, wide-eyed, into the line for food behind Saffron and Keahi.

Saffron piled her plate high with pork and taro rolls, pineapple and fish. She reached for a little cup of poi.

"You won't like it," Keahi said in her ear. She felt the warmth of his breath.

"I love it! I ate a whole banana leaf full of it, remember?"

"That was hand-pounded poi. This is . . . commercial stuff."

She gave him a defiant look and took a cup anyway. He shrugged.

Back at the table, Saffron tried the poi first. Keahi was right. Though she tried to slide it inconspicuously to the side, he noticed.

"I told you so."

"You were right. But this fish is incredible!" Saffron brushed away a bead of sweat from her temple.

"And the way you vacuumed up those malasadas yesterday, I think you'll like the taro rolls."

He was right. Saffron polished off a second one just as the show began. There were dances and songs, and she recognized the performers from backstage. The little princess did a dance that was powerful and graceful at the same time. Halfway through, Saffron removed her sunglasses and slid them into her bag. She couldn't bear to miss a single hue.

Keahi smiled at her and leaned over.

"I like seeing your eyes," he said.

After an hour and a half, Saffron sensed a change in the fast-paced show. She could tell the end was coming. That was confirmed when the two big men maneuvered the Empress' wheelchair out onto the stage.

In the flickering light of the torches, the Empress' silver hair gleamed. Her kind eyes were shadowed. The chicken still on her lap, she petted it in time with the rising beat of the drums from the side of the stage.

She began to sing.

Her voice was rich and full, the sounds of the unfamiliar words bright and dancing in the warm night air. She sang with a smile, and though Saffron didn't know the words, the meaning of the song was clear: it was a song of friendship and love, of family.

As it went on, more voices joined in. As if spontaneously, the men beside the Empress began to add deep, rumbling harmony. The drummers joined, softly at first, and then Saffron realized that some of the sound was coming behind her.

The servers at the buffet table were singing, too, and so was Keahi. Even a few members of the audience sang. At that moment, Saffron wished desperately that she knew the words, so she could have lent her voice to the exquisite harmonies that were reverberating around her. Even without singing, though, she was swept up and carried along on the song like a shell in the tide. She closed her eyes.

When she opened them, the Empress was gone, and the crowds were swarming out the gates.

"How did you like it?" Keahi sat across from Saffron at their front-row table and watched her expectantly.

"It was . . ." Saffron started to say *awesome*, then switched to *breathtaking*, then stopped altogether. She had no words for the spectacular feasts—culinary and visual—she'd just experienced. She felt aglow, tingling with the rhythms of the drums, the lilt of the languages, the colors, the textures of the costumes, and the poetry that was island dancing.

It was so different from anything she'd known before. The word *dance* didn't even seem to do it justice, because until that night, the word had conjured for her images of gliding figures in a formal ballroom and slouching middle-schoolers rocking from foot to foot and trying not to look at each other. *Dance* had, until that night, been a bride-and-groom boxstep, a casual swaying at a club with flashing lights, not this marriage of grace and passion, this spectacle of light and skill and precision that set her alight with awe.

"Spectacular," she finally said. "It's somehow more than a show. More than just dancing." It sounded childish when she said it, as if the words were a kindergartner's attempt at explaining the theory of relativity, but she had no other way to say it. She looked down, embarrassed.

When she looked up, Keahi was studying her with a new light in his eyes. "That's a great way to put it," he said. "It *is* more than a show. It's our stories and our families and ourselves all wrapped up in movements and colors and beats." He looked at her without speaking, his eyes burning with unsaid words. "Not many people get that."

Saffron heard her name. She turned to see the Empress.

"That was so beautiful," Saffron blurted, "I could listen to you sing all day."

The Empress's eyes crinkled. "I've got a gift for you," she said. Next to Princess on her lap was a bag from the little shop Saffron had seen earlier. She lifted it and handed it to Saffron.

Saffron pulled from it a skirt and top just like the Empress', only these were made of a vibrant jade fabric with designs in a darker seaweed color in bands around the bottom of the skirt and the bottom of the top.

Saffron beamed and tried to remember the right word, "a puletasi?" she said.

"It will be more comfortable for you around here. Trust me."

Saffron was beginning to feel more comfortable around here all the time.

THEY WERE STILL TALKING about the show when Keahi took her home. He got out of the car, and without formally deciding to, they were drawn toward the dark shore and the glistening ocean.

They walked along the beach, talking and looking out at the ocean. Saffron loved the rich hues of the night. Violets and crimsons touched the sky that everyone else saw as plain black. The shadows held rich umber and deep jade tones, and the day's bright aqua ocean had become a vivid, undulating sapphire. A full moon exactly the color of the Empress' chicken glinted off the water, and the breakers out on the reef sounded like distant heartbeats.

The bulk of the lava rock point loomed above them. It was darker than the night—a deep ebony cliff that rose and stretched away out into the ocean. As they neared it, Saffron reached out and felt it with her fingers as Keahi rolled his pant legs up and waded into the water. The point was sharp and pitted, jagged under her fingertips. The water hissed as it broke against the long point.

She wandered away from him, over the sand, silver in the moonlight, and toward the dense undergrowth at the base of the point.

She had been here in the day, and it seemed a dead end. But now, she was intrigued to see, the full moon illuminated a narrow passage into the black rock, behind a stubby bush.

"Keahi!" she called, "look at this!"

He walked over and peered at it. "Huh." He said. "I've never seen that before."

"Let's check it out," she took his hand, glad to have an excuse to, and tugged, but Keahi didn't move.

"I'm not sure," he said.

"Why?" Saffron was not used to being impulsive, and she liked the feeling. She didn't want to lose it so quickly. She let go of his hand and pushed past the springy bush, walking a few steps into the passage.

"Be careful," his voice was warning, "Some of these are lava tubes that go straight to the ocean. They fill up with water instantly if the tide hits them right."

A delicious thrill tingled up Saffron's spine. She took a few more steps. The moonlight didn't reach this far in, and there was perfect darkness ahead. She glanced back at Keahi, who was standing, shining, in the moonlight behind her.

The rough sides of the tube caught at her arms, and she turned back.

"Hold on," there was resignation in Keahi's voice, and she heard him move in behind her at the same moment that the tube was lit by the dazzling flashlight on his cell phone.

The tube curved sharply ahead, toward the ocean. Their hands found each other again, half from attraction and half from, Saffron guessed, anxiety.

It was quiet inside the passage, the roar of the waves a dull hush. The floor was knobbly, and Saffron had to step carefully around strange protrusions. She was glad to be wearing her boots. The walls were narrow, barely wide enough for them to proceed single-file, and sharp with waves of rough black stone. At one point, the tube dropped sharply before leveling out again. Keahi cleared his throat as they worked their way down the slope, evidently anxious about the adventure.

After the drop, they came to a place where the tube split and Keahi nudged her to the right.

"The ocean's the other way," he said, his voice tight, "this one's less likely to get us drowned."

He was right. After a hundred meters, Saffron saw a pale light ahead. The two emerged onto a secluded beach edged by the point they'd just come through and another, smaller point jutting out on the south of the crescent-shaped stretch of sand.

Saffron gasped. In the moonlight, it was glorious. Tall palms edged a freshwater stream that flowed out into the sea—picturing it, Saffron realized it must be the little stream that ran by the egg house. Flower-laden shrubs filled in below palms, making a solid wall of foliage edging the beach.

Keahi stood and stared, "I've lived here all my life, and I had no idea that this existed." He said.

They walked along the beach together. Saffron saw a dark shape ahead, high on the bank, and paused.

"Is that an animal?" she asked.

Keahi nodded. "It's a monk seal." He shined the flashlight toward it. A lovely mound of sleek brown fur lifted limpid eyes to gaze at them. He switched off his flashlight, and for a moment, everything was dark. Saffron saw the seal lower its head again.

"It's sleeping?"

"Yep. Probably just had a big meal, and now she's hanging out waiting for the sun to come warm her up tomorrow."

They skirted around it, leaving the big animal plenty of room. Beyond the seal, more shapes scattered across the sand. They moved forward to inspect them.

The shapes became clear as they approached. Plastic cups, a vase, and a crushed wicker basket with bold lettering: Oceanside Café.

Bud's Beachy Breakfast Basket had been found.

"What is this doing out here?" Keahi asked, gathering the items up. Something, probably the seal, had made off with any edible contents besides a plastic container of spoiled fruit chunks that lay scraped but unopened beside the basket.

A checkered picnic cloth lay rumpled but still spread out, its corners anchored by rocks and one side pulled askew by a passing animal or the wind. Atop it, a cutting board and thermos sat ready for use.

"I think Bud was going on a picnic the morning he died," she said. This must have been why he decided to bring the bolts to her. He knew about this place and had planned a rendezvous here early that morning.

The abandoned picnic seemed forlorn to Saffron. She didn't want to see it tonight, not when everything had been so bright. She took Keahi's hand and pulled him back up the beach, past the seal.

"I'll come out here tomorrow and clean it up," she said. "Let's not worry about it tonight."

Keahi didn't seem to mind. He sat on the beach and patted the sand beside him. Saffron dropped down, took off her boots and socks and dug her toes into the still-warm sand.

They watched the water together for a long time. The somber overtone didn't leave Saffron. She tried to think of a change of subject.

"So tell me about your hands," she finally said, reaching over to trace the line of his knuckles as he rested an arm across his bent knees.

"My hands?"

"Right. Your hands. Surgeon's hands?"

She felt him tense under her touch and pull away slightly. She knew that reaction. It was pain.

"I was a surgeon," he said, "back on the mainland."

This surprised her. "A surgeon?"

"Right," his voice, usually so warm, was distant now. "Pediatric surgery."

Saffron tried to picture the big man in a hospital somewhere. "Why did you stop practicing."

Keahi breathed a long, deep sigh. "I'm not sure you want to know that."

Saffron considered a moment. "I do." She thought she might like to know everything about him.

"I made a mistake and paid for it with a child's life."

Saffron felt a stab of horror. She looked out over the water, trying to think of what to say. Surely this happened to lots of doctors, but it wasn't something she'd ever dealt with. A bad day at *Every Detail Events* ended with a high dry-cleaning bill and a loss of deposit, not a funeral.

"Boy or girl?" Saffron wondered if she should leave the subject alone, but just as she liked physical things to be in their right places, she also liked her thoughts in the right places. She didn't like knowing only part of a story. There were too many ways to misinterpret.

"A little boy. Five years old." Keahi was quiet for a moment. "I like that you asked that," he said, drawing with a finger in the sand between them. The waves nibbled at Saffron's toes. "Everyone always asks what happened, as if they forget there was someone it *happened to*." Saffron didn't say anything. "He was five. Had just lost his first tooth." Keahi looked out over the waves. "He was so proud of that tooth."

The waves filled the silence whenever he stopped speaking.

"He had a tumor on his spine. I wasn't even worried about

it—it looked simple enough on the scans. I never even prepared his parents for the possibility that . . ." He trailed off, and they watched the sea a long time, "for the possibility of what happened."

Saffron didn't press further. She could feel the raw edge of emotion still in him. She had lived with an edge like that, and she didn't want to make it any harder.

"I'm glad you told me," she said.

"Well, now you know. No surprises." Keahi replied.

Chapter Nine

Mano was on Saffron's lanai the next morning with a box of malasadas, which they devoured with a cup of tea. The donuts were covered in crumbly coarse sugar, and they used little square papers from the bakery to keep their hands from getting too sticky while they ate.

He'd come with some ideas about new feeders and, Saffron was sure, to fish for information about how the date had gone last night.

Saffron smiled as she thought of the evening she'd spent with Keahi. The soft wind through the monkeypod branches above the lanai reminded her of the breeze on the secret beach last night, and how she and Keahi had talked until nearly one o'clock before making their way back through the lava tube. Mano listened to the account with rapt attention, brushing his fingertips across his silvery-white beard.

Hawaii's colors were soft this morning. Saffron noticed that she'd left her sunglasses inside in her purse, and she didn't bother to retrieve them. Instead, she allowed the early morning light to reveal every island shade to her.

Other things were different, too. This morning she had

sorted through her suitcase and finally admitted to herself that she'd brought nothing suitable to wear in Hawaii. Her slacks, skirts, and even her jeans were all heavy and dull. She'd extracted one of the muumuus from the closet, slipped it on, and felt like she was home. Now, the light material caught the morning breeze and cooled her immediately.

The breeze also caught one of the papers from a malasada and blew it off the lanai.

"I'll get it," Saffron hopped over the railing and tracked it down before looking up triumphantly.

But Mano wasn't pleased with her quickness. He wasn't grateful she'd retrieved the paper. He looked panicky.

"Come back up here, Ipo," his voice was sharp. One hand was tightly clamped over his silvery beard, and his eyes showed alarm.

Surprised, Saffron climbed back up onto the lanai. He pointed accusingly at her bare feet.

"Never walk near the lanai in bare feet," he scolded.

"Why not?"

"Scorpions."

"Scorpions?"

"That's right. They live under the boards, and sometimes they come out to catch the bugs in the grass like that. Always wear shoes. There are a lot of them down near the egg house. They're mostly out at night. Never even go down there at night in slippahs. Always wear boots or sneakers. And take a black light so you can see them."

"A black light?"

"That's right." He strode into the house and rustled around a bit. When he came back out, he was holding what looked like an ordinary flashlight. When he switched it on, though, it had two beams: a regular one and, when he pushed it again, an eerie purple one.

"Helps you see 'em. Scorpions shine under it." The roosters

set to crowing as Mano spoke. "But," he heaved a sigh, "I shouldn't be so worried. That bunch will probably keep the scorpions pretty well cleared out."

"Thanks for the warning, though," Saffron said. She didn't like the thought of stepping on a scorpion. "And it's good to know that the roosters serve some purpose besides keeping me from getting any sleep."

"Have you caught any of 'em?"

"A few. I have them in the egg house."

"That's all right. Just keep them as far as you can from the hens, or they'll fight. Did you put them in those far pens?"

Saffron nodded. The end pens on each side had wooden sides so the occupants couldn't see the chickens beside them.

"Good. That should keep them under control for a while. But you'll be wanting to advertise to get rid of some of them pretty soon."

Saffron nodded, "I'll make up a flyer."

"Now, I need to get back to town. Lotta carving to do today."

"Thank you for coming out."

"You're seeing a lot of the Kekoa kane lately," he said as he headed down toward the beach. Saffron guessed that that meant Kekoa men. She nodded.

"Laki me," she said with a smile.

The visit was a pleasant diversion. She hoped it would help her focus on the cleaning she still had to do. The more she saw of the dazzling Hawaiian scenery, the dingier the little bungalow looked. She needed to get it shined up.

Keahi had given her a quick hug before climbing into his car last night. She had carried the warmth of it with her into this morning. He had to work all day today, but he promised to come for a swim tomorrow morning, so she just had to fill twenty or so more hours before she got to see him again. Even after Mano left, she found that she was still too excited to settle into cleaning.

So she took a drive.

She stopped along Holoholo Street at a little building with bright fashions in the windows. A trendy twenty-something with aqua hair helped her pick out several new sets of clothes—comfy shorts and tees, a breezy top with butterfly sleeves, an aloha shirt, and some cargo capris. She bought a beachy wrap dress in a peacock shade that made her pink skin glow and her strawberry hair shine. She got a new bathing suit and a couple pairs of flip-flops. *Slippahs*, she corrected herself. The teal-topped owner of the shop, Kaila Monique, bundled it all into a reusable shopping bag sewn from scraps of bright aloha fabrics and invited Saffron back anytime.

Saffron wondered on the way to her rental car if she had spent too much on clothes she'd probably only wear for a few weeks, but she let the sweet scent of plumeria carry the thought away.

She didn't head back to the egg farm. Instead, she drove up along the North Shore.

Even from the highway, she couldn't help but watch the waves. They were mesmerizing, like nothing she'd ever seen before. The waves on her beach were tempered by a reef that Keahi had told her went about 300 feet out from the shore.

These waves were unbridled, rolling all the way in at their full strength. She nearly got lost in their undulations, the high swells that dwarfed the tiny surfers. Luckily, she pulled her eyes back to the road just in time to see Officer Bradley sitting in his patrol car beside a coconut stand. He gave her a stern glare as she drove by, but didn't pursue.

She drove until she found a little town called Haleiwa, where she had a sensational shave ice, and in a moment of audacity, allowed them to douse it with stripes of sweetened condensed milk. The result was a decadent, sweet concoction that she knew she was going to crave again.

Driving back, she kept her eyes dutifully on the road, but the ocean called her. Finally, when a wide stretch of beach opened up on the shoulder, she pulled off and parked the rental car. Saffron extracted her sunblock and smoothed it over her peachy cheeks, watching her tawny freckles disappear and reappear as she worked the thick lotion into her skin. When she was covered, she got out and walked to the sea.

The waves danced in front of her, and she was reminded of the performance last night. The ocean had that same power and grace, that same passion, that had been so evident to her in the dances of Polynesia. The waves were crystal blue, and the seafoam curled on them like jewelry.

There were a lot of surfers and boogie boarders, playing in the waves. Saffron watched a group of surfers paddle out—way out—and wait, riding out the smaller swells until, by practice and some innate sixth sense, they all knew that a good wave was coming. They pulled themselves up, and she watched as they rode the water toward the shore.

One of them was exceptionally skilled. He wore a vibrant green and black bodysuit, and Saffron kept her eye on him. He didn't just ride, he navigated the wave, working his board to the best position, cresting the wave, and cutting a straight line down the slope of moving water, leaving a trail of white wake behind him.

When the wave played out, he turned and paddled out again. Saffron sat in the warm sand and watched him conquer wave after wave. He rode inside the curls, on top of them, cut through them. His board was like an extension of himself. Saffron couldn't imagine being that in control on the unpredictable water. She'd never really liked large bodies of water, partly because you never knew what to expect. Too much chaos, she supposed.

But this surfer made the process seem neat and tidy, made it seem controlled and knowable.

Finally, the surfers began to make their way in, and Saffron turned to watch some young kids playing in the smaller waves near the shore.

"Hey!" a cheerful voice surprised Saffron. She turned and looked up into the dripping face of Bud's great-grandson, Nik. "How's my cousin?"

Saffron blinked. He was wearing a green and black wetsuit. It was him that she'd been watching. She'd had her eyes glued to him for the last hour. She pushed away a wave of embarrassment, telling herself that he wouldn't know that.

He did know. "You were diggin' my moves." He said, "I did that last pipeline just for you."

"You're amazing," she said, shaking her head. "It's like magic."

"That's what the judges all say," it didn't surprise her that he had competed. His skill was obvious.

"Do you surf professionally?"

He shook his head, "Not anymore."

"Why not?"

"Because competition with yourself brings out your best. Competition with other people brings out your worst."

Saffron sensed that there was more truth in that than she realized.

"Some words just shouldn't go together, you know?" Nik went on, "like Great Depression or military intelligence or professional surfer." He flopped down in the sand next to her and stretched, closing his eyes. He tipped backward and lay there sunning. She couldn't imagine the amount of effort it must take, working the water the way he had.

"I did compete some, but I only ever did it so that Grandpa Bud could brag about it," Nik's eyes were closed. "He loved to watch me surf."

Despite the blazing sun, a chill shook Saffron. Bud. Lani. Regret.

"I'm sorry," she said, though she wasn't sure which of her thoughts she was apologizing for.

Nik didn't open his eyes. "Thanks."

"I just regret not being there for him. At the end." Nik said.

That word again. *Regret*. That was the word Lani had used last night on the phone.

"Nik," she said, carefully, "did Bud date Lani?"

Nik opened one eye, gave her a long look, and then closed it again. "Oh, yeah."

"They were serious?"

"As serious as he ever was." Saffron didn't know what that meant but suspected it had to do with all the dates Bud had gone on. "Grandpa was quite the ladies' man."

Saffron remembered Mano saying so, too. Only, there was a different tone in his voice.

"It's kind of remarkable that you know your great-grandpa so well," she said thoughtfully, "I didn't even know my grandparents." *Or my father*, she thought but didn't say.

"He raised me, you know, and my twin sister, Naia."

"Really?"

"Yep. When our parents split up, my mom got remarried. Her new husband didn't want us around, so we lived with my dad. That was a rough time. We didn't have anything. Any money he made went to his various addictions. We didn't have clothes that fit, or," a touch of bitterness made his voice rough, "even food sometimes. Then my dad got put in jail, and we came back here to live with his dad until he was out. But then my grandpa died of a heart attack, so Great-Grandpa Bud took us in. When my dad got out of prison, Grandpa Bud said no, we weren't going with him. He knew about those rough times. Dad didn't put up a fight. Last I knew he was in LA."

There wasn't any sadness in Nik's voice. "Grandpa Bud was a great parent."

"Where's your sister now?"

Nik sighed, and now Saffron saw the sadness. "I don't know. Vegas, I think. She was supposed to be coming back when her husband came back, but he came without her, and she hasn't been returning my calls for a couple of months." She could hear that he was worried. "I flew out there, looked everywhere I could think of, but I never found anything that led me to her."

"But your brother-in-law isn't worried?" Saffron asked.

Nik grunted. "He keeps saying she'll be back. Sometimes I think that's why he's hanging around here—he knows she'll eventually come home, and when she does, he'll be here. Then she'll be back under his control."

"What's the deal with him, anyway?" Saffron asked, "Why is he here?"

"He wants the house. And the nest egg."

This sparked Saffron's memory. Bud had said something about that the day she'd met him. "Nest egg?"

"Yeah, Grandpa has been telling Naia and I since we were little that he had an inheritance for us. He called it his nest egg and said if we had it we'd never be left with nothing again. I think the thought brought him as much comfort as it did us."

Saffron felt anxious, thinking of the rough Derek, "will your brother-in-law get it?"

"It doesn't exist. Or maybe Grandpa Bud was talking about the house. We can sell that for a pretty good profit. Anyway, the nest egg's certainly not money. All of Grandpa Bud's account balances added up to a hundred and sixty-eight dollars. Derek was pretty upset."

"Not you?"

Nik looked at her, his clear eyes searching her face. "I'm a lot more upset that Grandpa died than that he didn't leave a nest egg."

Looking into his jade eyes, Saffron realized that she hadn't used her sunglasses all day. The bright water, the golden sand, this seemed a strange place for heavy topics.

Nik must have thought so, too, because he switched the subject. "Are you hungry? Let's go get poke!"

Saffron had seen the poke bowls advertised. Chunks of raw fish with various sauces and vegetables served over rice, she was intrigued but nervous about trying them. Still, Nik's enthusiasm was invigorating, and she wanted to spend more time with him. She tried not to admit to herself that she also wanted to hear more about Bud's involvement with Lani.

They walked to a little truck down the beach and sat at a table under an umbrella to eat. Saffron's bowl was heaped with rice, sliced onions, and chunks of avocado and translucent pink ahi. This was why she hadn't tried it yet. She couldn't get over her aversion to raw fish. She started by scooping a bite of plain white rice as Nik dug into one of his two heaping bowls. The truck had given them each a little container of pineapple, and she attacked it next, savoring the bright juices in her mouth. Nik pushed his serving toward her.

"Here, have mine, too."

"You don't like pineapple?" Saffron was incredulous. Maybe living here you got used to it.

"I'm allergic to it," Nik said, "I like the taste, but my mouth and throat swell up like a blowfish."

"I'm sorry," Saffron said. She'd hate to have to miss out on this.

After a few more bites, Saffron glanced at Nik, who had almost demolished his first bowl of poke. She was ready to try it now. She stabbed a piece of fish and popped it into her mouth.

It was different than she thought, the texture firmer than

she expected. The flavor of the brown sauce and the crunch of the green onions contrasted nicely with the meaty fish. She took another bite.

"How can this be so good?" she asked, smiling as Nik plowed through his rice.

"What do you mean?"

"It's raw fish!"

"You're in Hawaii," he said, "paradise. The sea and the land just provide sweet, delicious sustenance!"

She laughed. He may have something there.

NIK WAS BACK on the water, and Saffron was back in her car, driving South, back toward Maika'i. Glancing at herself in the rearview mirror, Saffron saw that her cheeks were glowing from the sun and the laughter. Nik was so carefree. So *fun*. She hadn't been with someone like him in a long time. He also carried the hollowness of recent grief, and Saffron identified with that, too.

Saffron let her mind wander back to that afternoon behind the shed. Bud had been killed. The details of his death made her feel sure of it. And even though no one else thought there was any reason to investigate the death of one very old man, she was going to. For Nik, for Bud, for herself. It would bother her for the rest of her life otherwise.

She thought about the people she had met. There was Mano, whose girl had, apparently, at some time, had a fling with Bud. But Mano and Bud were friends, weren't they? Why would Mano wait so long to take revenge?

Lani was the front suspect right now in Saffron's mind. She had as much as admitted her guilt.

And now there was Derek. Had the rumored nest egg driven him to murder?

Saffron felt, suddenly, very alone in this new place. She wanted to be back at the bungalow with Tikka purring in the corner. But that wouldn't help her find Bud's killer.

In order to figure out who had killed Bud, she needed to figure out what he had done that morning, who he had planned to meet on the secret beach with the picnic basket.

Maybe the police had asked some of those questions. Ahead was the ragged roadside shack that sold cold coconuts to tourists, and Saffron was pleased to see the patrol car was still there. She pulled over and walked up to the window. Officer Bradley looked up at her.

"Come to turn yourself in?" he asked.

"I throw myself on the mercy of the law," Saffron teased back. He was so detached, so cold. She didn't want to spend any more time with him than she had to. She asked bluntly what he knew about the day Bud died.

"It doesn't seem to have been a strange day for him. He was out the night before, stopped at home to change and shower. Nik said that he left before the sun was up. Walked out to your place. Must have just been working too hard. Died of a heart attack—well, died because the heart attack stopped his heart and he didn't get enough oxygen. So I guess he suffocated."

"But there was no autopsy?"

"Nope. He was really old, Miss. I know it was a shock to you, finding him and everything, but we've all been expecting it for a while. And I've got *real* crimes to solve."

"But isn't it just *possible* that someone killed him?"

"I've been in law enforcement long enough to know that anything is possible."

Saffron changed her approach. "So what makes you suspect someone? You know, hypothetically?"

"Well, I guess if you're looking at a specific person, you've got a who. Then I guess first of all would be the why. Why would they do it?" he scratched his chin, "Then I guess the how. How was it done? Then the when. When did they have an opportunity?"

"And if you knew those things, then you'd consider it a murder?"

"Well, I'd be more suspicious, anyway."

Just then a beat-up minivan streaked by them on the road. A flashing light in the patrol car signaled that they were going well over the speed limit. Saffron recognized that this ended their conversation. Bradley tipped his hat and sped off after the jalopy, leaving Saffron standing at the coconut stand, staring after him.

CHICKENS SCATTERED as she drove up the dirt lane into the yard. She was finishing off the cold coconut juice she'd bought at the stand when Bradley left. His words still rang in her ears.

Who? Why? How? When? Well, the when was clear. Sometime between the time Bud left his house and that awful moment when Saffron found him.

She climbed out of the car and let herself into the house.

The little chicken family was getting bigger. And louder. Saffron had barely slept last night due to their peeping and scraping, as well as Tikka's incessant obsession with that one spot on her wall.

Saffron grabbed a notepad out of a drawer and sat at the table.

Who? She wrote, then, hating herself for even thinking about it: *Mano*

Why? Jealousy. She looked at it a while, then added a question mark: *Jealousy?*

When? Thursday Morning.

How?

This one was the tricky one, especially without an autopsy. A heart attack. Had Mano scared Bud? Had they fought, causing strain on Bud's heart? And Bradley had mentioned suffocation, too. That seemed odd. She wished she was a doctor, or that she knew one.

But she did know one. And Keahi didn't know what she'd been thinking. She could ask him a simple question. Saffron pulled out her phone and texted Keahi: *Can heart attack cause asphyxiation?*

His response came quickly. *Asking for a friend?*

She half-smiled as she traced the words on her screen's keyboard: *Sure*

This time she had to wait a few minutes for the reply. *Yes. Or asphyxiation can cause a heart attack. You working too hard over there?*

She glanced at her pad, feeling guilty for even asking him when it involved her accusing his tutu of murder. Keahi thought she was the one having the heart attack.

While she tried to think what to write back, her phone pinged with another message.

Symptoms can be different for women. Having any dizziness? Jaw pain? Shortness of breath?

Saffron didn't want him to worry. *No, I'm fine.*

Go to the ER if you're worried. I'll come meet you.

Fine, really. Just curious.

There was a long stretch. She looked at the clock and realized he was at work, probably backstage in all the chaos. She wondered briefly where he would carry his phone when he was in costume.

OK. I'm on in a few. Check on you later?

Sure. Break a leg.

His response had got her thinking. A heart attack could result in asphyxiation or vice versa. It was a chicken and egg problem. That was significant because though it was hard to cause a heart attack, there were many ways to cause asphyxiation. She wrote some down next to *How*.

Smothering
Choking
Exposure to fumes

That was all she could think of for now. She realized that she'd be a terrible murderer. And maybe not such a great detective, either. Imagining Mano performing any of those tasks was absurd.

Still, Saffron knew Bud hadn't died naturally.

She pulled another slip of paper out and wrote again:

Who? Lani

Why? Saffron thought a moment. Bud had been a ladies' man. *Jealousy?* This seemed a common theme in Bud's life.

When? Thursday Morning. This jogged her memory. She *had* seen Lani Thursday morning. At the diner, saying she could kill Bud. A chill went through Saffron. Though she immediately felt foolish. An old woman? A murderer? She imagined trying to explain that to Bradley. He'd laugh her back to the mainland.

But she had heard the woman on the phone. That meant something. Maybe if she could define the *How?* Then she could figure out what.

Saffron jotted down another suspect: Derek. Nik had revealed the motive: Bud's fabled nest egg.

But that probably meant that anyone in line for that nest egg should be a suspect. She wrote Nik and Naia on another piece of paper, even though that was unlikely.

She shoved that aside. Of the three, only Derek had the cruelty to actually go through with it. She knew Nik, and she'd seen his affection for Naia. Surely neither of them would do something so awful.

Derek, though. Of him, she could believe it. She thought of the first time she'd met him, of his sneer. She felt sick as she wondered if he had come to the cafe straight from the farm, stopping for breakfast after he'd killed Bud. And what had Bernadette said after the confrontation? That it was as if Derek had *wanted* people to notice that he was there.

Tikka tapped on, and her babies made a ruckus while they searched around in the sand of the box for spilled treats. They were creating an amazing amount of dust these days. She admitted to herself, reluctantly, that they would need to go out to the egg house soon. They needed more room, and she needed some sleep.

She slid the papers into the notebook in her purse, then went to the closet and pulled out some old work boots she'd found. Slipping them on, she trudged down to the egg house and looked over the pens. There were a dozen pens, six down each side. The first, second, and third pens on the right side of the building were full from the efforts of her early days of chicken-catching. Ten fat hens in each pen. The last pen on either side of the aisle, by the back doors, held roosters. Catching them was tougher, so she had only about a dozen. Mano had told her that if she kept the hens away, she could probably keep the roosters together, and he'd been right—they seemed to get along fine. They did cause a deafening ruckus, though, and she was glad to have them farther from the house. Mano had also said that he'd let people around town know that she had some roosters available.

The rest of the pens were empty, and Saffron looked them over, trying to think which would be best for the little family. She settled on the first pen on the left side. It was right next to the workstation, so she could easily watch Tikka's family while she gathered and washed eggs. She closed the door to the outside run, worrying about predators, and filled up the feeder. She twisted the screw on the water line that started water flowing into the automatic nozzle and made sure it was adjusted low enough that the babies could reach it. Smoothing the sand with a rake one last time, she went up to collect the new tenants.

Tikka crouched again when Saffron reached in to pick her up. She was calm and content on the ride down to the egg house, fluffy and soft in Saffron's arms.

"This is going to give you more room," she explained as she put the chicken in the pen. Tikka tapped at the ground, scratching in the deep sand. Saffron went back to the panicked babies.

They had grown more used to her. Some of them didn't run when she lowered her hand in and caught them gently.

It always surprised her how light and tiny they were under their baby feathers. She loaded them all in a box and carried them down to their mother.

It was nice, seeing the little ones running and flapping their awkward little wings down the length of the pen. Tikka investigated the pen, then found the water. She called to the chicks, and Saffron watched them crowd around the automatic water dispenser and sample it until they'd all had a drink.

Tikka seemed to be watching them, too. When she was satisfied, she visited the feeder, using her alerting chirp to show the brood where to eat. She stepped aside as the chicks crowded in.

Tikka tipped her head and stared at the side of the feeder. She bobbed her head, then struck at it, making the same hollow tapping that she'd loved to make in the brooder box.

Saffron remembered how the Empress had said chickens could see better than humans. Maybe Tikka could see something Saffron couldn't. She thought back to the sand on the counter that Tikka had thought was so fascinating. Like the Empress had said, she and the chicken certainly had differing ideas of what was important. Either way, she hammered on at the side of the feeder while her babies ran in fluttering circles in the big pen. They'd never known such luxury.

A light afternoon rain had begun. It speckled the brown eggs as Saffron carried them back up to the house. Time for some inside chores.

Saffron grabbed a poi malasada and walked back down the hall to the nursery. The donut was sensational, this one filled with a bright pineapple custard. She thought briefly how Nik couldn't have one because of his allergy. No mango, either, he'd said. That seemed like torture, living in Hawaii without being able to enjoy the fruits of the islands.

The nursery seemed soft and quiet in the hush of the rain outside. The cloud cover had dimmed its bright blue walls to pale gray, and it seemed a good time to go through more of the details Uncle Beau had locked away.

The suitcase sat open on the floor, and Saffron sat back down to finish her exploration of its contents. She looked again at the picture of Uncle Beau and Aunt Ila, with Bud and Keahi's grandma.

There was no doubt that they were involved. Glenda's lips on Bud's cheek, his hand on her knee, the light in their eyes. Saffron set it aside.

She tossed a few old programs in the trash and some receipts from the nineties. She put other photos—Beau's and Ila's wedding, Ila with her new baby, in the pile she'd started before with the marriage certificate.

Near the bottom of the case was a manila envelope. Saffron pulled from it a yellowed paper. "ARREST REPORT" was emblazoned across the top in bold letters.

There followed a section with a case number and arresting officer's name, then sections stating the defendant's information, the charges, and an incident description.

Mano was the defendant.

The charge was assault.

The victim was Bud.

Saffron read the incident description with interest. Mano

had apparently attacked Bud as he was leaving a movie theater with Glenda Iona, who Saffron was willing to bet was Keahi's grandma. Mano had left Bud with two cracked ribs, a broken nose, and, Saffron's eyes widened, bruises around the throat from choking. He had threatened to kill Bud. The then-young men had both been detained at the town jail, but only Mano had been charged. Uncle Beau had posted his bail, according to this paperwork.

Saffron let the paper fall to her lap. Well, that took care of the *why* question. What it didn't explain was why *now*.

Chapter Ten

T he nursery shone in the late afternoon light, and Saffron was proud of herself. The bungalow looked more livable every day.

She hauled a massive bag of garbage to the pile outside, where Mano assured her that someone would eventually come to take it away.

Looking over it, she thought of the secret beach and the trash she had meant to go back for. It didn't take her long to make her way down to the beach, and she noted that the late afternoon high tide was lapping at the upper edge of the water line.

She'd just made it to the first curve in the lava tube when she stepped high to avoid a jutting lava protrusion and set her foot back down into water.

Cold seawater sucked her flip-flop off, and she nearly dropped her phone as she shone it ahead into the steeply declining tunnel. Glassy water bounced it back to her. She hopped backward, breathing hard, trying not to imagine what would have happened if she'd gone further and slipped or dropped into the water-filled passage.

Keahi was right. This was no place to be at high tide. The delicious recklessness she'd felt last night had fled, and she scrambled out of the tube as quickly as she could, hopping and rubbing her hands raw trying not to put her bare foot down on the rough floor. She was grateful to emerge onto the soft sand.

Saffron made her way back to the house and got more sturdy shoes. This time she grabbed the flexible diving shoes she'd found in some of Uncle Beau's beach gear. She had an idea about another way to get to the secret beach.

Saffron made her way to the egg house and pushed her way through the bushes behind it. The rain had stopped, but the foliage was slick with droplets, and by the time she reached the stream she was soaked.

That made wading down the stream an easy decision. Though there were places where the dense shrubs on either side of the stream had laced themselves together over it, and though there were downed palm trees to be ducked under or climbed over, Saffron soon found herself splashing out onto the secret beach with feet numb from the cold stream water.

The monk seal was gone, leaving only a trail of churned

sand that led to the water. Saffron followed the path, stopping only to lay her cell phone on a rock, and walked into the ocean. She let its warmth embrace her and floated, clothes and all, in its gentle undulations.

She looked back on the beach as she floated in the surf. It was aglow with gold. She looked back on it as she drifted in the water. There was only one word for it: paradise. And for the first time in her life, a feeling of belonging washed over Saffron, a sense that this place, with its flowers and waves and cultures, was home. She felt protected by the jutting arms of lava rock that shielded this beach, enfolded by their substantial presence. She floated a long time.

When she climbed out, the light was nearly gone. She set about gathering up the remains of Bud's picnic. The basket was beyond repair, so she gathered it, along with the cups and cutting board and wrappers and container of fruit, into the center of the picnic blanket. Removing the rocks from the corners, Saffron tucked it all into a manageable bundle. As she lifted it, a flutter caught her eye.

On the far side of the beach, caught between the trunk of a fallen palm tree and the husk of its coconut, was one last scrap of detritus from the picnic. Saffron could see it was paper, perhaps a napkin? She crossed to it and plucked it from the trunk.

It wasn't a napkin. It was a note. Scrawled in erratic handwriting and streaked with rain and salt spray, the only word Saffron could make out was "Lani."

SAFFRON HAD NO MORE luck with the note when, after she had lugged the bundle back to the house and dumped it on the trash pile then taken a hot shower, she sat peering over it in the bright kitchen.

Was Bud meeting Lani? Was he meeting someone else, who'd left him this note about Lani? What if it was a warning to Bud about Lani? Perhaps Ed had slipped it into the basket to warn Bud about his sister's fury?

One thing was for sure, the note Saffron had hoped would solve the mystery had only served to deepen it. She tucked it in the drawer of her bedside table and curled up in her surfboard sheets exhausted from the hike up the stream bed.

The next morning dawned clear, and Saffron woke to realize that she'd had her first good night's sleep in Hawaii.

She was ready when Keahi showed up at the door with breakfast in hand.

"One of these days, I'll feed you," she said, taking the warm tinfoil packet he offered. "What is it?"

"Honu sandwich," he said, "or at least that's what my mom always called them."

Saffron unwrapped it to find a roll with the corners of a fried egg sticking out of it. "Honu? Is that some kind of fish?"

"The word means sea turtle," he must have read her horrified expression, "no, no, it isn't made of a sea turtle. It just looks like a little turtle, see?" She saw it now, the floppy egg white sticking out and making turtle-like flippers under the dome of the roll.

"Sorry," she said as she took a bite and they began to walk down to the beach.

Keahi's laughter was as warm as the morning sunshine, "I'm always surprised what assumptions people make about other cultures."

Saffron ducked her head. Her cheeks were hot. "I'm sorry. I didn't mean to offend you."

Keahi waved a hand. "No offense. I learned a long time ago that if people don't talk about things they don't understand, then they'll never come to understand them."

"But talking about them reveals my ignorance. I'm always

making missteps and wrong assumptions. There's so much I don't know about Hawaii."

"You'll learn," he said lightly, "as long as you aren't afraid of making mistakes."

He certainly made it easy not to be afraid. Saffron ventured a question.

"You don't eat sea turtles, then?"

"No. They're sacred, at least in my family. Tutu—my Grandpa Mano—would never allow it. It's a tradition from his mother's side." He was chewing, "He believes that they protect us. I think his love of them is what spurred the invention of a look-alike sandwich in our family."

Saffron liked that. "We could all use more protection," she said.

"I wish I'd been here to protect you from having to find Bud," Keahi said. "How are you doing with that?"

She didn't know what to say, exactly. "I didn't even know you then," she said, and the thought was strange to her. "I'd only just met Mano."

"Then I wish he could have been here with you," Keahi said.

Saffron saw an opportunity. She had to be careful, but maybe he could give her some information on Mano. "Do you know where Mano was that morning?"

They had reached the lava tube and Keahi had entered it, shining his cell phone flashlight along the dark floor. The water was gone, back out to sea until the tide rose again. Keahi's tone was precccupied when he answered her question. "I'm not sure." He stopped and stooped down. When he stood, he turned to Saffron, holding up the shoe she'd lost last night.

"Is this yours?"

Saffron told him about her adventure the evening before.

Keahi grunted. "You be careful. You could lose more than your slippah down here."

"Slipper?"

"You call 'em flip-flops. We call 'em slippahs."

She loved the warm sound of the word.

"I'm serious, though. This place can be dangerous."

But when they broke out of the dark passage onto the crescent beach, danger seemed a world away. Everything, Saffron noticed again, seemed far away when you could see nothing but the points, the palms, the sky and the water. They swam until they were exhausted, playing in the gentle waves.

"This is the first day in Hawaii that feels like a real vacation," Saffron said.

"Then you're doing Hawaii wrong," Keahi teased. "Every day is a vacation in Hawaii."

Saffron sighed, "I'm not sure I even know how to vacation anymore," she said. "The DC Metro area is busy all the time."

Keaha had a faraway look, "I remember that life," he said. "I practiced in Boston."

"Boston?" Saffron heard the surprise in her own voice. She looked at the turquoise water playing across his strong shoulders and tried to picture him in the city.

"Listen, Metro, I'm not the only one who seems a little out of place somewhere. Until the last couple of days, you've gone around here looking like a tiger in a tide pool."

"Hey!" she splashed him, but he took a few vigorous strokes away from her.

When he was safe, he called back, "Wearing boots to a luau!"

She tried to catch him but he was too fast, and she was too tired to exact revenge for his teasing now.

They pulled themselves onto the sand, and Saffron felt how warm it was beneath her. Keahi stretched out beside her chuckling.

"This beach is a gift," he said solemnly, "There aren't many places left like this on the island, where you can go and be completely alone."

"Sometimes I don't like being alone," Saffron said.

Keahi studied her. As always, he seemed able to look right into her soul. "Saffron, what's bothering you?"

She felt the muscles of her face tense. She couldn't tell him, of course, what was bothering her.

He slid closer on the sand. "Is everything okay?" His amber eyes found hers, "I saw the locks you put on the doors. Are you not feeling safe?"

"I'm not," she confirmed carefully.

"Why? Has someone been bothering you?"

"There was a break-in," Saffron said carefully.

Keahi's eyes widened. "What?"

She tried to downplay it, hearing Bradley's voice in her own as she spoke, "Probably just kids on a dare. It was the first night I was here."

"Somebody creeping around your house in the middle of the night?" He sat up, "No wonder you're edgy." He slid closer to her, his expression protective.

She felt close to him right then, as if, somehow, he had taken part of the burden of knowledge that she had been carrying.

"Did you call the police?"

Saffron hesitated. "I did, but . . ."

Keahi made a sound of frustration. "Didn't do anything, did he?"

"He came out, but he thought it was no big deal."

"I'm glad you've got the locks on. You call me if anything else happens."

"I will," Saffron promised.

Keahi was watching her closely. "There's something else."

"No, I'm fine. Really." She tried to make her voice light.

"You're tense," he said, running an electric hand across her shoulders, "and your eyes are troubled."

Saffron watched the water. Its constant shush was calming, and the secret beach made her feel safe somehow. She spoke carefully. "Well, I've seen other things at the farm that have me . . . concerned."

He nodded encouragement.

"There was a handprint on my door frame." Saying it out loud made her feel foolish all over again. "Right where someone would put it to look through the windows of my front door."

She could see that he found that concerning, too. Was it because he had lived in the city, knew what it was to live on guard?

"Bradley thinks I'm a nuisance," she admitted.

"Bradley thinks everyone's a nuisance. That doesn't mean there's nothing to worry about."

"See," she said, turning toward him, "I think there is something. I think something happened, and I don't know why or who did it, but I'm afraid about what else might be coming."

"What is it? What do you think happened?"

There in the easy morning sunshine, with the whisper of the palms and the shush of the waves, Saffron finally said her suspicion out loud. "Keahi, I think Bud was murdered."

Keahi's expression didn't change. He was taking her seriously. "What makes you think so?"

"I don't know. I'm still trying to figure that out. There was no autopsy, but they say he died of asphyxiation from his heart attack."

"Why do you doubt that?"

Saffron told him everything. About the tracks and the wheelbarrow.

Keahi's eyebrows were drawn together. He asked some follow-up questions. "What did his skin look like?"

"Cesious," she said immediately. The color was forever burned into her memory.

Keahi's eyes were puzzled. She realized she had used too specific a color word.

"Grayish-blue," she amended, though the words didn't convey the true dinginess of the shade like cesious did.

He nodded. "Any visible bruising? Wounds?"

"I didn't think to look," Saffron said, "I was a little shocked. But none that I saw, and I think they would have noticed anything very obvious." Her mind was churning with the suspicions she'd been carrying. She closed her eyes against the incessant shush of the waves and tried to focus on all the pieces of evidence. How did they fit together?

Keahi's voice interrupted her thoughts, "Who do you think murdered him?"

Saffron's eyes flew open. Did he suspect that Mano was on her list? Words poured out, and she recognized that she was trying to cover up for that traitorous thought.

"I don't know. Some people had something to gain, like Derek and Nik and Naia. And Bud made people angry, it seemed. Lani hates him, and I heard her talking about something she regretted. Her brother hates him, too."

"Ed?" Keahi interjected.

"Yes. And last night I cleaned up out here and I found a note with Lani's name on it, and the basket came from the Oceanside Café. Lots of people seem to have had a motive and an opportunity."

Saffron thought she'd covered well until she glanced up to see Keahi peering at her closely. "There's something else. Someone else? I feel like you're holding back somehow. Tell me everything, and maybe I can help you figure it out."

Saffron didn't respond. She couldn't tell him. She couldn't accuse his grandfather.

Saffron waved it off. "No, really. Bradley's probably right.

He thinks I brought too much of my city girl suspiciousness with me from DC, and he's probably right."

"I think you're an intelligent person. If you're concerned, we should explore the possibilities."

She shook her head. "I'm sure it's just an over-reaction."

Saffron couldn't look at him. She gazed over the golden sand toward the other point. He stopped pushing and let the silence settle between them.

Finally, he spoke up. "The house looks good, though."

"Thanks," she responded.

"It's a monstrous job. I wish I weren't working so much. I'd help out more." She heard him shift beside her, "I could haul stuff off for you."

"There might actually be some of it you want," she said. "I should have thought of asking you before. I've got some great pictures of our grandparents together, and—" Saffron stopped, the picture of Keahi's grandma kissing Bud flashed through her mind.

"Sure, I'll take a look—"

She cut him off, "On second thought, maybe I should go through it a little more. There's a lot of junk, I could put things aside for you."

Keahi was peering at her, and his tone was reserved when he spoke. "That was a switch. Is there something you don't want me to see up there?"

"No!" She could tell her voice was too bright, too enthusiastic.

He still had that sincere concern for her that made her want to tell him everything. "What did you find, Saffron?"

"Nothing. Nothing important." She could try to hide it, but maybe she should just tell him the truth. He was reasonable, and he was growing more suspicious every minute.

"I just, I found this picture of your grandma and Bud and an arrest report where Mano had fought him—"

Keahi's eyes widened, and his head jerked back a little as if he'd been slapped. "What?"

"See, it's nothing. I just don't know that it's really an *heirloom* or anything you'd want to see."

His eyes had narrowed. "Wait, wait. You asked me earlier where Tutu was that morning. Why did you ask that?

Saffron backpedaled, "I was just . . . curious."

"Why? Why are you curious about my grandfather?" He was suddenly on his feet, and she knew he had made the connection. "He's on your little list of suspects, isn't he?"

Saffron's stomach was a stone. "Keahi, I just wondered. I mean, I know that Mano wouldn't. It's just when I saw that picture, and found out that they fought—"

"Yeah, forty years ago, maybe," Keahi said. He paced around the beach. "That's crazy. How could you even think that?"

"Well, not him, maybe, but I'm telling you, Bud's death isn't right."

Keahi snatched his slippahs from the sand. "You don't know anything about my grandfather," he strode off down the beach and Saffron scrambled to her feet and went after him. She followed him all the way to the mouth of the lava tube, where he paused to jam his shoes on and then ducked inside the tunnel.

"Maybe he didn't mean to. Maybe it was an accident?" Saffron called after him. She was making things worse.

Keahi turned. She could barely see him in the dark passage. "Not everyone in my family is a murderer," he said, pain in his eyes, "just me." He disappeared into the darkness.

Saffron leaned against the rough wall of lava, feeling more alone than she ever had.

She hadn't shaken the feeling hours later when she drove into town. The hotbed of Maika'i information was the Paradise Market bulletin board. Saffron tried not to think about Keahi as she stood in front of it. A four-by-eight sheet of cork inside the front door of the market held flyers of all descriptions: full-color announcements of services: "Jim's Plumbing: we'll clear you out," hand-drawn pleas: "Missing Orange Cat. Please return. We love him!" Even business cards were stuck under the pins and along the edges of the board. There were 3x5 cards and a marker if you didn't have writing supplies of your own. Saffron's flyers were hot off the presses from Papaya Printing, and she felt they were pretty eye-catching. The realtor had suggested an open house, and Saffron thought she could have it ready in two weeks. On some level, the thought bothered her. There was still so much to be done here. But after her disastrous morning with Keahi, the sooner she could get out of here, the better.

Anyway, *Every Detail Events* was speeding along through its schedule without her, and she'd had three calls from Trish today about details. Saffron felt a little panicky whenever she thought of all the clients she had left behind.

She also had a nice flyer advertising her roosters. Her pens were filling up fast, and it would be harder and harder to keep the hens away from them.

The third folder was for the baby's crib and changing table. The thrift store didn't have room for them right now, and Saffron had realized she wanted them to go to someone who would be able to use them. It seemed what Uncle Beau would have wanted.

She tacked them up and perused a few more ads, tearing off one about house painting before she left. She'd been thinking about touching up the lanai.

"Saffron!" A cheery voice called to her. She turned and saw Sandy approaching. "How's our resident chicken farmer?"

"Good. Just cleaning things up."

Sandy waved her hand. "Oh, that place! I don't know how Beau even got around out there. It was a catastrophe. I have heard that you've tidied things up very well, though!"

"You have?" Saffron was still unused to the small-town grapevine. In DC, not even her next-door neighbors knew what she was up to.

"Oh, yes. We've seen lots of things around town that people tell me used to be Beau's." Sandy's face folded in sympathy, "or Ila's. I bought one of her vases, myself. From Consuela down at Tiki Thrift and Trade."

Saffron smiled.

"Do you have any jewelry?" Sandy's stacked bracelets flashed as she asked. "My father was a jeweler, and I've got a bit of a sweet tooth for the stuff."

Saffron shook her head, "Not much yet. But I still have one more room. I'll keep an eye out for you."

"Thanks, honey. Are you getting enough to eat out there?"

"Oh, I eat at the cafe a lot. I've been too busy to cook much."

"Well, you be sure and eat. You've got a big job out there," Sandy eyed the flyers, "and not much time to finish."

Saffron realized that was true. Time was ticking. She snatched a couple more groceries while she was there, then loaded them into her car.

When she reached into her purse for the keys, a sharp edge of paper caught her finger, and she pulled it out with a gasp. She opened the door and sat down in the driver's seat, rooting through her purse to see what had caught her.

It was the slips of paper with her suspects on them. She sat in the car for a moment, looking over them: Derek, Mano, Lani, Nik, and Naia. Keahi's reaction was still fresh in her mind. She hadn't gone about that the right way at all. She shook her head in disgust. Why couldn't she just let this go?

Leaning over, she popped the glove box open and stuffed the papers inside. They had no proper place in her purse, and they weren't getting her anywhere, anyway.

When Saffron arrived back home, Mano was sitting on her lanai. His silver beard and hair made a neat frame around his serene expression.

Saffron's shoulders tensed up. The words from the arrest report snaked back into her mind, and she tried to seem casual as she approached him. She wondered if Keahi had told him the terrible thing she'd said. But the details of Bud's death still bothered her, and Saffron knew, even if Keahi didn't, that even people you admired could make awful choices. After all, she'd found, she still couldn't rule Mano out completely.

He held up his cup of tea. "Just having my traditional cup honoring Beau."

"Of course! You're welcome to it." She sat in one of the big, low lanai chairs. It was the kind that made it impossible not to be relaxed.

"You've been to town?" he asked.

"Right. Putting up some flyers for an open house in a couple of weeks, and for the baby crib, roosters . . . There's a lot of stuff around here that needs a new home."

"Any luck finding the shark box?"

Saffron shook her head. "Not yet," she said. For the first time, she wondered what was in it, and why it was so important to him. Maybe there was something about it he was trying to hide. Saffron had to know. She tried to think how to bring up Bud without sounding suspicious or sounding morbid. Saffron needed him to talk about his friend, needed him to talk about what had happened between them.

"The place is looking good. I saw that you cleaned out the back bedroom."

"Yeah. It's a little hard going through the stuff from Uncle Beau's past. There were some sad times, I think."

Mano's heavy lids closed, leaving little crescent moons above his round cheeks. "Mmmmm. Sad times."

"Why didn't he ever remarry?" she asked.

Mano shrugged. "Sometimes, for a man, there's only one wahine—one woman. *The* woman. That was how it was for Beau and Ila. He just gave everything he had to that love, and when she died, he didn't have anything left to give. I know people don't think it exists anymore, but true love is real, and sometimes no one else ever measures up to the true love."

"You sound like you know about that. Was that how you were about . . ." Saffron realized that she didn't know Mano's wife's name.

"Glenda?" He took a deep breath. "Yes, I was."

This seemed like as good a chance as Saffron was likely to get. "Where did you meet Glenda?" she asked.

"Fifth grade. She moved here from the big island. We were best friends from the start."

"Wow. That's a long courtship."

"Yep. I chose Glenda over college. Went to work for my father, carving, asked her to marry me. Best choice I ever made. We were a good match. We didn't fight. We cared about each other. We raised our keiki. Inseparable for forty-six years."

Saffron sank into thought for a moment, "Honestly, I can't even imagine how that would be. I can't even seem to stay in a relationship for two years."

"You just haven't found the right one yet," Mano said. His eyes sparkled as he took a long drink, then feigned nonchalance. "Hey, what about Keahi? I think he had a nice time the other night."

Saffron jumped. She didn't want to tell him how quickly

she had messed that up, that after this morning Keahi may never speak to her again. And once Keahi told his tutu what she'd said, Mano may never speak to her again. She had him talking, and she couldn't let the moment get away. "I did, too," she said. "But tell me—you really never fought? Never disagreed?"

"Oh, I didn't say that. We disagreed. We just never let it get to a fight."

"So she never went on a shopping spree or told you not to hang out with your friends?"

"Sure. But Glenda was more important to me than money or my friends."

"That picture of all of you looked like fun. The one on the beach? Did she like your friends?"

Mano shrugged. "I think sometimes she did."

"She liked Uncle Beau?"

"Yeah. He was like family to her. She even called him cousin. I think she felt as sad for him as the rest of us did. She was good at showing compassion."

"Did she like Bud?"

There it was. The flicker of discomfort she had expected. "Mmmm. Sometimes." Mano shifted, and she felt a change of subject coming. She jumped in with another question before he could speak again.

"Because I remember you saying that he was kind of a ladies' man, and that seems like it could get . . . Complicated."

Saffron couldn't believe what she had said. She felt immediately that she had crossed a line. She waited for him to grow defensive, to be angry. But Mano turned his smiling eyes toward her. He looked at her.

"Don't let other people's stories scare you. Every love is its own journey. Yes, Bud's curse was his charisma. I think sometimes he didn't even know he was getting girls interested." Mano took a long drink of what must be, by now, cold tea.

"But sometimes he knew very well. And he shouldn't have done some of the things he did."

Saffron willed herself not to lean forward. She didn't speak for fear of interrupting him.

"Glenda fell for him once. Just after I turned down my scholarship to the University of Hawaii and asked her to marry me. He just couldn't help himself." Mano laughed, but there was no anger, no bitterness in it, "I can't blame him. She was the most beautiful girl."

"She dated him?"

"Yep. For a couple months. Gave me back the ring and everything. It wasn't a good time. I guess we did fight then." Mano closed his eyes and turned his face out toward the ocean, smoothing his beard.

"How could you stand to be friends with him after that? And how could you forgive her?"

Mano opened his eyes and kept his gaze on the water. Saffron tuned out the cries of the birds in the monkeypod tree above them and the soft breathing of the ocean to focus on him. "It's like I told you before, about letting go. People always think that they'll get more satisfaction out of hating someone forever, out of punishing someone by withdrawing their love. But the truth is, that never brings satisfaction. It always brings heartache for everyone, especially the one carrying the anger."

Saffron had to admit that this did not sound like the opinion of a murderer. They sat in silence for a while, listening to the sound of the waves.

"Beau had a lot of sadness in his life that he didn't deserve. Bud had a lot that he probably did deserve, but neither kind ever gave me any pleasure. And I loved Glenda. When she realized that she and Bud weren't good together, that their relationship destroyed rather than built, she came back to me, and I was happy to put it behind us."

"You forgave them?"

Mano nodded. "Let go. Move on. Be better. That's how you find happiness."

It was good advice. Saffron wasn't sure she had any of those steps down just yet.

Mano sighed. "Long time ago. When you get to be my age, things just look a little different."

There was one more question that Saffron had to ask. "Where were you the morning that Bud . . . That I . . . That I found Bud?"

Mano shook his head. "My daughter and I went down to Honolulu to the swap meet. Wish I had been here. Maybe I could have helped him."

She spoke quickly. "I wish that, too. I was supposed to go to his house and get the bolts for the feeders. I had no idea that he'd bring them out here. I wish I had been here when he came."

"If he had told me, I could have sent someone to check on him. The walking club was always offering to keep an eye on him." Mano laughed, a subdued chuckle, "of course, most of the women around here would have been happy to do that."

This made Saffron think. "Was Bud dating Lani? You know, the sister of the cook who works at the Oceanside Cafe?"

Mano laughed again, this time a short bark. "Ipo, Bud was dating everybody. He took them all out. That thing that I told you before, about some of us having eyes for just one wahine? That was not true for Bud. He was playing the field until the very end. I think he had two dates the night before you found him. Too much playing around. That many women's gotta be hard on the ticker." Mano patted his chest, laughing, "He never slowed down, though. Pushing a hundred and still charming the ladies." Mano wiped his eyes with the back of his hand and stood. "Well, we've got some chickens to catch. If you're going to have this place ready by the open house, we'd better not spend all day on the lanai drinking tea."

Looking up at his smile, bright as the mounded clouds in the azure sky behind him, Saffron saw the absurdity of her suspicions. Mano was not a killer. She sat a moment more, letting his words sink in. *Too much playing around. That may have been what did him in in the end.*

Chapter Eleven

Saffron had learned a thing or two about rounding up chickens.
First, that grabbing them one by one was a lot harder than merely walking behind them and shooing them where you needed them to go. As Mano filled the feeders in the egg house, she made her way through the rain-damp grass. She waved her arms, and a little flock of about fifteen chickens scrambled out of their hiding places in front of her. The hens, their full skirts abounce, waddled along, protesting. The roosters alternately ran and turned to face her in shows of bravery. None of them were as pretty as her lanai rooster, Curry. She had never been able to catch him yet, so he still roosted on the railing and crowed her awake every morning.

She'd blocked off the walkway in the egg house and opened the fourth pen on the North, so as they careened and flapped inside, they funneled naturally into that pen. Mano stood still in the work area and watched them pass. She stepped into the enclosure, closing the door behind her. Now was the tricky part. She had to separate the roosters, and the second thing she'd learned, as a nasty gash on her arm testified, was that roosters could be tricky.

She had taken to using a thick woolen army blanket. She threw out some grain, then, as the chickens obsessed over finding their favorite bits, she tossed the blanket over the rooster she wanted and bundled him up like the stork would. Then she took the weighty bundle to the rooster pens and set him free.

There were four roosters in this batch, so that meant well over an hour of wrangling. But in the end, when the fat, happy hens were hopping onto their perches and investigating their nest boxes, Saffron felt that same sense of accomplishment that she'd been feeling at the end of each mammoth farm task.

"Getting good at this, now," Mano said, "you may not want to leave after all."

Saffron shook her head. "I'm a lot better at herding wedding guests than I am at herding chickens."

She'd also learned that some chickens couldn't be herded. As she walked back out, she grabbed a tin can with a few grains in it. She saw several hens grouped together under a big bush with long waxy leaves. They stuck their heads out between the foliage to watch her, looking like ladies in hilarious hats. Saffron stood still beside the door of the egg house and shook the can.

She'd been working on this for a few days, shaking the can, getting them to come to her, then tossing the feed to them. This time, having learned the game, they barreled out of the bushes and came bouncing over to her. She stepped back, into the egg house as she had yesterday, and the hens followed. This time, instead of tossing the grain directly to them, she tossed it into the next open pen. The hens didn't hesitate. All ten of them dashed after the grain and Saffron closed the door behind them.

Saffron sometimes envied chickens' ability to forget. Once

they were inside, they didn't rush back to the door to look out forlornly. Instead, they busied themselves scratching and pecking, almost as if they'd already forgotten their old life out in the bushes.

There was still something she didn't understand.

"Mano," she called, "I've been wondering: How did the chickens get out of their pens in the first place? The pens are all in good repair, and the doors were open when I got here. Did someone come and let them out after Uncle Beau died?"

"Beau let them out years ago. They were so well trained back when he was running the place that he let them come and go from the pens as they wanted to. He just left the doors open and kept the feeders full, and the hens came into the egg house to eat and drink and lay their eggs."

"What about the roosters?"

"No roosters back then. Beau didn't keep any. The hens slept here and came in to lay their eggs, but spent their days outside running free. After he died, the food ran out in the feeders, and they went wild. Didn't come in anymore. I guess they found enough berries and centipedes and scorpions." Mano turned the crank on the feed bin, sending feed rattling down the long pipes and shooting into the feeders.

"If Uncle Beau didn't keep roosters, why are there so many of them now?"

"Where there's hens, there's roosters. Beau didn't keep any, but I'm sure you've noticed that there are plenty of wild ones on the island. When he wasn't here to keep them away, some of them moved in, and once the roosters come in, more roosters are sure to follow." He waved a hand.

All the hens were eating, and the babies had learned that the sound of feed in the pipes meant eating time. They were crowded around their feeder, peeping, and pushing.

Saffron stopped to say hello to Tikka, but the hen was transfixed by a particular place on the side of her feeder and didn't pay any attention to her former roommate. She was tapping on the side just as she had tapped on the box in the kitchen, incessantly, obsessively. Saffron peered at it. From what she could tell, there was nothing unusual about that spot, but the Empress had said that chickens see things differently.

She went to the work area to gather the eggs. Cranking the conveyor brought dozens of them riding along down to the work area like swaying bubbles on the surf. The hens were really getting going now. From what she'd read in the chicken book, it might have been because of the constant access to high-protein feed, which they didn't have in the jungle, or the absence of stress caused by predators.

A rough voice burst into the shed, over the ruckus of the roosters.

"You selling?"

Saffron turned to see Derek and two other rough young men that Saffron didn't recognize standing in the doorway blocking the light. He was holding up her flyer from the grocery store.

"I—uh . . ." Saffron found herself standing between him and the roosters.

"We want some roosters," Derek said, taking a few casual steps into the egg house.

Saffron wanted rid of her roosters, but she suddenly didn't want them to go with Derek. "What are you going to do with them?"

"What do you care?"

"They're not free. I'm selling them. Five—no, ten dollars each."

"Ten dollars! That's stupid. There are roosters all over the island."

"And yet you're here."

One of his friends leaned over and mumbled something in Derek's ear. Saffron could hear them murmuring.

"Three or four hundred, probably."

"Alright," he turned back to Saffron, "okay. We'll take them for ten."

From the darkened corner of the work area, Mano spoke up. "And do what with them?"

Derek scoffed. "What do you care, either?"

"Derek," there was a forced calm in Mano's voice, "you've already served four months in prison for that stuff."

"What stuff? You wanna tell me my business?" He walked toward Mano, with his hands lifted and spread wide.

Mano didn't flinch. "Cockfighting. We all know what you're here for. It's illegal, bruddah." There was something beautiful about the way the old man stood, unyielding and unconcerned, and about the way he was trying to talk Derek out of doing something self-destructive. It rattled the thug, who was used to getting his way, apparently.

The younger man backed down. "You keep 'em, then. They're costing you, anyway." Saffron wasn't sure if that was just a statement of fact or if it was a threat. He turned and walked out of the egg house.

Mano followed him, and Saffron followed Mano. They walked behind the young men all the way up to the house. On the lanai, Curry was pacing, making his warning sounds. He flapped down and met the thugs in the center of the yard.

Derek spoke loud enough for Saffron to hear from where she followed 50 yards behind him, "Look, here's a wild one! I'll just take it." She broke into a jog. Derek was going for Curry, and remembering that glint in the thug's eye, she had no doubt he'd snap the rooster's neck before she could get to them.

"No!" she shouted, and Mano moved quickly, too.

But Curry was quickest of all. He didn't run from Derek. Instead, just as the man leaned down to snatch at him, Curry flapped into the air, his claws raking, his beak snapping. He landed a long slash on Derek's cheek, then fluttered up and over him, deftly avoiding the others and landing high in a nearby hibiscus.

Derek looked back at them, the angry gashes on his leathery cheek beginning to trickle blood, and swore. Then he and his friends piled into their old jalopy and peeled out of the driveway.

"Get rid of the rest of the roosters," Mano said, "but hang on to that one."

THE SUN WAS SINKING when Saffron and Mano made their way back toward the house, satisfied that all the chickens were now gathered into pens.

All but Curry, of course. He greeted them with a low cluck as they climbed the back steps. Mano pulled a handful of grain from his pocket and threw it to the rooster. "Good rooster," he said, smiling, "so ono."

"Do you want some dinner?" Saffron asked as they stood watching Curry snatch up the little treats, making a cluck that sounded very self-congratulatory.

"I could eat," Mano said, with his characteristic openness.

Saffron opened the back door. A rustling inside made her freeze.

"Someone's in there," she whispered, taking a step back and holding the screen door so it wouldn't squeak.

Mano froze, too. "Derek?" he said aloud.

That was precisely what Saffron was afraid of. Suddenly, the thought of Derek as a suspect seemed very possible. He was violent, angry, and he'd had a perfect motive—Bud's nest egg.

A light voice trilled from inside, making them both jump. "Hello! Are you two coming in or not?" It was a woman's voice, and when Saffron stepped into the kitchen, she saw Sandy at the counter, putting a dash of seasoning into Saffron's new pot on the stove from a little yellow jar that said "pineapple powder." On the counter sat a lovely woven grocery basket like the one Saffron had seen her bring to Fumi's. The table was set, and a plate with what looked like rolls sat in the middle. Saffron was surprised to see that they were not purple.

Mano smiled, "You scared us, Sandy."

"I'm sorry. You were out in the bushes when I came, and I got busy making these and didn't have time to come tell you I was here. I just thought Saffron would enjoy a home-cooked meal after all her hard work, and you get to benefit, too!"

The kitchen was filled with the yeasty warmth of baked bread and a bright scent that Saffron couldn't identify. She went to look over Sandy's shoulder into the pot.

"Soup?" It looked like chicken noodle, only the noodles were long and translucent.

"We call it chicken long rice. Mung bean noodles, chicken, and ginger, plus my signature ingredient," she tapped the little yellow bottle. Pineapple—that was the bright smell. Saffron breathed it in.

"I'm going to go clean up," Saffron said, suddenly ravenous.

She showered and changed as quickly as she could, hearing the voices of the two visitors down the hall as she came out of her room.

Things seemed brighter inside now, with most of the rooms clean and the chickens settled into their tidy pens. There were a hundred and twenty-four of them altogether, hens of every color and shape. The rooster pens were full, and Saffron wondered what she would do with them, but she was a lot closer to having the place ready to sell than she had been this morning, and that felt good.

Mano was talking when she walked in, "the way he struts around town bullying people . . . He's getting out of control."

Sandy shook her head. "I've been afraid of him for a while. I hate it when he comes into the market. I know he and those thugs steal things, I just don't feel brave enough to confront him, and you can't count on Bradley, can you? I don't know what we're going to do about that poor excuse for the law. It's almost as if he wants more crime around here."

"Good way to keep his job," Mano said, and the bitter way they laughed told Saffron he was only half joking.

Sandy was ladling noodles into three deep rice bowls, which she moved over to the table as she gestured for Saffron to sit. Sandy took the kettle from the stove and poured it into their cups. A warm, sweet fragrance mixed with the scent of ginger in the air.

The meal consisted of much slurping. The long noodles snaked into Saffron's mouth, creating a burst of warmth and flavor that was just right after a long day's work. The tea—pineapple rooibos, according to Sandy—paired beautifully with the soup. Saffron took a roll and bit into it. To her surprise, it was filled with savory barbecued pork. She ate it and then another.

"Mainland girl discovers manapua," Mano said. Saffron looked up, aware suddenly that she had not been listening. "You like those, huh?" He asked, smiling.

"I *love* these," she said, taking another for emphasis.

"I was just telling Sandy about Derek's visit earlier."

Saffron nodded, "It was a little scary."

"I don't know what Nik's going to do. I think that Derek's got him scared, too. And he has to live with him."

"Nik's a good kid."

"And Naia. Where is she? She didn't even come for the funeral. That tells me something is very wrong."

Mano was quiet, finishing the last of his long rice and then patting his beard dry with a napkin.

Sandy changed the subject. The two talked about Keahi

and how he was doing. Saffron heard them skirting around the details of his previous life and taking special care to mention all his accomplishments from the time he was a child. Half of her wanted to tell them they didn't have to try so hard, that he wasn't going to want to see her again, anyway. But that would take more explaining, and that explaining would probably lose her Mano's friendship, which she had come to value very much.

The sunset outside streaked the windows with pink, and here in the warm kitchen light, Saffron felt safe. But the spectre of Bud's death still hung over her. She wondered if she'd be able to leave it in Hawaii, or if the weight of not knowing would follow her home. And now, with Derek's latest visit, she wondered if anyone else was in danger by her not saying something.

"Can I ask you both a question?" she said.

"Of course," Sandy said. There was empathy in her eyes.

"Has Derek ever—hurt anyone?"

The two exchanged a look that answered her question. "Okay, so that's a yes. Do you think there's a possibility that he did something that caused Bud's death?"

Sandy's eyes widened, "You think Bud was murdered?"

Saffron waited before answering. "I think it's possible," She said finally. "And I heard . . ." she didn't want to say who just yet, ". . . someone talking about regretting what they'd done to him."

Both of them leaned forward slightly.

"Who?"

"Well, I don't want to say, but I'm trying to figure out who's the most likely, and if Derek could have done something—scared him or choked him or something—that brought on the heart attack. Ruling out Derek would leave Lani as the only suspect. "

Sandy stirred her soup thoughtfully. "I'm not saying he couldn't do it," she said, "but I don't know why he would."

Mano blurted out an answer, his voice uncharacteristically brusque. "Money. The kid makes no secret that he's here for Naia's inheritance. He's so afraid of it going to Nik that you can see it in his face."

"Did Bud ever talk to you about a nest egg?" Saffron asked.

Mano nodded, "He's been saving a long time for those kids."

"But the money's gone," Saffron blurted.

"What do you mean?" Sandy asked.

"His accounts were empty. Nik told me." Mano eyed her, and she wasn't sure whether he was more disturbed about the money being gone or that she'd been talking to Nik. "When I ran into him on the North Shore," she added hastily.

Sandy stood and started clearing the table. "Well, let's face it. Bud did spend a lot on . . . Entertainment." She said the last word delicately.

Saffron and Mano both stood to help with the dishes as well. Mano seemed genuinely sorry when he spoke again. "He worked hard for that money. I hope Derek didn't get his hands on it after all."

Chapter Twelve

Tikka's little brood loved coming out to free-range in the yard. Saffron would open the door to their pen, and they'd come tumbling out, falling all over themselves and tripping Tikka as she bustled around them. She was always keen to follow Saffron up to the house and scratch in the shade of the monkeypod tree while Saffron worked inside.

Lately, Saffron had been rushing in and out so much that she hadn't had a proper chance to sit and watch the ocean. She'd decided today to try her hand at cooking again. She didn't want to get all her meals at the Oceanside—since Bernadette still wouldn't let her pay, it felt like taking advantage of the woman's generosity. The old Betty Crocker cookbook she'd found in the kitchen was a bit overwhelming, though, so she messaged one of her favorite caterers back home for help.

Delicious Eats replied quickly with what they claimed was their easiest recipe. It was pulled pork, and reasonably straightforward, though it did require Saffron to dig out a crock pot from the depths of the lower kitchen cupboard. It would need to cook for the afternoon, so she decided to take a towel and her chicken-keeping manual and go enjoy the beach a while before she sold this place and headed back to DC.

The sand was warm and soft where she lay. The waves hushed in and out, making a background for the chapter about exotic chicken breeds she was reading.

She saw the Empress' chicken staring out at her. Apparently called a silkie, it was known for its docile nature, extra toes, and blue earlobes.

It made her think about the Empress' assertions on chicken eyesight. She turned to the section on chicken anatomy and found that the old woman had been right.

A breeze through the palms above her drew her attention, and Saffron looked up. The teal water, the blue sky, the vibrant green palm leaves, the warm husks of coconuts that had washed up on the beach, all struck her suddenly and forcefully. It was, without a doubt, the most beautiful place she had ever seen. She laid down the book and sat watching the sea.

THE SAVORY SMELL of the pork had filled the bungalow when she returned, but the meat was far from ready. She could see that it would be very late evening before it was done. She ate a malasada on her way through the kitchen to tide her over. She was going to have to find a place in DC to get those when she went home. She'd come to love them. She changed into the soft, loose pants she'd bought and a tee shirt with a pineapple on it. She pulled her hair up and glanced in at the third room. It was the last room she needed to attack before she was ready to freshen the paint and stage the bungalow for the open house.

The warm tones of koa wood caught her eye. Peeking from under a stack of old towels was the corner of a small wooden box. She knew before she reached over and plucked it out that it would be the box that Mano had asked about. Carved koa wood, with an arched shark on the top, it shone rich, deep seal brown.

Saffron opened the box. On a bed of velvet laid a beautiful pearl ring. The pearl was stunning. The size of a cherry, it gleamed honey gold against the indigo lining of the box. Was this what Mano wanted? He didn't seem the type to want jewelry. She pulled out her phone and called him.

The old man's voice was excited, "You found it?"

"Yeah. It was pretty accessible, actually. Just in a box in the last room—I guess it was an office? Anyway, I just hadn't worked on that room yet." She bit her tongue and didn't say, "nobody has"!

"Thank you. My father made that box, years ago. I gave it to your uncle when we were young, long before my father died. I don't have much of his carving. I'd love to have it back. I'll be happy to pay you for it."

"There's no need for that. It's rightfully yours. Did you know that there was a ring inside?"

The line was silent for a long while. Just as Saffron was about to ask if he was still there, Mano spoke again. "I thought there might be."

His voice was somber. "We bought them for the girls. Long time ago. I figured that Beau had put Ila's there after the accident. You should keep that. It was your aunt's. Bud's is probably long gone. He's had lots of sweethearts since then."

Saffron was quiet, thinking of the whole lives that had been lived in this house long before she was even born. "I've never seen a pearl like this," she finally said.

"Golden pearls are not the most rare, but ones of that size and perfection are very hard to come by. We bought them from a Filipino fisherman in Honolulu one night. Had them made into rings, gave them to our girls." Mano chuckled. "They were the talk of the town. Lotta girls wanted those rings. They wanted the rings more than they wanted us, I think. But we sure felt like the big men then."

Saffron liked thinking of her new friend back then, dazzling his sweetheart with gifts.

"Long time ago," he finally said.

"I'll bring the box by your place later," Saffron promised.

There was a hopeful tone in Mano's voice when he said, "Or I could send Keahi over after his show. The luau's not very far from your place."

Saffron thought about that while silence stretched on the line. She didn't know if Keahi would even come, but if she was honest with herself, she wanted a good excuse to see him again and try to make things right. She tried not to let the jitters in her voice give her away when she said, "That would be fine, too."

When she hung up, she looked at the pearl ring for a long time. It had meant something to Uncle Beau. She would put it away for now.

She thought of the burglar. She was glad he hadn't found it. She pulled a chair from the kitchen table, moved the teacups on the top shelf, and tucked it away with the gold coins in the secret compartment at the back of the cupboard for safe-keeping.

"I'M SORRY" didn't seem like enough, and *"That was a stupid assumption"* seemed like it might just make Keahi think about her accusation again, which was something Saffron wanted to avoid like a scorpion sting. She tried not to be nervous while she staged the nursery. The crib had never sold, so she was setting it up with fresh linens in hopes it would appeal to a

buyer with a young family. She set the picture of her grandparents and their two young sons atop a shelf on one wall, and Uncle Beau and Aunt Ila's family picture when Warren Wayne was still a newborn, next to it.

She still hadn't worked out what she'd say to Keahi when the lights of the SUV shone in the front window. She waited for Keahi's light tap on the front door before she gathered the box and met him there. His dark eyes were unreadable when she opened the door, and he took the box wordlessly. She realized as he turned that he wasn't going to say anything, that he was going to get right back in his car and leave. She went through every apology she had composed all day, but none of them were right. When he reached the stairs, Saffron blurted out the only thing in her mind.

"I really like Mano," she said and meant it. Keahi stopped but didn't turn back around. Saffron kept talking. "He's talented, he's so kind. He's funny."

Keahi grunted.

"Listen, in the last few days, I've learned what kind of a friend Mano is."

Keahi turned toward her, regarding her with a cautious warmth in his expression that kept the words tumbling out of her mouth. "I see now what he'd do for anyone he cared about, and I—I know I was wrong, and I know you were right. I didn't know him. I see now that he'd never do anything to hurt anyone."

Keahi had shifted his weight to lean on the railing.

"He wouldn't," he said stubbornly, the words coming out tight, as if he'd been wanting to say them for days.

"I know," she said, and then, because she could see it was enough now, "I'm sorry."

Keahi sighed and tipped his head back. The branches of the monkeypod tree growing beside the lanai framed him. "I know. I'm sorry, too. I'm . . . protective of my family."

Saffron was talking before she thought. "I forget that about people sometimes, because my family wasn't really like that. We didn't really have a lot of loyalty."

"That's not what I've heard about your father," Keahi started.

Saffron hugged her arms around herself. "Actually, he's the mascot for having no family loyalty." Should she tell him that she had no idea what had happened to her father? That he had never contacted her, had never sent so much as a birthday card? That she had no idea whether he was even alive?

Keahi didn't press the issue, "Our families shape us in lots of ways," he said, and she let her arms relax.

"Anyway, it's been a lot quieter around here without you coming by," she said, barely admitting to herself how nice it was to have his solid presence beside her in the warm evening air.

"I'll bet."

"Do you want to come in for a minute? I've got some malasadas . . ." She let her tone drift up tantalizingly, trying not to reveal that she'd been picking them up every day just in case he came by.

"Dobash?" he asked, narrowing his eyes. The chocolate ones were his favorite. She nodded, and he threw up his hands in mock defeat. "Well, I can't turn that down," he said. "I had to fill in for another performer tonight, and by the time I finished, they'd packed up the kitchen, so I didn't get any dinner."

Saffron rethought her plan as she ushered him into the kitchen.

"Listen," she said, "another thing my family taught me was that you can't have dessert if you don't eat your dinner." She gave him a stern look.

"Seems like a fair rule," he said. The smell of the pork hung in the air around them.

"Will you eat some dinner with me?" She asked.

Keahi pretended to think for a while, "well, I guess. If it gets me a Juno's malasada."

It was strange to be cooking again. Saffron had been eating out and using caterers for so long that she felt unsure and hesitant when she looked around to see what she should start with.

The feeling faded, though, as Saffron sliced the ciabatta rolls she'd bought at the Paradise Market. She took one of Uncle Beau's mismatched plastic cereal bowls and mixed her special DC mayo: a sweet-and-spicy concoction she'd invented when her mom was at work, and she had to fend for herself with whatever was in the fridge. She told Keahi about it as she mixed.

He looked doubtful, "Mayo with lemon juice, vinegar, and soy sauce?"

She slathered the mixture on the rolls, topped them with the pulled pork, and fished two pickles out of a jar to set beside the sandwiches. Keahi did not jump in immediately.

"Is this the kind of thing you serve at your fancy weddings?" he said, a teasing gleam in his eyes.

She scoffed, "no way. This is from the house menu. Only VIPs get this kind of fare. Anyway, mayo with soy sauce isn't something you ask a bride to eat in her three thousand dollar silk and satin wedding gown."

Keahi chuckled, "I guess not."

"This outfit, however," she indicated her tee and sweats, "is perfect for it."

Keahi didn't answer. He had taken a bite and was chewing slowly. He took another and gave a long approving grumble.

"I told you it was good."

He swallowed, "No argument here."

Saffron felt the warmth between them. Her mistaken accusation had cooled their mutual affection, but it hadn't drowned it. She liked his natural humor, his quick smile. She liked that, like her, he was familiar with both laughter and tears.

THE NEXT MORNING, Saffron was aglow from inside as she sat in the late morning sun and stirred the paint for the hallway. She nearly dropped her phone in the bucket when she got a call from Rose, the real estate agent.

She said she had good news. Bud's old neighbor, Sal, had finally made an offer. It was rock-bottom, less than the price the seller was asking for her little DC office space, and much less than she needed to take *Every Detail Events* to a competitive level.

As badly as she wanted to sell and get out of here, she couldn't see selling for that little.

"Let's wait for the open house," she said, "maybe that will turn out better."

An hour later, when the hall was finished, and Saffron was ready to move on to the kitchen, Saffron passed the doorway that led to the living room, and she jumped. A man's face was framed in the little window at the top of the door. It took her a moment to realize that it was Sal. His hand was on the wall outside, steadying him as he peered into the house, and she instantly knew who had left the handprint.

He must have left it the day he came skulking around the house, the day that she and Mano had been working on the feeders. The thought made her both angry and uncomfortable at the same time. She opened the door. Sal, usually so neat, was rumpled. A three-day beard made his face ragged, and his hair was unkempt. His hand was wrapped in a bandage, and his eyes were snapping.

"We seem to have a misunderstanding," he said, sliding a shoulder into the doorjamb. "I hear you declined my offer."

"I did," Saffron had dealt with unhappy customers. She knew how to stay calm. "It was too low."

"For this place?" he threw his hands wide and pushed past her into the living room. Swinging his arms in erratic gestures, he said, "Look at it! It's a dump!"

"If you're not interested, that's fine. I'll find another buyer." Saffron kept her voice level. He was obviously overwrought.

"I am interested! I want it. I've finally got that cesspool next door, but I need a bigger property as well." His voice was petulant. He was a very different man than she'd met before. He raised his hands into claws and closed them around the air as if choking her from across the room. "Why can't you see that this place is nothing to you, but it means my business. My marriage, probably my life."

Saffron thought that was a little dramatic, and she was still absorbing his first comment. "Wait. You bought Bud's house?"

"Didn't you hear? The sister came back, and she and Nik agreed to sell it to me. I knew they would, once that old man was out of the way." Saffron stared at him. Sal had just made her suspect list.

And Naia was back? This seemed big news. Of course, Saffron hadn't been to the cafe today, so there was no way she would have found out.

"Listen, I'm buying this place. If I have to tear up every other offer myself, I'll get it," he laughed, a high, rattling sound. "I'll do whatever it takes to get this place on *my terms*."

Saffron stepped back, pulling her phone from her pocket. "Is that how you felt about getting Bud's place?"

"Oh, I knew I'd get it sooner or later. The kids didn't want it. Once the old man was out of the way . . ." He was looking down the hall. "I could do a lot with this place."

Saffron tried not to think about the tracks, about the wheelbarrow with its terrible burden. She tried not to let her mind go through the list:

Who: Sal
Why: To get Bud's house
When: That morning
How:?

She didn't know how, but she knew he was tall enough and strong enough, to easily overpower an old man. What if he had choked Bud? The image of his clawed hands in the air made her back up even more.

"I'm going to call the police now," she said evenly, stepping out onto the lanai. She tried not to think what they would think receiving *another* call from the farm, and she hoped Sal didn't know that Bradley probably wouldn't come anyway. "Or you can just go." She waved at his car. "Feel free to talk to my Realtor if you'd like to make another offer."

He stormed out, throwing up his hands.

As she watched him climb into his luxury car, she saw that the back seat was filled with stuff: blankets, pillows, an open cardboard box, and clothes. Sal drove away, and Saffron lowered the phone without dialing. She'd handled it. She wouldn't bother calling.

Saffron needed to get out of the house, and she was hungry. She also needed to find out the lowdown on Sal's erratic visit. Saffron realized that she could really use an ono burger.

Business was slow, so Bernadette sat down at the table and answered all of Saffron's questions.

"Ohhh," she said, shaking her head, "big trouble with his wife."

Saffron had heard of the wife but had never seen her. "What is it?"

"Well, Heather, that works at the bank? She says that all the properties are in the wife's name, and she's taking off with a man from the big island who's got properties all over."

Saffron nodded. No wonder Sal was so desperate.

"He's always been crazy, though. Yelling at his neighbors, coming and spending lots of money at a time, then being broke the next week. I don't even know what brought him here in the first place."

The bell on the door jingled, and Lani entered the café and walked straight to Ed. He set about putting together a take-out order for her. Saffron remembered hearing Lani at the luau. She was still a suspect, even if Saffron did like her better than Derek and Sal.

She looked around, then leaned close to Bernadette. "What was between Lani and Bud?"

Bernadette shot a quick look at the cook, who was thoroughly engrossed in his work.

"Oh, they were lovers a long time ago. Then, he Budded the whole thing up, carousing with other ladies. But they were gettin' back together. I know it, because," she reached out and pulled Saffron's head forward, leaning in to hiss in her ear, "I seen them the night before he died."

Saffron made her face look shocked. She wasn't supposed to know that. "Really?"

Bernadette eased back into the chair. "Really. He was telling her sweet things every time I come by. And he said he had a ring for her, and he was goin' settle down with her for the time they had left."

"What about all the others?"

Bernadette shrugged. "He said he was goin' break up with all of 'em. Said he was done runnin' round."

"Do you think he meant it?"

"I don't know. I know they left together, and I watched 'em walk to her place," Bernadette waved a hand toward the wide back windows. They looked out on a steeply eroded bank that dropped down to the ocean. For the first time, Saffron noticed a little house alongside the café.

"Is that her house?"

Bernadette nodded, "used to be a nice beach here, too, but we had a king tide here last year that nearly took all of us down with it. We kept five or six feet of bank behind us so we could build them stairs down to the water, but the French doors in Lani's bedroom open right onto a thirty-foot drop."

This was an interesting detail, but Saffron was impatient to hear more about Bud and Lani, "You think he was really going to settle down with her?"

"Seems like. And I know I've never heard him say anything like that before," Bernadette said, "mostly he just told the ladies how pretty they were and how lucky he was, you know, flattery. I never heard him make no promises. But when he came by the next morning, real early, he picked up a Beachy Breakfast Basket. I guess he was up to his old tricks."

Saffron tried to look shocked again, "What? You saw him the morning he died?"

"Yep. He said he was having a picnic."

Saffron suddenly remembered the voices. The morning she'd left for her first meal here. She'd heard voices but hadn't seen anyone on the beach. Maybe Bud and his date were slipping back to the secret beach at that very moment. The thought made her sick. Maybe she could have stopped it.

Saffron thought a minute, and Bernadette heaved herself to her feet to go check on the only other customers in the cafe. Before she left, Saffron said, "Who were they? The other women?"

"I could make you a shorter list of who they weren't," Bernadette said. "But here lately it was mostly Lani, Mattie, Sarah. Charlotte. Sandy. Rose. He asked me out once, but I knew better. I knew he was a fool." She glanced up, "no disrespect," she added quickly.

That was quite a list.

It seemed that any one of those women would want to do

away with Bud. But Lani was still the only one who Saffron had heard admit it.

"Guess he liked women who were active," Bernadette said. "Almost all of em's members of the walking club."

Saffron realized that she'd been missing a great opportunity. Tomorrow morning, she'd join the Walking Wonders.

Chapter Thirteen

Saffron didn't know what she had expected, but breaking a sweat to keep up with the 60-plus crowd wasn't it. The Wonders were hoofing it along the beach, leaving a churned-up trail of sand in their wake.

This morning they were out in full force: Sandy Vaughn and Mrs. Claus were in front, followed by a forceful woman wearing a vibrant pink spandex outfit whose name, Saffron learned, was Jan Lin. She walked with the warm and reserved Consuela Limon. Fumi was next to Saffron, and they were followed by the thin and sour Miss Vinny Dingely and a chattering woman named Tilly Allbey. Saffron's heart sank as she saw that they all wore toothy sneakers that could have easily matched the tracks in the mud by the shed. None of them seemed like killers, though, as they filled the morning air with bright conversation.

Sandy led out, setting the pace with Mrs. Claus. The group had met at the park next to the thrift store, and Saffron had barely seen those two women since. For a plump lady, Mrs. Claus could really move. It gave Saffron hope. She had settled into a pretty good clip with Fumi in the middle of the pack, and Fumi had been revealing all the greatest new kitchen gadgets as they walked. Saffron tried to pay attention as Fumi rattled on about orange zesting, but behind them, Tillie Allbey the platinum blonde bombshell was chattering away to the very thin Miss Dingely about something much more juicy.

"Well, nights are a lot quieter in this town, I'll tell you."

"I know," Miss Dingely replied, "I wanted to see that new movie last night, and I sat around for an hour waiting before I realized that he wasn't going to call. I just had to make my own plans and call Jan to go with me."

"I find that I'm not even doing my hair anymore some days," Tillie said. Saffron glanced back. The blonde had obviously done it today. There was no way hair could have that much height without some serious attention. "What's the point? Just going to get windblown walking with all of you anyway, and who cares what you think of my hair?"

"I don't know what we're going to end up doing."

"The only real entertainment is watching the neighbors now." Tillie's tone was conspiratorial.

"Oh?" Miss Dingely asked, "interesting stuff over there?"

"Well, not as interesting as when Bud would work in the yard without his shirt, but they are keeping it pretty exciting even without him."

"What's going on over there?"

"Fighting. Terrible."

"Really?" The thin woman seemed disbelieving.

"I'm telling you, I heard screaming. It was a fight like you've never heard."

"What were they yelling about?"

"Naia." There was a long, pointed pause. "She's back."

The gasp that followed was half shock, half exertion. "Did you see her?"

"I saw her. Poor little skinny girl, slipping into the house as meek as a little gecko."

"I'm just glad she's still alive. After that husband of hers served his time in prison, I didn't think there was any other explanation for her disappearance."

"Well, I learned about that, too. She's been in Vegas, all right, but according to the yelling, she's been in state protection. Something about an illegal arms deal she saw."

Disbelief made the other woman's voice high. "I swear I'll never understand why people live in that desert nest of sin."

Saffron felt a tug on her shoulder. She blinked, looking down into Fumi's wide eyes. "Do you?" Fumi was asking.

"U-understand why people live there?" Saffron fumbled, trying to sort the last few sentences of conversation out in her mind.

Fumi cocked her head to one side, her arms pumping furiously as she tried to hold her place in the pack. "Do you know why it's so important to use the right zester?"

Saffron shook her head numbly.

"Because if you zest too deeply, you'll end up with the pith. The pith is bitter."

"I imagine it is," Saffron nodded, trying to tune an ear to the conversation behind her as Fumi went on.

"What were they shouting?"

"Nik was saying that he knew Derek had been busting into places, and he'd told Bradley about it. He said he had evidence. Derek was actually threatening him."

"Those poor kids. They just never had any stability, did they? Bud gave them all the home they ever had. Now Naia's back in a bad situation, only this time Bud's not here to help her out of it."

"And I'm scared of that Derek. There's no telling what he'd do."

"He's a loose cannon, for sure. And he only came here to get his hands on Naia's inheritance."

Fumi was still rattling on, "You want the oil from the peel because it has that great flavor. But not the pith."

"The pith is bitter," Saffron said absentmindedly.

"That's right!" Fumi sounded pleased. As the group rounded the gentle curve of the beach, Saffron caught the last phrase of Platinum Blonde's conversation.

"Now Derek's trying to unload some stuff that I know isn't his. He was throwing things into the car, and I heard him say he was going to the swap meet at the stadium."

Saffron couldn't wait to reach the thrift shop parking lot. Once the walk was over, she would head straight for Nik's house.

Fumi was finishing another question, " . . . Separator?"

"I'm sorry?" Saffron asked.

"Have you tried the Yolk-less egg separator?" she asked again. Saffron detected a note of mild annoyance in her tone.

"I haven't."

"Oh, they are sensational. That Sal brought me one as a trial a couple of weeks ago," she looked down and shook her head quickly. "I don't like to think about that day, but that was the day he brought it by."

"What day?" Saffron was interested now.

"The day Bud died," Fumi said quietly, casting furtive glances around. "He'd picked it up in his travels, and he thought I'd be interested. I was—"

"What time was this? When did he come to your store?"

Fumi shot her a sidelong glance. Saffron read it immediately as defensiveness. "Very early. Long before I opened. But he knew I was up because we'd met when I went out for my coffee and he was checking out a worn-down bakery property across the street."

"He was in town that morning?" Saffron saw her suspicions crumbling. The *When* column didn't match up if Sal was in town that morning. Saffron had also seen him at his house later when she'd gone to Bud's. She whispered a silent apology to him while Fumi went on.

"Well, there are a lot of egg tools you're going to need to familiarize yourself with. The Yolk-less is a great tool when you're baking, and you are just using egg whites or just yolks. It works on suction."

"Mmm-hmmm." Saffron tried to focus.

"And then there's egg slicers, egg wedgers, egg tappers, egg cups, poaching cups, the newest thing is boiled egg peelers. There are some pretty great ones out right now, they make peeling a boiled egg a snap! You should come by the store, and I'll give you a demonstration." Saffron admired the passion that Fumi had for her business. It was evident that she adored kitchen supplies.

The group had slowed, and the bright-pink clad woman ahead of Saffron turned.

"Are you ladies talking about eggs? Because I want to know when I can get out to Hau'oli Ka Moa and pick up a couple dozen. Are your hens laying?" Jan Lin had starkly arched eyelids and straight brows that framed her deep brown eyes. Her straight black hair was streaked with silver and styled in a no-nonsense rounded bob. She ran a little cell-phone store called Ring Up 808, and word was that she was a genius with any hand-held device.

"Oh yeah," Saffron said. "I've got eggs coming out my ears."

"Well, you should be selling them!" Jan scolded. A hint of her first language—Chinese—shadowed the words as she shook a finger at Saffron. "You've got a customer base right here!" She turned again and raised her voice. "Who wants eggs from The Happy Chicken?"

A ripple went through the group. Saffron caught several affirmative answers on the wind.

"Well, let's go out there now!" Jan said, calling up to the

front, "we're going to the Egg Farm!" Sandy, at the front of the pack, turned with a question in her eyes, but Saffron watched the women between them ferry the message to her, then she tossed the OK sign back at them and veered off the beach toward the road.

The women seemed utterly at ease with their new destination as they trekked two by two down the narrow edge of the road. They kept up their conversations—Fumi was expounding on the different makes of egg peelers just now—and didn't seem at all upset by the cars that whizzed by or the crumbling edge of the highway that they walked on.

But the two miles out to the farm were a little more than they had bargained for. When they made it there, they all collapsed in the lanai chairs and on the living room futon. Saffron was glad that the kitchen and living room were sparkling clean, even though she hadn't been expecting company.

The fresh paint in the hall made the place look and smell new.

She brought out all the soda, cold water, and pineapple juice she had in her fridge. The women seemed grateful. They were grateful, too, for the broad shade of the monkeypod tree and the cool breeze that blew onto the lanai from the open doors of the air-conditioned house.

They each collected one or more cartons of eggs. Saffron ran out halfway through.

"I'll be right back!" she said, "I'll get today's crop from the egg house."

"Take your time!" Jan Lin called from the futon.

Saffron slipped out the back door, leaving bubbles of cheerful chatter drifting out into the warm Hawaiian morning.

Her cheeks ached from smiling. She thought, as she cranked the conveyor and gathered the eggs, that it had been a long time since she'd been social. She threw parties for a living, but she was never a guest or even a host. She was always behind the scenes, watching that the punch bowl stayed full and the canapes made a perfect grid on the serving platter. The last time she'd even had people over to her apartment was the last Christmas before she and Reggie broke up. It felt nice now to share cold drinks and have the Walking Wonders exclaim over the transformation of the bungalow.

When she came back, they'd infiltrated the whole house. Sandy and Mrs. Claus were in the bedroom admiring the koa wood headboard. Saffron didn't mind. She liked that they appreciated it. Saffron caught a tantalizing word as she came in. "Lani."

She froze. The women hadn't yet seen her. They stood close together, their backs to the door, and Saffron tried not to breathe as she listened.

"She's been going all over town bashing him," Sandy was saying in a confidential tone.

"What's she saying?"

"Oh, you know, the same old thing: he was a player, a cad. He wouldn't commit. Nothing none of us didn't know anyway. But she's also been insisting worse things. I heard her in the market yesterday telling someone that she's glad he's dead!"

"Oh!" Mrs. Claus was clearly disapproving.

"She's not stable," Mrs. Claus said. "And now, this girl," Mrs. Claus waved her hand at Saffron's suitcase told Saffron that she was the girl, "comes in and uncovers the key piece of evidence in the mysterious disappearance of Lani's late husband. What do you think will happen if Lani comes to the open house and sees this?"

"Well, it won't be pretty. That's for sure. What was the story, anyway?" Sandy asked. Saffron wondered how long she had been living in the community. She seemed unsure of many things that the other Wonders knew.

"Well," Mrs. Claus leaned in more, "This bed was carved

by Mano's father. It was for sale in that big window at the secondhand store, which used to be Maika'i Furniture, which Lani's husband owned. Then, after the scandal, the building was sold to become a flower shop, then when that flopped, they moved the secondhand store in. But back then it was the furniture store."

"And?" Saffron felt as impatient with the extraneous details as Sandy sounded.

"And, Lani and her husband were always fighting. They'd have arguments out in public: at church, in the grocery store. He wasn't a calm man, and Lani matched him shout for shout. But anyway, word had it that Lani wanted this bed. But she and her husband were fighting about something, and he sold it. Or, at least we thought that was what happened. But he was mean enough and spiteful enough, he could have tossed it off a cliff into the ocean just because she wanted it. We had an Elks club dinner that night, and they started arguing about it, and even though people tried to get them to settle down, they just got louder and louder. She accused him of selling it to spite her and insisted on knowing who had bought it, but he wouldn't say. We all just sat there staring at them until Lani threw a plate at him and screamed that one day he was going to just disappear, too, and they'd never find his body."

Sandy made a low, amazed sound.

Mrs. Claus's next words were spoken slowly, with an edge of delighted revelation. "And that's exactly what happened. He didn't open the store the next day, and nobody *ever saw him again*."

Sandy threw up her hands and then clapped them to her cheeks in amazement. "That *is* suspicious."

"We learned a long time ago not to ignore Lani." Mrs. Claus began to shift, and Saffron saw that they were going to discover her. She made her voice work just before they turned.

"I'm back!" she said brightly. The women didn't seem to realize she'd been there all along.

"I hope you don't mind us taking a look around? It's been such a long time since this place was presentable."

"Not at all. I'm trying to get it ready to sell. The more people that see it, the better!"

"Oh," Mrs. Claus sighed. "We used to have the nicest bridge parties here." There was a note of genuine wistfulness in her voice. "Back when Beau and Ila were newlyweds." The old woman shook her white curls as if freeing the memory before she switched subjects. "You found more eggs?" Mrs. Claus said hopefully.

"Oh, yes. We've got plenty of those. I put them in the kitchen."

"Well. I'd better run down and get mine before Vinny gets her hands on the rest of them," Mrs. Claus said, slipping past Saffron. Sandy followed, leaving Saffron standing alone in her room.

Walking back down the hall, she found a knot of ladies in the nursery, hushed voices and solemn faces testifying to the fact that they'd been discussing the accident.

Consuela Limon rushed up and embraced Saffron as if the loss had just happened.

"Oh, it was such a tragedy!" she said, squeezing Saffron with ample arms.

Tillie Allbey, the platinum blond, stepped over, too, and patted Saffron. "We're so sorry about your aunt, darling. And your little cousin."

"And they waited so long for him, too!"

This set of a gale of agreement from the women. "Oh, that baby was beautiful!"

"Beautiful!" they said.

"Just precious!"

"Those big eyes!"

"I never saw a baby so sweet!"

"And when they were lost, oh, we grieved!"

"Didn't we?"

"We all grieved."

The hugger patted Saffron on the back and released her. "We tried to help that uncle of yours, but he was stubborn."

"Stubborn is right," the women agreed. "Stubborn and hurting."

"Wouldn't even let your father comfort him."

Saffron's interest was piqued. Her father?

"Did my father come back then?"

"Oh, yes, child. Came back and took care of Beau."

There were sighs all around.

"Took care of him?" Tillie said, "I'd say *saved* him."

"What do you mean?"

"Slate did everything for Beau for a long time. Cooked, cleaned. I even remember seeing him spoonfeeding your uncle," the woman clucked. "Washed his face. Beau's sorrow was just too much. Put him back in a childlike state. Your father had to do everything for him for years and years."

This was new information to Saffron. Though she had spent her whole life pretending, for her mother's sake, not to be interested at all in her father, she felt now the return of an old hunger, a curiosity about who he was and why he had left. Her stomach felt twisted. She had hated him for so long. But now she was finding that he had gone to take care of Uncle Beau. No wonder her uncle had felt such deep debt to his brother. No wonder he had come and paid for Mother's medical bills. No wonder he had left her this farm. It was penance for his brother's sacrifice.

Saffron swallowed. Her mouth tasted bitter. She gazed at the crib and the family photo. Could the brothers have known that the end result of all their efforts would be the loss of both their families?

When the women had finished their reminiscing, Saffron finished distributing the eggs. The Walking Wonders filled the hibiscus bowl with cash and checks. Those who didn't have money on them borrowed from their friends, even though Saffron tried to insist that they not worry about it.

"We'll pay you. We love these eggs!" Tilly the platinum blond said. "And we'll bring the cartons back next week. Beau gave us cards, and every time we brought the container back to refill, he marked it down. After 10 refills, if you still had the carton, he swapped it for a new one full of a free dozen! I still have a full card I didn't get to cash in."

Saffron had to admit that was a smart marketing strategy. "I'll honor it," she said.

This seemed to please the women, and as the group started back to town, Saffron found herself a little disappointed that the Walking Wonders' visit was over.

"We'll make this our usual Tuesday route!" Mrs. Claus said. "That way we can get our eggs once a week!"

Saffron was surprised to find that she liked that idea. She reminded herself that soon she'd be back in DC and they'd be picking up the eggs from the farm's new owners.

On the way back, Fumi told her about a device that made "Golden Eggs," which were scrambled in the shell before hard-boiling, combining the yolk and the white. Saffron had to admit that they sounded intriguing. She'd grown to enjoy Fumi and her encyclopedic knowledge of what you could do with kitchen gadgets and a supply of fresh eggs. Saffron found herself a little sorry that since she was heading back to DC after the sale, she wouldn't get a chance to test out some of the kitchen store's toys.

By the time the Walking Wonders made their way back down the beach to the park next to the secondhand store, they were all worn out. Even Saffron found herself leaning against the hood of her car for longer than usual.

"You come by the store now, all right?" Fumi said, walking off toward the main street.

"I will," Saffron promised. She did want to see what a golden egg looked like.

"Today?"

Saffron grasped at a thought that had been skirting the edges of her mind with more intensity the closer they got to town. It was Nik, and his apparently returned sister. She shook her head. "I'm not sure I'll have time today. I have to go check on someone."

Fumi didn't seem upset. "Soon, then!"

Saffron waved after her. "Soon!" she promised, then turned to unlock her car.

Chapter Fourteen

The first time Saffron saw Naia, she knew exactly who the girl was. Naia had Nik's same wide-eyed charm, with a heartbreaking shadow of persistent fear in her eyes. She had long, thick, black hair that spilled down her back, and the painfully thin air of someone who had not been looking after herself for a long time.

She stood half-behind the open door, eyes wide as Saffron handed her a pineapple-shaped basket of eggs and introduced herself.

The girl took them, thanked her, and began to maneuver the door closed. Nik's boisterous voice stopped it.

"Saffron!" he said, throwing the door wide. Naia stepped behind him as he enveloped Saffron in a hug. "You met my sister!"

Saffron hugged him back, drawing the smell of sunshine and sea that Nik seemed always to carry with him. "Yes," then to Naia she said, "I know Nik's so glad to have you back." She followed the pair into the dark living room. Heavy woven drapes covered the windows, and the room was paneled in dark faux wood. The floor was shining black tile with a matted brown rug over it. The whole place felt oppressive. No wonder Nik spent so much time at the beach.

The girl peered out from her waves of hair and nodded slightly. "It's good to be home." She shifted. "I just wish I'd made it before . . ."

Naia didn't have to finish the sentence. Bud's absence hung over the twins like a blanket. Now that her eyes had adjusted, Saffron could see that the paneled walls were lined with four-by-six inch photos in cheap frames. Bud and his children, Bud and his grandchildren, Bud and these two, all much younger than they were now. The rest of the photos were of the twins. Nik and Naia as children, Nik and Naia in formals, standing awkwardly by their high-school dates, Nik and Naia in graduation robes. It was easy to see that they had become Bud's life.

"But we're going to the swap meet today," Nik said, "to eat some barbecue and find Naia some new threads." Saffron noticed the other girl's worn cardigan and threadbare slacks. "You should come with us!"

Saffron shifted. "Aren't Derek and his friends coming? I

don't want to crowd you." Mostly, she just didn't want to see the sneering Derek again.

Nik waved a hand. "They left a while ago. It's just the two of us. And I'm sure Naia would love to have another girl's opinion on clothes. I'm not much help unless you're buying a wetsuit."

Naia gave a small, generous smile.

"Come on," he urged. "I'll show you all the sights," He slid a hand up her arm and caught her gaze with his. Saffron felt her concern fading. It was easy to see he had inherited Bud's charm. Saffron wondered if it was genetic. One last entreating smile from Nik and Saffron heard herself agreeing.

THE SWAP MEET WAS MASSIVE. A giant ring of booths and aisles surrounding the Aloha football stadium, it was hot and sticky there from the beginning. Saffron found herself distracted from the racks of bright sundresses by trying to keep an eye out for Derek as she walked.

They stopped near the beginning at a booth called Saltwater Sodas, where brightly colored tubes crisscrossed the back wall and shining silver cylinders bore names such as "Coconut Cream Craze" and "Cherry Bomb." Saffron chose "Orange You Glad" and sipped it as they entered the festive atmosphere of the market.

They found some great skirts and tops in the first few booths. After several more shops of island wear, Naia had slipped away on her own. Nik got a phone call and waved Saffron on.

"Let's meet at the barbecue truck," he pointed in the direction of a raised walkway with green railings. "I'll text Naia. It's a couple of aisles past that walkway," he whispered before turning back to his conversation.

Saffron agreed, and they used gestures to settle on a meeting time about an hour away. Saffron set off to explore the labyrinth of lights, fabric, music, and food, wondering if she'd run into Derek or Naia along one of the aisles.

Saffron jumped when she heard a familiar voice call to her. She turned to see Mano sitting under a white pop-up canopy. Spread around him were ukuleles, carved bowls, cutting boards, even a beautiful wooden rocker like the one at the bungalow.

Saffron ran her gaze over the delicate carving, the rich grains of the wood. "You made these?" she asked, not disguising the awe in her voice.

Mano nodded and took a stack of bills from a customer before handing over a plastic bag heavy with one of the beautiful bowls.

"They are beautiful!"

He smiled and gave her a little nod of thanks.

"I didn't know you set up here."

"We do the booth every Wednesday, Saturday, and Sunday," Mano said. "Although I only take Wednesdays. My kids and grandkids usually take the other days."

Wednesdays. So he had been out of town the day Bud died. He'd been here. That's why he felt guilty.

"There's a few of us from Maika'i that come down here," he said.

Saffron had to check her watch. Nik would be expecting her to meet him in less than an hour. She needed to get back on Derek's trail. "Mano, does anyone here deal in secondhand stuff?"

Laughing, Mano waved an expansive hand. "The short answer is yes. But I thought you were trying to get rid of things, not buy more."

"I am. But," Saffron leaned in close to him, "I think someone's been in my house. I suspect they may have taken some things and brought them here."

He looked alarmed, "What did they take?"

Saffron squirmed. "I don't know, really. It's just a hunch."

"Well, it can't hurt to look. Some of the bigger second-hand guys are in the next section over. HI Enterprises does a lot of trades and stuff." He shook his head, "And you be careful."

Saffron thanked him and headed for the next section. HI Enterprises was run by a trim, elegant woman whose nametag read "Eva" and whose piercing gaze seemed more likely to drive customers away than to attract them.

Saffron was impressed with the collection of vintage pieces the woman had laid out on the table: candlesticks, china, vintage glassware, it was an event planner's dream.

But Saffron wasn't shopping. She was snooping. She started with some general small talk and then tried to move toward the woman's suppliers.

"This is a great piece. Do you know its provenance?" She held up a cut-glass tiki tumbler.

"That one came from an estate sale on Maui. Most of the stuff was worthless, but there were a few nice finds. In fact, most of what I've got out today is from there."

"That s an art, finding jewels in the midst of junk." Saffron meant that. "Do people ever bring things to you?"

Eva's eyes narrowed. "Sometimes. But I'm pretty careful who I buy from. Why? Do you have stuff to sell?"

Saffron shook her head. "Not right now, but I might sometime."

There was nothing here, and Saffron was running out of time. She said her goodbyes and began working her way back to the food truck where she was supposed to meet Nik.

The swap meet was a maze of bright flowers, colors, and smells. Saffron couldn't help accepting a wedge of sweet pineapple from one booth, a squirt of homemade tropical lotion from another. She ran her fingers over rich, bright fabrics woven with plumeria and hibiscus flowers and stopped to admire a whole booth of vintage Hawaiian advertising posters in warm teals and greens.

She was nearly to the truck when a flash of silver in a tourist's hand caught her eye. Saffron stopped and moved closer.

The booth where the tourist was shopping was different than the others. The canopy overhead was a black tarp, held up by two flimsy poles. There was no table, no display racks, only a van pulled up sideways at the back. The canopy was attached to it, but only loosely. Everything about it suggested an easy setup and a quick getaway. Saffron peered at the tourist, who was arguing with a man standing in the shadows under the canopy.

The man was small and wiry, with a scruffy beard, jeans, and a smudgy red tee. Saffron noticed as she approached that there was something unusual about his face. It had a jarring asymmetry: one gaping pale eye and one withered socket. She tried not to look at it as she approached, but he was watching her.

The tourist thrust forward the object he was holding. "I don't want it then."

The one-eyed man took the item without comment and didn't seem to notice the departing customer. Saffron came under the tarp and held out a hand. Wordlessly, the man handed it to her.

It was a silver frame with intricate, intertwined patterns surrounding it. It was an exact match to the one she'd found back at Uncle Beau's. And if there had been any doubt about where it came from, the picture of her grandparents staring back at her removed it.

"Forty-five," the man said, wiping a shaky hand on his jeans.

"Where did you get this?" Saffron asked, glancing at the other things he had laid out inside the open side doors of his van. A plastic container of watches, a pair of lamps, an old doll staring crazily up at the canopy.

"Junk seller," the man said. "If you'd have found him first, you coulda bought it for thirty. But I gotta make a profit, you know."

Saffron peered at him. He was not as old as he looked. Maybe fifteen years older than her. "What if I told you it was stolen from my house?"

The man shrugged. "Wouldn't surprise me. Seems to be how my luck is going lately." He waved a dismissive hand. "If you say it's yours, I believe you. You can take it."

"I will. But I don't just want the frame. I want some information."

"Like what?"

"I just want to know if you can tell me anything about the person who sold it to you."

He squinted his eye as if studying the air. "Little white guy, shaved head. Thirties. Tough, you know. Prison tats on his right arm, scar on his lip . . ."

That was enough for Saffron to know who it was. "That's what I thought. Would you be willing to tell that to the police?" His answer was evident, though he didn't speak. He shifted backward, ever so slightly, like a baseball player getting ready to head for second. She held up a hand. "Don't worry. I'm not calling the cops. I'll sort it out."

"It's not that I don't want to help. It's just—" he glanced around, "I've bought other stuff from him, and I swear I didn't know it was stolen. But I don't think the cops would care. They'd put me out of business."

Saffron eyed the van doubtfully. It didn't seem like much to lose.

"I just do this on Wednesdays," the man explained, "I have an actual store that I run the rest of the week."

"Store?"

"Pacific Pawn. Honolulu. We get a lot of stuff that we don't exactly know where it comes from. If I insisted on knowing everything, my shelves would be empty, and I'd be broke." He made a fast sound through his nose that Saffron thought was a bitter laugh, "Well, broker than I am."

"He's brought you other stuff?" she pressed.

"Yeah. Just the odd piece here or there. Nothing sensational, although he claims to have a big item coming in that he claims will make us both rich. Course, he says he's got a big payday coming anyway, so I'm not sure he's too realistic. I'm just trying to run a business, you know?"

Saffron nodded, thinking of the office space she wanted and *Every Detail Events* back in DC. "I do know. I have a small business myself. It's not always fun."

"Thanks for not making it a big deal. I'll steer clear of him from now on."

"Probably a good idea," Saffron said, "and thanks for giving me this back." She glanced down the row and saw Nik standing at the truck, looking around. He hadn't spotted her in the midst of the crowd. She started toward him, but the man's voice stopped her.

"Hold on," he said, "Just a minute."

Saffron turned back to see him rummaging in the van. He emerged holding his hands in front of him. In them was what looked like a green bowl. She went back under the canopy to meet him and inspect it closer.

It wasn't a bowl. It was a helmet. The dark green paint had flaked off it in places, revealing a dull gray metal underneath. It had a worn woven chin strap with brass hardware that drooped down into it and drew Saffron's eye to a long object nestled in the helmet. The knife from her living room. The shape of it was just as she remembered from the shadowbox: long and curved, coming to a cruel point at the end. The handle was covered in black leather and had wide ribs that led down to a round metal piece with a starburst symbol on it. It was nothing special: obviously military memorabilia. *The knife that saved my grandfather's life,* Saffron thought.

"I knew it. They're yours, too. He brought them at the same time. Go ahead and take them."

Saffron looked at the shabby man. She looked at his van and his tee shirt and, again, at his missing eye. The knife and helmet were a piece of the puzzle. They showed that Derek had been robbing her house. But they weren't sentimental to her, and they weren't beautiful or appealing for her business. She laid the knife back in the helmet and held them out to him. He raised his eyebrows, which pulled the drooping lid of his missing eye up and made a tiny black cavern where the eye should have been.

"I'll take the picture, but you keep these. Go ahead and sell them. I probably would have taken them to the thrift shop anyway."

"Thanks," he said, taking them.

"At least that way he didn't rob both of us," she said.

The man gave Saffron a genuine smile. "You ever need anything, you come on into Pacific Pawn, and we'll take care of you," he said.

Saffron smiled back. It was always nice to have connections. She reached into her purse and pulled out a card. "Do me one other favor, will you? If he does ever show up with that big score, give me a call. It may be from my house."

The man nodded his agreement, and they parted as friends.

. . .

Nik swept Saffron up in a warm hug as she approached, and she tried not to enjoy it. Naia hung back, much less enthusiastic than her brother, and Nik bridged the distance between the two women by spreading his arms wide and throwing one around each of them.

"Now we eat!" he declared, his green eyes dancing.

And they did. Nik took them all over the market, getting barbequed chicken kababs, deep-fried bananas, and shave ice for dessert. Along the way, they stopped to look at a beautiful display of white LED pineapple lights that Saffron could imagine using in an evening reception. She seriously considered buying some for the open house, but it made no sense to buy more lights when she had so many back in DC, and adding on the cost to ship these back to the mainland made little sense when she'd probably never have anyone who wanted to use them there, anyway.

Naia was quiet, lagging behind and barely looking at any of the booths. She only nibbled at her food and didn't join in the conversation unless Nik spoke to her directly. Most of the day she seemed lost in her own thoughts.

But Nik's enthusiasm swept them from booth to booth, from aisle to aisle, and before they left, he had decorated both girls in sweet ginger leis and plumeria hair clips. On the way back to the car, he took Saffron's hand.

They rode his bright chatter back to the car and all the winding way back to Maika'i. He stopped to let his sister out at their house before driving Saffron home.

"So you're still glad you sold the house?" Saffron asked.

Nik nodded, resting an easy wrist on the steering wheel. "It's time. I need to get a smaller place. Somewhere there's not so much room for company."

Saffron knew what that meant, and she didn't blame him for wanting Derek and the others out.

"Nik," she said carefully, "I need to tell you something."

He shot her an encouraging glance.

"I think Derek broke into my house. Maybe more than once."

Nik's jaw tightened, and he shifted his hand to grip the steering wheel. "I believe that," he said simply.

"I found some of the things he stole at a booth today." She said. "And the guy gave me Derek's description. But I probably can't prove it, because the man said he wouldn't speak to the cops."

"Sounds like his general mode of operation," Nik said, his voice hard.

"I just didn't want to . . ." Saffron trailed off, suddenly unsure why she was telling him this. The rolling waves made a bright backdrop behind his sandy hair, and she could see in the tense lines of his shoulders exactly how he felt about his brother-in-law. "Hurt you, I guess." She finished lamely.

He looked at her quickly, shaking his head. "It doesn't hurt me." They drove in silence for a few moments, palms and monkeypod trees whipping by the windows. "It just makes me mad." He said, "Like everything he does."

Saffron thought for a moment, then built up her courage. "Nik, he's been at my house at least twice in the middle of the night. I'm not usually a panicky person, but . . ." She tried to think how to phrase it, "Is Derek dangerous? Is he more than just a thief? Should I be really worried?" She was rambling. "Would Derek hurt me?"

Nik pulled the car into the driveway. The bungalow sat like a monk seal, stretched out on the beach in front of them. He slid a hand over hers. "Derek would hurt *anyone* who got in his way," Nik said. With his other hand, he rubbed the back of his neck, as if treating a memory of pain. "Even my sweet sister isn't safe." He sighed deeply. "She hasn't ever been safe, since the day she met him. Honestly, until she walked into the house, I wasn't even sure she was still alive."

Saffron put her other hand over his.

"So honestly, yes. I think you should be really worried. And now," he smiled wearily at her, a new shadow in his playful eyes, "I'm worried, too." Nik was open. He was honest. It was disarming for Saffron, whose whole life had been about making impressions and presenting perfection. His voice was heavy when he asked, "Do you know what he wants?"

"I don't know. Valuables, I think. He's been pawning or selling the things he's taken so far. But the guy at the swap meet said that Derek kept mentioning a big score, something that would bring them both a lot of money. I can't imagine what that would be."

"There's not a lot of big scores on the island," Nik said, "real estate, of course, and a few antiques. Jewelry. Maybe some electronics."

Jewelry.

"Wait here for a minute," she said, slipping out of the car. She ran into the house, closing the door behind her. She wanted to show him the ring but didn't want to show him its hiding place. She left the lights off as she got the pearl ring out of the secret compartment on the top shelf. She held it in her closed fist as she walked out and leaned down to the window of his car.

"Come in, would you?" She asked, "I want to show you something."

"You move pretty fast for a mainland girl," Nik said. She was glad to see the twinkle back in his eyes.

Inside, she opened her hand. The rich sphere caught the light. "I suspect this is worth—"

"Wow," Nik said. "That's awesome." He took it carefully and turned it around. "Is it real?"

Saffron nodded. "Haven't you ever seen your great-grandmother's? Mano said that he and Uncle Beau and Bud all got them and gave them to their sweethearts."

Nik shook his head. "I've never seen anything like this."

"I wonder what happened to it," Saffron thought aloud. "This one was in a carved box that Mano's father had made. I gave him the box back, but when I think of it being buried in all this stuff, and when I think that if I hadn't been looking for the box, I might not have ever seen it, it just makes me sick." Saffron shook her head, "Mano says his wife was wearing hers when they buried her, and I guess they gave this one back to Uncle Beau after my aunt's accident. I guess your great-grandmother took hers when she left—" Saffron stopped abruptly, knowing how it felt to have something like that come up from your family's past.

"It's okay," Nik said. He must have sensed her discomfort. "It was a long time before I was born. But I will say that the story goes that she left everything that would remind her of Grandpa Bud—even her kids. I don't think she took it with her."

"Do you think Derek might know about the rings?"

"I don't know how. I've lived here all my life, and this is the first I've heard. He's only been here a year or so, since Grandpa's first cardiac event. Unless someone told him, I doubt it."

Nik slid the ring on her finger.

"And you think I move fast." She teased.

Nik blushed and pulled back, but Saffron caught his hand. "I'm joking."

"I wouldn't mind if . . ." Nik cleared his throat, "if I didn't like you, Saffron."

She couldn't take her eyes off his face. The clear green eyes, the turned-up mouth, his sandy, unkempt hair. When he slid close to her on the couch, she found it easy to lean into his embrace.

Chapter Fifteen

Saffron dreamed of Keahi and Nik, of the beach and city streets, of blood and pearls.

She woke up torn and turned, as she always did in turmoil, to her to-do list.

She was detained from starting on it by a couple of cars full of locals looking for eggs. As she handed out cartons, she realized that the customers were coming by in a steady stream now. The avocado fridge was practically emptied out every day, and at 5 dollars a dozen, she was making good money. She'd make over a thousand dollars this month just on eggs.

And she could use it. In a week, Saffron would be having the open house of the decade. She'd called Trish and had her prepare a shipment of decorations. She'd also called and talked her favorite caterer into shipping a selection of foods that would travel well. Everything was set to arrive two days before the event, and Saffron just had to focus on making the house shine before the big day.

Today she was working on the final bedroom, which, from what she could tell, was never actually used as a bedroom. The furniture that she could see through the piles of clutter seemed to suggest an office: a rolltop desk, a low table with a typewriter, a wheeled chair stacked with yellowing ledgers. It was where she had found the shark box, but she hadn't gotten much further since then.

The acorn-colored matchstick blinds were down, and they looked as if they hadn't been rolled up for decades. Each shaft was bleached on the back and top where the sun had reached in, and the fronts and bottoms were a more vibrant shade. Saffron first charted a course to get to them.

She'd have to start with a stack of fruit crates that looked to contain old records.

Pulling one from the top box, Saffron smiled at Elvis wearing a crimson aloha shirt, an orchid lei, and a sharp flattop haircut. He was holding a ukulele and smirking in front of an azure sea. Saffron looked around and spotted, on a long koa wood credenza, a square shape she thought might be a turntable.

By standing on her tiptoes and leaning a hip against the wall, Saffron could just reach the cracking plastic cover. She pulled it off to see a pristine turntable beneath.

She leaned back, got her balance, and shoved some of the boxes toward the center of the room. The whole pile shivered as if it might fall in on itself, but it settled back with no more than a couple of creaks, and she had a little pathway to the credenza.

She placed the album on the turntable and switched it on. The familiar sweeping crackle of a needle on vinyl filled the air, and she smiled with satisfaction as the King's warm voice filled the room.

After days of silence in the house, it was a welcome change to have the smooth music for company. She lifted another box and found it full of beautiful carvings. She knew at once that they had been made by Mano. There were tikis and turtles, a surfer atop a graceful wave, and several delicate plumeria and hibiscus flowers. They would have to come home with her. They were beautiful, and they'd be the perfect reminder of the new friend she'd made in Maika'i. She lifted each one out and rubbed the dust off them with the corner of a blue and green aloha shirt with a palm frond pattern.

ELVIS WAS CROONING *Hawaiian Sunset* just as the sun was sinking into the waves outside the window. Saffron jumped as she heard a tapping on the window. She was ready to curse Curry, but looking up, she saw it was Sandy peering through the window.

Saffron tried to calm her pounding heart as she walked toward the front door.

Sandy was smiling widely, her veneered teeth gleaming, framed by her cherry-red lipstick. "I did knock first, before prowling around at your windows."

"I'm sorry," Saffron said. "I didn't hear you."

"Many a woman's gotten lost listening to the honey voice of the King," Sandy winked as Saffron gestured her into the living room. "I don't blame you. I'm just popping by with a little business proposal."

"Oh?" Saffron asked.

"I wanted to ask you something," Sandy said, "about the eggs? I still want some for my own use, but I also wanted to see if I can buy more?" Saffron liked the Aussie twang in Sandy's words, "Your price is great, and I can mark them up nicely because they're local and organic and whatnot. The locals will always come here, but the tourists will snap them up at the market. I'd love to start out with twelve dozen a week or so if you've got them."

Saffron smiled and led Sandy into the kitchen.

"When I first came, I couldn't figure out why an old bachelor would need two fridges," Saffron said, opening the avocado-colored door. Sandy laughed when she saw the neatly stacked cartons filling the fridge shelves awaiting the morning rush.

"Well," she said, holding out her arms, "fill me up."

Saffron spent the next few minutes carrying eggs out to Sandy's car. The woman was delighted to hand over her money, and Saffron invited her in for a drink after they were done.

"I can't believe what you've done in here," Sandy said. "It's remarkable."

"I know," Saffron said honestly. "It was quite a mess."

Sandy took a sip of her raspberry ginger ale, "I suppose you're going home soon? After the open house?"

Saffron nodded. "I need to buy my return ticket. I haven't gotten around to that yet. But I'm hoping for a good offer from the open house, then I can sign the papers and head off."

"No chance you'll stay in Hawaii?"

Saffron opened her mouth to say *no*, but Nik's face, and Keahi's, and Mano's, flitted through her mind and she found that it didn't come out as easily as it had a few weeks ago. "Probably not," she managed.

Sandy peered at her for a minute. "It gets to you," she said. "It really does." Her eyes were clouded, and Saffron wondered what she was thinking. "I never thought I'd stay so long."

"How long have you been here?" Saffron asked.

Sandy considered a minute. "ten years," she said.

"Where did you move from?"

"Australia."

"That is a change."

"You said it."

"Do you miss it?"

A shadow passed across Sandy's face, fleeting, but unmistakable. "No," she said firmly. "I don't miss it."

"Do you have family back there?"

Sandy put her glass down and stood, walking to the bookshelf as she tossed her answer over her shoulder. When she spoke, it was as if she hadn't heard Saffron's question. Sandy walked along the bookshelf, running a finger across the spines and stopping to pick up a brass paperweight in the shape of the islands. She turned it over absentmindedly.

Saffron knew what avoidance looked like. She'd seen the same coolness, the same false casualness, in her mother whenever people had asked about Saffron's father. She knew what scars looked like, and she knew not to pick at them. She changed the subject.

"I've had a lot of egg customers lately," Saffron said. "The Wonders every Tuesday. And other people from town."

"How are your roosters?"

"Gone. People have taken them a few at a time, too, as they've come out from town. I'm sure they mostly ended up in recipes, but at least they aren't starving or fighting. They were getting a little rowdy, all in the same pen. And, it leaves more room for anyone who buys the place to keep a few dozen more hens."

Sandy shot her a strange long look as if trying to decide something. Then she shook her head slightly and said, "The egg farm was quite an institution when your Uncle Beau was running it. It's been sad to see it all run down, dark and closed up, and all those pretty chickens going wild. I notice you have one out there now," Sandy peered out the window, leaning down to get a better view, "with a bunch of little chicks."

"That's Tikka," Saffron said. "I read in my chicken keeping guide that it's good for the hens and babies to free-range, so she can teach them about what's edible and what's dangerous. Also, my porch rooster, Curry, was getting lonely and tapping on my windows all the time. So, I've been trying to let Tikka and the babies out for a few hours each day. They like scratching and pecking, and Curry gets a good distraction by pretending to protect them all." She peered out, too, and saw the round mother hen leading her babies to a nice patch of weeds in front of Sandy's car. "And, truth be told, I like watching them. I find it very calming."

Sandy hummed. "I can see how it would be."

"Of course, the ocean is calming to watch, too. And the palms when the wind is making them sway. It's not hard to see why this is paradise."

"Sure," Sandy said. "Like I told you, I couldn't leave once I made it here."

"Listen, I was wondering," Saffron tried to approach the topic delicately, "About Lani." She saw a wave of surprise move over Sandy's face.

"What about her?"

"Well, is she . . . Okay?" Saffron asked.

"Define okay," Sandy said. Her voice was light, but Saffron could tell that she had raised her guard. Did Sandy know something that she wasn't comfortable saying about Lani? Maybe it was due to the conversation she'd had with Mrs. Claus last week.

"I just mean that she seems . . . Upset. A lot of the time. She seems . . . Angry."

"She's had a difficult life," Sandy said simply. "And I don't really know what all she's been through. I've only been here ten years or so, and she and I are not close. She talks a lot, but she doesn't say much."

"I've heard . . . Things about her first husband." Saffron said. "And I've heard her say things down at the cafe about Bud."

Sandy's expression was guarded as she picked up a book and flipped through it absently. "She did seem prone to . . . *turbulent* relationships, from what I can tell." The comment hung heavy in the air for a moment, then Sandy seemed sorry she'd said it. "But that's true of most of the women that Bud interacted with. He was like a hurricane. Women just got swept up by him, and he left a lot of wreckage in his wake."

"Did you date him?"

"Oh, honey, everybody dated him," Sandy said, "but I didn't have a problem with his seeing other people. I wasn't looking for more than a good night out once in a while." She waved a dismissive hand.

Another question sprung to Saffron's lips, but before she could ask it, the silence in the room was broken by a buzz from Sandy's phone. She checked it and held up a hand in apology. "I guess I'd better take this, and I should get on my way."

She scooped up her handbag as she answered, and Saffron opened the door and saw her out. As Sandy climbed into the car, Saffron focused on shooing Tikka and her babies out of harm's way. Curry placed himself between the brood and the little convertible, strutting and flapping with his neck feathers—which Saffron had learned were called hackle feathers—raised. He was issuing what Saffron had come to know was his standard warning sound: *tuk tuk tuk*. He seemed pleased when Sandy's car backed away and fled down the long driveway as if he'd scared the beast off. His sound changed to a long, proud *bawk* that ended in a crow.

Tikka calmly nosed at a wayward chick, directing it back to her side. Saffron would have liked to name them all, but to be honest, she usually couldn't tell them apart. Only the little yellow one, who she called Sunny, had a formal name. She hoped it was a hen so she could keep it.

Saffron went back to the third bedroom. The break had been beneficial. She could see more clearly now what needed to be kept and what could be tossed out into the trash pile. She hung onto the records: they'd make a subtle statement piece in the room for the open house, and she might even end up shipping some back to DC. They'd make great decor for a hip vintage wedding or maybe even a 50th-anniversary party.

She jumped when she took the lid off the next box. Staring up at her was a garish red rooster statue with its mouth open, and its neck stretched out as if it were crowing. It was red-glazed ceramic, and not as bad when she pulled it out as she had first thought. In the box, she found a matching hen with round chicks peeking out from beneath it. As a group, they were quite charming. She carried them, one at a time, over to the credenza, where she started *Blue Hawaii* again. This time, the needle found the bouncy instrumental intro to a song that, according to the album cover was called "Almost Always True." Its hollow percussion and bright saxophone made Saffron dance back over to the box. She pulled out a few more items just as Elvis started singing.

Uncle Beau had apparently collected chickens inside as well as outside the house. Maybe that was why Tikka and Curry felt so at home in the kitchen when she'd arrived. Saffron found herself holding a delicate teapot shaped like a setting hen. Saffron loved how its feathers flared out to make the bottom of the pot, just like Tikka's did when she was sitting on her nest.

Decor was something that Saffron had always understood. Though her mother was an austere woman who believed that owning things was too materialistic, Saffron had kept a secret stash of beautiful things that spoke to her soul. Maybe it was that part of her that understood Uncle Beau's desire to surround himself with his treasures. Maybe she was so afraid of that part of herself that she couldn't stand for things to be out of place. If her mother was right, and things were dangerous, then Uncle Beau was a perfect example of that.

Still, everything she pulled from the box was a new delight. A pair of brass paperweights shaped like a rooster and a hen, a trivet with a pen-and-ink drawing of a speckled chicken, a metal rooster with individual feathers made from shaped pieces of shining steel. When she finished one box, she dove happily into another. This one, along with the next, contained a pale blue and white china set—complete service for eight—that was etched with graceful drawings of chickens in every phase of life: scratching, sitting, stretching, flapping. It was a true work of art. Even the teacups had sketches of eggs on straw in the bottom of each, giving the feel that each was a little nest.

A dive into the third box revealed hand sculpted paper mache chicken Christmas tree ornaments and another family of statues. This time, they were beautiful wood carvings: rooster, hen, and three little chicks. Saffron knew immediately that they had been carved by Mano. She wasn't surprised when she turned them over and saw his name etched into the bottom.

But they were a slightly different style than the examples of his work she had seen at the swap meet. There were more chisel marks and a certain roughness that she recognized as early work. It was fascinating to see how his style had refined over the years. Saffron carried them out to put on the mantel in the living room. Arranging them was calming.

She thought of Tikka and Curry as she set them up. She put the rooster toward the end of the mantel, over the built-in bookshelf, to stand between the hen and the outside. That's where Curry would position himself, she was sure. And she arranged the little chicks around the hen, with one brave one halfway between the pair.

She liked the thought of both hen and rooster watching over the little brood. It would have been different to grow up with both her parents.

Back in the third bedroom, she was pleased to see that she'd made some real progress. There was a wide spot where she could see the grimy center of the floor, and she kept working through boxes of chicken decor until the room was brashly decorated with poultry and all the empty boxes were piled outside on the lanai.

Saffron sat down heavily in the wooden rolling desk chair. It felt sturdy and substantial, and she realized how weary she really was. She considered going to bed, but the room was so close to clear that she pushed on, chasing the hope of seeing it clean and tidy before she hit the sack.

She turned the key sticking out of the lock on the rolltop desk and pushed the slatted top up and back. A beautiful, neat scene greeted her inside. It was such a contrast to the rest of the room that she froze for a moment and took it in.

This had, apparently, been her uncle's business desk before it disappeared under the clutter of his grief. The inside was all intricate compartments, drawers, and slots. Beautiful fountain pens that must have belonged to Saffron's grandparents lay in a gracefully curved tray. Rubber stamps with the name of the egg farm sat lined up in one compartment, while stationery and a checkbook stood at the ready in another. Envelopes and postage stamps featuring old presidents lay on the desktop, available for use.

Saffron looked through the drawers. There were love letters from Aunt Ila in there, as well as the papers from Uncle Beau's time in the Navy.

Wanting to put the desk as right as she could, Saffron got a cloth and dusted the rolltop. As she was finishing, the dusting rag caught on something. She tugged it free, and a little hidden compartment inside the desk snapped open. She was again amazed at the number of secrets this house held.

Saffron sunk into the chair and extracted a pile of papers, some coins, and a gold locket. Saffron popped it open. It held pictures of her grandparents. She sifted through the coins. Most of them were silver and more modern than the ones in the secret compartment in the kitchen. The papers were standard important documents: birth certificates, her grandparents' death certificates. Saffron was leafing through them when a half sheet of paper slipped from the stack she was holding and fell, graceful as a feather, to land with a soft shush at her feet.

Saffron laid the papers down. Lifting the fallen sheet, Saffron's gaze fell on the bold type at the top: **Certificate of Adoption**. She scanned the document as fast as her eyes could move, then laid it down reverently on the desk.

Her cousin, little Warren Wayne, had been adopted. Admittedly, Saffron had not had much contact with this side of the family, but it still came as a shock. She couldn't help but wonder about the story behind that little piece of paper, and as she began to dig, she found more and more about it.

In the big drawers were medical records from the first few years of Aunt Ila and Uncle Beau's life. They told a story of pregnancy losses, of hopes dashed on the rocky shores of disappointment. The paper trail was incomplete, though, and Saffron found no details about her cousin's birth parents or the circumstances of his adoption. She stopped searching when she saw the certificates of death haphazardly stuffed into the side of the drawer. They looked to be the last addition to the family archive.

Saffron sat back, considering the complexity of her uncle's life. It was strange to think of him as a child, a young man, a husband, a father, a widower. She let her mind wander to her own father and thought how strange it might be to, someday, see him this way, too.

For now, there was still too much hurt there, still too much confusion over his leaving, over why he never came back, over where he went after he left here. Saffron knew more now, but still not nearly enough.

Saffron thought about her little cousin. She thought about the pictures of him she'd found, of his parents gazing lovingly down at him, of his baby smiles. She thought of his perfect nursery, his little crib, the delicate clothes. He'd been loved.

And, tragically, his time here had been short. She didn't know what possible good her insatiable curiosity could do him now. She put the locket, coins, and papers back. She placed the adoption certificate on top and slid the hidden compartment closed on any other secrets it wanted to reveal.

Chapter Sixteen

The warm night was still draped around her when Saffron woke. She checked the clock. 2:26 am. She lay trying to figure out what had awakened her. Tapping. On the window.

Saffron looked out to see Curry's wide eyes and tilted head

peering into the window. She opened it a crack, and he flew away from her, down onto the worn boards of the lanai.

About to scold him, Saffron paused when she heard a ruckus in the still night air. A cacophony from the egg house. She sprung out of bed and snatched the special flashlight from the kitchen counter. She remembered what Mano had said, and went to the living room to dig a pair of Uncle Beau's work boots out of her thrift box. They were too big, but at least she felt assured that she wouldn't be getting stung by a scorpion.

She flew down to the egg house to find one of the doors ajar. Saffron froze for a moment, listening. There were no voices on the night air, no light inside. Maybe she'd left it open when she and Mano had gone up to the house after their long day.

The chickens inside were squawking, making a terrified sound. She went in. Movement in the corner of her eye made her swing the beam down the center of the aisle. Rats. Three of them, scuttling along the walkway toward the back door, which was also ajar. This scared Saffron, as she hadn't been out the back door in days. She suddenly felt very exposed. Saffron chased the rats off down the aisle. They ran out the back, and the chickens began to calm. They settled back onto their roosts as the rats scuttled away and Saffron closed the back doors. She was trembling in spite of the warm night. She heard tapping and spun to look back down the aisle, the way she had come. It took her a moment to realize that the sound was, once again, coming from Tikka. The little chicks were scratching at the sand and Tikka was staring at her feeder, tapping away.

Saffron squatted down and looked at her. The little yellow chick, whose feathers were coming in white, shone like a moonbeam under the black light. It was a treat for Saffron to have another range of colors to explore. The black light gave her a whole new visual world.

"You're a crazy bird," Saffron said to Tikka, trying to shake her own anxiety. "There's nothing there . . ." She stopped talking. She'd looked at this feeder before, and had never seen anything. Now, under the black light, Saffron could clearly see something new. Right where Tikka was pecking were several dark streaks. They looked like droplets that had fallen on the side of the feeder and then been wiped away.

They weren't the only interesting thing in the pen. Besides the chicks, various spots and specks glowed bright under the black light, giving the place a psychedelic feel. But those streaks didn't fluoresce, they absorbed the light, making them seem ominous. Could they be glue? Some kind of varnish? She walked along, looking at the other feeders, but none of them had such prominent dark streaks. It was far more common to see bright flecks and smudges.

Maybe it was the dark, or maybe it was her recent preoccupation with murder, but Saffron's mind kept going back to a single word: blood.

"You're freaking yourself out," Saffron said aloud. "Calm down."

But she couldn't stop thinking about them. Even as she closed the doors—tight this time, so no egg-eating rats could get back in—she saw those dark streaks in her mind.

The walk back to the house was tense. Saffron shone her blacklight along the ground and switched it to the regular flashlight to inspect nearly every hulking shadow. They were all bushes, their colorful flowers muted in the night, but not erased. "There's nothing to worry about," she said aloud. "This is paradise." But her heart still hammered and her flashlight still swept the path, trees, and yard. She was relieved to see the steps of the back lanai. She was so focused on getting into the house that she barely heard Curry's warning.

When she did, she spun to see a dark figure moving around the corner of the house. He must have just come out the open back door. She bolted inside and locked the door, hoping no one else was inside. She flipped on every light as she rushed to the front door and peered through the high window.

The figure fleeing off the lanai was small and wiry, running down the long driveway. The moonlight reflected off the smooth eggshell of his shaved head. It was, without a doubt, Derek.

She looked around. The room was ransacked. Books pulled off shelves, the roosters tipped over, the cushions pulled off the futon and chairs. The nursery was the same: the carefully-made crib torn apart, the closet open, but she must have startled him before he hit the office or the master bedroom because they remained untouched.

Saffron's hands shook as she pulled out her phone. The screen read 3:44. All Saffron wanted to hear was the calm, deep tones of Keahi's voice. She dialed her phone with shaking hands.

His voice was loose, sleepy, "Saffron?"

"Derek was in my house," she blurted, and then, though she didn't usually cry, she heard her voice choking with sobs as she explained.

She heard rustling and a car engine on the phone.

"I'm coming," Keahi said.

Though he stayed on the phone with her until she saw him get out of the gray SUV, the seven-minute journey seemed, to Saffron, to take much longer. When she opened the door, and he was standing there, solid and reassuring, she reached for him.

He righted the futon, and they sat close together on it. Saffron told him the whole story, then stopped him from going out to look for Derek. He was placated by calling the police. Bradley wasn't on duty, but the dispatcher took all the details and promised to send Bradley to Derek's house for questioning. She said she'd have him drive by every hour to make sure they stayed away.

Keahi didn't think that was quite enough.

"I'm staying," he said. "I'll sleep out here on the futon. You don't have to worry. I'll be right here." He guided her back into her room. "Get some sleep."

She climbed into bed, and he spread the covers over her. He tucked her in with such tenderness that she half expected him to kiss her forehead, but he didn't. He just moved to the doorway. As he switched off the light, Saffron was very glad he was there.

The next morning, over re-warmed manapua, Saffron thought again about the streaks on the feeder.

"Keahi?" she asked, "do you know anything about black lights?"

"Not much," he said.

"Do you know why some things wouldn't glow? I mean, they would look darker than what's around them, but still really distinct?"

"Blood does that," he said, chewing. "It looks pretty unique."

Saffron felt panicky and vindicated at the same time. She was pleased that she'd identified it correctly, but *it was blood*.

"Can people having a heart attack bleed?" She asked.

"Not usually externally. Unless something else is going on. Why?"

"I think I found blood on the feeder that was in the shed."

At this, Keahi looked intrigued, "Really?"

"Well, I don't know for sure, but the streaks didn't glow like everything else. I think I need to go down and look around the shed," she looked into Keahi's amber eyes, "but I don't really want to."

She knew what he'd say before he spoke. "I'll go with you."

Together they made their way down through the egg house. Saffron carried the blacklight. She stopped to show him the feeder.

"Looks like blood to me," he said, "from what I can remember. We just did a little bit on forensics in one of my survey classes."

The path to the shed seemed shorter with Keahi at her side. It was still early, and the sun had not yet fully pushed through the dense trees. The morning was warm, but Saffron felt a chill as she pulled open the shed door.

With the new information about Derek, she felt a new determination to find his connection to Bud's murder. If she could, then maybe he'd go to prison, and Naia and Nik could be free of him. The thought brought an edgy twist to Saffron's stomach. But to even get Bradley to take this seriously, she knew she'd have to have more than circumstantial evidence.

The shed door creaked when she opened it, and its musty dry smell washed over her. It was dark inside, and she switched on the blacklight and shone it around. Keahi stood at the door behind her, blocking what little morning light tried to seep in.

The wild nest was ablaze under the black light, its eburnean eggs like little moons. But everything else was dark. Saffron saw no glowing arachnids scurrying around on the dusty floor. The feed barrels stood unmoved. Saffron peered around. The dust had begun to settle where the feeders had been, and Saffron leaned down to look them over.

It was then that she saw it: under the dust where the feeder had been, on the wall, on the barrels. Dark spots in a splatter pattern: blood like she'd seen on the feeder, only this hadn't been cleaned up. These droplets lay untouched.

"Keahi," she said, her voice tight.

"I see them," he said. "Don't touch anything."

She looked around more. Nothing seemed out of place on the workbench, but when she leaned to look underneath, she saw a glowing screwdriver that had been kicked far back under the bench. Its tip and shank were stained dark all the way to the handle.

Saffron pointed. She could find nothing to say except, "look."

"Come on," Keahi said, pulling her backward out of the shed, "we need to call 911."

WHEN BRADLEY FINALLY CAME, she told him about all the evidence against Derek. She told him about the break-ins and the stolen goods. She told him her suspicions about Bud's death. For once Bradley seemed to take her seriously. He said they'd bring Derek in for questioning and also called in a forensics team from Honolulu. They spent some time in the shed, gathering samples of what they confirmed was definitely blood of some kind.

"Could be chicken blood," one of them said. "The previous owner probably did some slaughtering here." They'd have the results, they said, in a week or so.

DEREK HAD DISAPPEARED. Nik and Naia hadn't seen him, and Bradley couldn't find him. It was as if he'd known they were looking for him and completely disappeared. Saffron thought about it as she swept and polished the floor in the office the next day. Once it was clean, she retrieved the folder the lawyer had sent with a request for her to verify that the valuables were all in the house after her uncle's death. Now that all the rooms were clear and she'd sorted all the clutter, she could finally say for sure what was here and what wasn't.

Scanning the photos, Saffron recognized some of the collectibles and some of the books. Around the sixth page, she uncovered a series of photos that showed Mano's shark box.

He'd been right. A photo showing the inside of the box featured two identical pearl rings. The paperwork listed both of them, and Saffron gasped to see their value. She never would have guessed they were worth that much. A thought struck her. Was that ring the nest egg Bud had meant to leave for Nik and Naia? It certainly seemed to be the most valuable thing the old man had owned besides his house.

It was the only discrepancy that she could find. Two rings were listed, yet only one remained. Sometime between her uncle's death and the day she'd discovered the box, someone had taken the other ring.

And Saffron suspected that she knew who. He'd disappeared. If he had found the ring, Derek would never have any reason to come back. Though outraged that he had stolen from her house, Saffron did find comfort in the idea of his never coming back.

She glanced up to see Curry gazing in the window at her. "You'd like that, too, wouldn't you, boy?" she said, "If he never came back." He tipped his head as if trying to read her lips. Saffron stood and walked out, lazily dialing Trish to check on the supplies she'd ordered for the open house.

Before she could finish dialing, the phone rang. Saffron didn't recognize the number, but she often got calls from clients, so she answered. The gravelly voice on the other end was familiar.

"Hi. This Gary. From Pacific Pawn, that you met the other day at the swap meet?"

Saffron was surprised. The man went on. "That fella you were tailing the other day? He left me a message that he wants to meet me. I think he's probably got that big score. He wants to unload it, and then he says he's going back to the mainland."

Saffron wondered if Naia knew this, or if Nik did. She knew how hard it would be on him if Naia left again, especially now, in the wake of Bud's death.

"He said he'd call back and set up a time," he said. "I'll call and let you know when he wants to set it up, but I thought I should let you know that he called me." She thanked the man and hung up.

Nik answered on the second ring. There was music in the background, and he was shouting as he tried to understand what Saffron was trying to tell him.

"I'm sorry," he said, and Saffron could tell that he hadn't heard her, "I'm at a beach music festival. You should come!"

Saffron could see that it was the only way she'd get to tell him. She got the name of the beach and went to meet him.

The festival was loud, and torches lit up the performers. A small stage had been set up to keep amps out of the sand, and Saffron saw Nik standing with his sister over to the left of it. He waved as she approached. Naia melted into the crowd as Saffron reached them.

There was no hope of a conversation next to the stage, so Saffron took Nik's hand and led him back across the beach to her car. He seemed happy to climb inside with her. The music was muffled as they closed the doors, and Saffron felt she could finally breathe. She took a deep breath and told him what the man had said.

The news snuffed the carefree light out of Nik's eyes, and his voice was tight when he spoke again, "Thanks for letting me know."

Saffron was worried about him. "What do you think we should do?"

"Have you passed the tip on to Bradley?" Nik fiddled with the door handle, then with the knobs on the silent radio.

Saffron nodded. "I told him I'd call when I find out where and when Derek wants to meet Gary."

Nik played with the latch on the glove box as he answered, "That seems like the right thing to do. And probably the only thing, too, for now."

The glove box popped open and papers spilled out. Nik was apologizing as he picked them up from the floor mat at his feet, but Saffron waved it off. "Don't worry about it." She was absentmindedly watching a wild rooster cross the beach in front of the car.

It was the little noise Nik made that first drew her attention. Glancing at the paper in his hands, Saffron felt a sense of horror. She snatched at it, but he pulled it away. She could see her own handwriting from here:

WHO? Nik (The only one who knew Bud was coming to the farm)
WHY? Blackmail? To save his sister? Derek forced him to kill Bud?
WHEN? That morning

NIK STARED AT THE PAPER. Saffron reached for it again, but he held it away, like a dangerous item he didn't want her to touch.
"Nik, that's not—"
"What is this?" Nik held it up, and his green eyes searched Saffron's face.
"I was just thinking," Saffron began, "It was before—"
"Thinking I killed my great grandpa? What kind of a world do you come from? What kind of sick person would do that?"
Saffron held up a hand, trying to stop his words. She felt defensive. That was a long time ago, and they had real suspects to talk about now. "Look, I was just making a list of people who might have a motive." It was like Keahi all over again.
Nik's voice was shaking with emotion when he looked into her eyes, "Grandpa Bud saved my life. He saved my sister's life. There is nothing," here his voice cracked, and he closed his eyes, swallowed, and started again, "*nothing* in this world that would ever convince me to hurt the people I love."
Saffron believed that. She saw his commitment to it in every line of his tense form. Nik made a fist and crumpled the paper. "I guess we don't have the connection I thought we did."

"But we do—"

"If we did, you could never think that about me."

Saffron caught his arm and made him look at her, "Nik, listen, I'm sorry about the paper, about thinking it could be you, but I didn't even know you then!"

"You don't know me now?"

"Yes! And you're not on the list anymore. But I can't just pretend. I *found* him, Nik. He was helping me. I want to help him."

"Nobody can help him now." Nik's tone was flat.

"But we can. Don't you see? I really think Bud was killed. I think someone did it on purpose, and if that's true, don't you want to know who it was? Don't you want justice?"

Nik looked into her eyes a long time without speaking. The late afternoon sun fell across his face, showing hollows in his cheeks and eye sockets that Saffron hadn't noticed before. When he did speak, Saffron saw in his eyes a depth of experience that she was familiar with. "True justice, for anyone, is really rare. People don't get what they deserve. You can spend your whole life chasing that, or you can just make the most of your own life. Even if you're right that someone killed him, what difference does it make now that . . ." Nik's voice broke, "now that he's dead?" He pulled his arm free and reached for the door.

"Nik, wait."

"I don't want to think about it anymore. I just want to go on with my life." He swung the door open and sprung out of the passenger's seat, slamming the door behind him with finality.

Saffron watched him go, the sting of his words still reverberating in her mind. She wanted to go after him, but bitter experience had taught her that rarely changed someone's mind. Instead, she looked away as Nik disappeared into the shade of the palms next to the beach.

Saffron saw his point. She knew that he'd waited for justice for himself, for Naia. He was probably right about chasing it. But he was wrong about something. You couldn't go on living your life if you knew there was danger and you didn't do anything about it. Though she had eliminated a couple of people on those scraps of paper, there were still some that were very likely murderers. Someone had killed Bud. She was going to find out who it was and, if she could, stop that person from hurting anyone else.

LATE THE NEXT MORNING, Saffron was on her way to a neighboring town to meet with a lawyer over the paperwork.

She tried not to think of Nik as she drove. Instead, she soaked in the island morning—bright as lemon-merengue pie. Her sunglasses had been relegated to the drawer of her nightstand. She found that not only did she not need them, but she didn't want them anymore. She looked forward to the brilliant colors and didn't want to miss a single one.

She stopped at the post office first and walked in fully expecting her boxes to have arrived. But Nelly hadn't seen them. Now it was time to panic.

She was dialing her phone as she walked out of the post office, and she walked right into Keahi.

"A little distracted?" he asked, reaching up and tucking a strand of her hair behind her ear. She liked the warmth of his hand and his smile.

"My open house just turned into an empty house," she said. "My supplies didn't arrive from the mainland."

Keahi narrowed his eyes and shook his head. "Supplies?"

"Yes. I had a dozen lighted Mason jars coming, along with four hundred dollars' worth of blooming cherry blossom branches. And the imported cheeses and french bread from Pierre's were supposed to be here, too. I have no party."

Keahi was chuckling.

"It's not funny. This party has to be perfect. I have to sell this house!"

"Okay, okay, relax. You're in Hawaii. We can put together a party in ten minutes."

"That's impossible," Saffron said.

"Every day is a party in Hawaii."

"No, you said every day is a *vacation* in Hawaii. It can't be both."

"See, that's what you've got to learn, Metro: every day in Hawaii is whatever you want it to be." He grinned, and Saffron forgot about impossible for a moment.

"I'd love it if you could, but I still don't think it can be done."

"Okay. I like a challenge. Let's say this: if I can put together a party by tonight, you'll agree to give me another date?"

Saffron knew she needed his help, but she didn't want to make it too obvious, "If I do take you up on that, you have to realize that we're not talking about a hotdogs and chips kind of party. I've got to make the people who come to this open house want to stay—to picture themselves living there and buy the place. This has to be high-class."

"High-class is my middle name," Keahi said. "Only it's in Hawaiian, so you wouldn't pronounce it right."

Saffron had to admit that she wanted him to win this bet.

THE VISIT to the lawyer took longer than Saffron had expected, and as she came into town going a little faster than she should, she wondered if she should stop by the Paradise Market to search for something to feed the guests she hoped were coming tonight. Truth be told, she didn't really trust Keahi to have all this covered.

Bradley was sitting in his squad car beside the bridge, and he snapped on his lights as she went by.

He didn't follow her, though, just waved an arm out the window in a downward sweep that meant *slow down*.

The warm Hawaiian evening had fallen when she pulled up to the farmhouse and sat staring.

The lanai was transformed. Gauzy fabric floated above, making a canopy just below the massive monkeypod branches that shaded the lanai. Twinkling white pineapple lights just like the ones she'd seen at the swap meet cast a starlight glow over the neat tables and chairs.

Saffron walked up in wonder. Keahi was coming out the French doors with his arms full of enormous exotic flowers. His smile was as wide as the sweep of the ocean beyond the lanai.

"I win, right? I see it in your eyes."

Saffron tried not to cry with relief. "You win." She managed, "how did you do all this?"

He shrugged behind the bouquets, "the Laki Luau was pleased to loan their favorite employee some stuff from the storage, and these," he indicated the flowers, "are left over from last night's performance. Don't look too close, they're a little wilted."

Saffron could see no such thing.

"Hot stuff, comin' through!" A voice called from behind Keahi. He shifted past Saffron, and she smiled to see Sandy toting a tray of finger foods.

"Is that—" she could hardly believe her eyes.

"Hawaiian Bruchetta," Sandy beamed, "Betty, from the walking club, makes it. I brought a few baskets of groceries, and she worked the magic." She offered the tray to Saffron, who picked up one of the warm little creations. The purple poi bread she loved so much had been sliced and toasted, topped with a smoky cheese and finely diced pineapple, mango, onion, and garlic. It was savory and sweet, and Saffron barely stopped herself from grabbing another. She half-wished nobody would show up so she could eat the rest of them.

"Well, that should bring the town running," Saffron said.

"We'll get this place sold for you," Sandy said, bustling past and making room for Mrs. Claus—Betty—to pass through with a beautiful white china tray etched with pineapples. It held tiny poke creations, cucumber slices with chunky ahi and avocado poke, drizzled with a translucent amber sauce that made Saffron's mouth water.

"These look amazing!" She didn't try to hide her admiration or her relief. With these appetizers, the breezy decor, and the warm, sweet air of Hawaii drifting in, this was a party to rival any she had thrown in DC.

She beamed a warm smile to Keahi, who was tucking the last flowers into the glass containers. He met her eye and smiled back. Saffron fought the urge to rush over and hug him.

A light, cheerful sound rippled through the evening air, drawing Saffron's attention. She turned to see that the koa rocker had been brought outside, and Mano sat effortlessly strumming a ukulele.

He had begun a gentle song that sounded like water to Saffron. The first pair of headlights swept past them as he began to sing, and the party was underway.

Chapter Seventeen

The stream of cars began and didn't end. They parked all down the long driveway and made their way up the lanai steps, exclaiming about the success of the cleanup.

The rest of the Wonders arrived, and they cut straight inside to exclaim over the office, the nursery, the bathrooms. They pulled Saffron from room to room, telling her all about how it had looked when Aunt Ila was here, and about how glad she'd be that it was put right again.

They commented on Mano's carvings, which she had placed throughout the house, and on the charming chicken decor she'd used, too.

"Your grandmother loved chickens, too," Tilly Allbey tossed her platinum hair, "a lot of this stuff was hers. I remember these," she gestured to the garish red rooster and his hen on the office credenza, "from when I used to visit as a little girl."

Saffron was only half-listening. Outside the window, she saw Nik's station wagon nosing into the driveway. She excused herself.

Slipping down the stairs, she saw him helping Naia out of the car. Naia passed Saffron without making eye contact and waited at the top of the steps for her brother.

Nik caught Saffron's eye.

"I'm sorry," she said quickly. "I know you wouldn't. I—"

He held up a hand, and she saw the pain in his eyes. "It's okay. Thanks for caring about him. I'm not mad anymore."

He reached over and squeezed Saffron's hand. She stepped forward, and they embraced. Nik's smile, when she stepped back, looked weary. He glanced at Naia, and his handsome face was etched with worry.

"I'm glad you came," Saffron said weakly.

"Sure. I wanted to support you," he still wouldn't quite look at her, "Plus, Naia hasn't wanted to do much since she got home, but she seemed really interested in coming out here."

Saffron looked around. Naia did seem eager. She was already in the house, peering intently at the bookshelf in the living room. Saffron smiled her thanks at Nik as he moved up onto the lanai. Tilly Allbey met him there with a plate of cake.

Saffron saw how Nik had moved on from Bud's death. He was able to focus now on the living, to give his attention to his sister, who truly needed him, rather than fixate on the past. Saffron asked herself if she had been too obsessed with the old man's passing. He *was* old. Why was everyone else able to accept that Bud had just overexerted himself and died a natural death? Why was she so sure he hadn't? Why, even now, when she should be focused on the party, was she still eying her guests, cataloging each of them by their likelihood of being a murderer?

But Saffron knew the answer to that. It was because of the shoe prints. And the ruts. Because of the missing pearl ring and the break-ins. Because of the blood.

IN A LITTLE TOWN LIKE MAIKA'I, everyone came out to everything. Even an open house. Saffron knew that most of them were there out of curiosity rather than a genuine interest in the property, but she made them all welcome anyway.

The bright sound of Mano's music wove through the house, and his rich voice filled it with warmth beyond the Hawaii evening. The little white lights that Keahi had strung cast a glow like starlight on the lanai, where the groceries from Sandy's warm woven baskets had been transformed into delectable finger foods, and the flowers from the Laki Luau loaned their sweet scents to the air.

The bungalow looked charming with its new coats of paint. Its shining windows were like eyes into its bright interior. Saffron saw Lani wandering through with her brother. She tried to calm her pounding heart. The disappearance of the ex-husband, the phone call, her obvious anger toward Bud, if it wasn't Derek, it was her.

Lani barely looked like herself. Her hair was fixed, arranged into a shining springy style that set off her face. She wasn't wearing her usual jeans and tennis shoes. Tonight, she wore a colorful lavalava and strappy sandals.

The cake was running low. Saffron took the big platter into the kitchen. Sandy's empty grocery baskets had been arranged neatly here and there. She moved one of them over to the counter and set the cake plate down so she could begin filling it with more squares.

"Let me help you with that," a voice said from across the kitchen. Saffron didn't need to look to know it belonged to Lani.

"Sure . . ." Saffron handed off the knife and stepped back. As she did so, Saffron caught a glimpse of Lani's hand. On it was a beautiful golden pearl ring, the match to Uncle Beau's.

All Saffron could think was that she'd been right. This old woman had killed Bud and taken the ring. Saffron was transfixed by the thought.

"Don't seem so surprised that I'm willing to help. I'm not always crabby."

"That's not why—" Saffron stopped herself. "Your ring is beautiful," she said carefully.

Lani looked down at it, then her eyes darted to Saffron's.

"Thank you," she said, her tone guarded.

"I think my uncle had one like it."

There was a visible tremor in Lani's hand as she gripped the cake knife. "He did." She said softly. It didn't sound like a question.

"Where," Saffron started, then stopped. The sounds of the party faded away. It was as if she and Lani were the only people in the house, "Where did you get yours?"

"Bud."

The sound of the word startled Saffron.

"He gave it to me the night before he died," Lani said. "When he asked me to marry him." Her voice was edgy and angry.

"Marry him?" Saffron tried to keep the surprise out of her voice.

"That's right. The lying scum asked me just like he did forty years ago. He said we'd be together the rest of our lives. And just like then, I believed he was serious." Lani was breathing hard. So Bud had been the one who'd taken the ring. Probably when he'd come to the house that first day, but maybe even before. If that's what Derek was after, he'd been looking in vain. Saffron didn't know whether to step toward Lani or step away from her. The old woman was getting more and more angry. "I fell for it again, because I apparently never learned."

Saffron made her voice gentle, "Never learned what?"

Lani's head snapped up, and she spent several breaths looking out the window without speaking. "That Bud was a cheat. He went out the very next morning with another woman. The very next morning. He left my house as the sun came up, and my brother called to tell me he'd picked up a Beachy Breakfast Basket from the Oceanside Cafe. He was going on a date before I even had a chance to call the reverend."

Saffron was on her toes, leaning forward. The hatred in Lani's voice was born of love and betrayal. It was the bitterest kind. Saffron had her why. And then Lani removed any doubt.

"I'm glad he's dead," she said. "He'll never hurt anyone again."

Saffron was trembling. Lani's anger filled the kitchen. She had the when, the who, and the why. Bradley could sort out the how.

"I'll be right back," Saffron said, looking around for Bradley. She stepped out onto the lanai. Bradley was talking to Betty Claus. Saffron cut through the crowd and approached him.

"I need to tell you something," she said.

"Sure. By the way, you're some kind of miracle worker. The way this place used to look—"

A loud crash drowned the sound of his words. Saffron spun to see Lani leaning on the doorframe, her brother next to her, the tray of cake spread across the lanai.

She rushed over to help, stepping carefully over blobs of frosting. Had Lani seen her talking to Bradley? Was she trying to draw attention away?

But the woman was obviously abashed, apologizing profusely as Ed helped her back inside and onto a chair.

"Now just rest. You can't be trying to carry things like that."

"I was just trying to help," Lani snapped at him. Then she turned to Saffron. "I'm so sorry. I've made such a mess of that beautiful cake."

"It's okay," Saffron searched the woman's face for a sign of deception but found none.

"I've been making a mess of everything lately," Lani said, a bitter edge in her voice. "I even managed to let Bud slip away just when I'd won him back."

"That wasn't your fault," Ed said, "the man died." For the first time, Saffron really saw Lani's brother. She saw the white on his knuckles as he gripped the chair arm. She saw the fury in his eyes. Saffron's suspect list got longer.

Lani was still talking. "But I lost them all. I lost Carson."

"Your husband was a coward," Ed spat. He seemed to have forgotten that they were at a party. "Couldn't face the truth that you didn't love him anymore."

"No," Lani said quietly, "I just hurt him too deeply. When I found out about the baby—"

"Lani!" Ed hissed as if he'd suddenly noticed the growing crowd around them.

"No, Ed, don't stop me. I want to talk about my baby. Bud and I talked about him for the first time the night before Bud died. It felt good, Ed. I never should have hidden it in the first place. That's what started all the sadness—the lying."

"Stop talking." Ed's voice was a plea. "Lani, please."

"This was his home, Ed. My baby. I saw his crib in there. I saw the happy family picture. I'm glad I gave him to Ila. I'm so happy he had a family. But I shouldn't have believed that Bud and I would be able to forget, that I wouldn't love them both even more after that. I shouldn't have believed that Carson and I could pretend to go back before Bud."

Saffron felt frozen in the moment, fixed only on the stream of Lani's broken words flowing into the room.

"Carson couldn't pretend. He couldn't bear to see my baby." Lani's voice was high and trembling. "When he caused the accident that killed Ila and the baby, it was because he was so deeply hurt. He thought that would take it away, but it only added to the pain. After he caused that terrible accident, he couldn't live with himself anymore. He took his own life. That was three lives gone because of my lies, Ed."

"It wasn't your fault!" Ed's voice dripped venom. "It was Bud. Bud used you and everyone else. He never loved anyone."

"He loved those keiki," Lani corrected him. "Nik and Naia. That's why I did what I did, and I shouldn't have done it. I never could hold on to him. I can't hold on to anything." Her voice was desperate, fueled by embarrassment and grief. She reached up and grasped Saffron's wrist.

"I'm so sorry. I'm sorry about your party, and I'm sorry about your aunt."

Saffron barely heard the words. Lani was Warren Wayne's biological mother, and Bud, his father. That should have been the most shocking thing, but Lani's grip on her arm blocked out everything else. Though the woman was in the throes of emotion, her hand circled Saffron's wrist with no more strength than a child's.

"Are you . . ." Saffron tried to think, "are you well?"

Ed spoke this time. "She's not well. I tried to convince her to stay home, but she wouldn't listen. She's got Guillain-Barré syndrome. Her muscles are as weak as seaweed. She could never have carried that cake plate more than a few steps, much less all the way out to the lanai." Then, to his sister, he said, "you should have known that."

Saffron jumped in. "I'm sorry," she said, and she was. Not only for the woman's illness but also for her own hasty judgment. "How long have you been dealing with this?"

"A long time. But it's only been the last few years that I've lost my strength completely. Just about the time they started the walking club." Saffron followed Lani's gaze and saw Jan and the other Wonders cleaning up the mess on the lanai. She could see from Lani's wide eyes and the way she was pressing her lips together that she wished she were one of them. She was lonely.

"That's why you're not in the club?" Saffron said, "Because of your illness?"

Lani didn't respond, but the answer was clear.

If Lani couldn't take a leisurely walk, if she couldn't carry a cake plate, then there was no way she could have gotten the wheelbarrow through the mud patch with Bud's body inside. It was ludicrous to think of the weakened woman maneuvering such a load. Saffron felt even worse now.

"I shouldn't have done it," Lani blurted.

Saffron asked a question with her eyes.

"I burned all the photos I had of Bud, but they really belonged to Nik and Naia. I regret it now, but I was just so angry. And if I have to go to jail, I will."

That was what she had done. When she couldn't bear the weight of her love for Bud any longer, Lani had tried to erase him from her life, just as she had forty years ago.

"Take me home, Ed," Lani said, and Saffron didn't stop them.

Betty and Sandy were standing beside Saffron, their eyes wide and their hands over their open mouths. Sandy recovered first, and her eyes were filled with pity.

"Lani," she called, "you need to rest. I'll bring you by some of the leftovers later."

It seemed a small gesture, but Lani seemed to appreciate it. Betty shook her head.

"None of us even knew," she said to Saffron. "to think they've hidden that for forty years."

"That's a long time to carry a secret," Saffron said softly.

Chapter Eighteen

The party settled back down when Lani was gone, but the conversation buzzed with the new revelations. Saffron fetched more cake and thanked the Walking Wonders for all their help, who then helped themselves to the newly-filled cake platter.

Saffron wandered around the side of the house and down the back steps. She didn't feel like talking to anyone. How had she been so wrong? Maybe Bud hadn't been killed at all.

Tuk, Tuk, Tuk. Curry's warning call caught Saffron's attention immediately. Were the rats back? She went toward the sound, wishing she wasn't wearing slippahs. The egg house was a dark shape in the night as she slipped down toward it.

A low snarl snaked around the corner of the building.

"I'm not taking my hand away until you understand. I want that money. I need it. If I don't get it, I'm dead. You don't mess with these guys. They want their money."

There was a sound like crying. Saffron peered through the wire of one of the screened windows, trying to keep her breathing quiet.

Derek stood behind Naia, one hand pinning an arm

behind her back and one hand wrapped around her mouth. The girl shook her head.

"I know things, and I have friends. And if you're not worried for yourself, then you'd better be worried for that brother of yours. I've had plenty of opportunities to get rid of him, but I've kept him around. Now you know why. Leverage. So you will get me that money."

He eased his hand off, "I don't know where it is," Naia mumbled. "I don't know. I just know it was at Uncle Beau's."

"That's what the old man told me, too. But he wouldn't show me where."

"It was his money."

"How can you still be sticking up for him?" Derek ran a hand over his right side, "after what he did to me?"

"He must have been afraid," Naia began.

Derek stepped forward again, grabbing her wrist. "He stabbed me with a screwdriver!"

That's where the blood had come from.

"He was the violent one, not me. It's not my fault that he was out here. I didn't even know he would be here. I just came around the door of the shed, and he was inside."

"What were you doing?" Naia showed a spark Saffron hadn't seen in her before.

"I was looking. Looking for that money. Looking for that stupid ring. It was supposed to bring a lot of money." Saffron supposed that was the big score he'd told the pawnbroker about.

"But you couldn't find it, so you killed him?"

"I just told him I wanted the ring, and he said he'd given it away and I'd never find it. But I'm gonna find it. Believe me."

"Is that what you told him?"

Derek's face scrunched into that slow sneer that Saffron had seen before, "He's a fighter, that one. I can see why he lived so long."

"Stop it," Naia's gaze was on the ground, as if the words hurt her. But Derek went on.

"You don't want to hear how he chose his money over his life? You don't want to know that he just wouldn't believe me when I told him that I could make him talk?"

"So you attacked him?"

"I told you, he attacked me first," Derek's laugh was dark and bitter, "I think he wanted to kill me."

Naia's voice was a controlled scream. "What did you do to him, Derek?"

"I told you—nothing. I was just putting on a little pressure, trying to get the old man to talk. I grabbed him—that's all. But then he got that screwdriver and stabbed me, and I pushed him down and ran out." That explained the blood spatters in the shed. Bud must have wiped the feeder down after Derek left, leaving the streaks soaked into the wood, but either he didn't notice the other splatters, or he died before he had a chance to clean them up.

In the wan light, Saffron could see tears running down Naia's cheeks. "I can't believe I got him mixed up with you."

The man's voice had a low, mean sound, "girl, you're *all* mixed up with me now. And if we don't find that money—"

Naia interrupted him, and Saffron could tell by the way she started strong and then trailed off that the girl wasn't used to doing so. "Stop talking about the money! The man raised me, Derek, *saved me*. And you killed him. Don't you love anyone? Can't you see that good people are worth protecting?" The last part was so quiet that Saffron had to lean forward to hear.

Derek missed any meaning Naia was communicating to him. "I told you, I didn't kill him. He was alive when I left the shed." Derek was sputtering now, some of his confidence flagging, "I just shook him up."

That would explain the heart attack, Saffron thought.

"I even came back to check on him,"

"To harass him some more, is likely," Naia said, and Derek moved forward and took hold of her again.

"Either way, he was dead then," there was a sick pleasure in Derek's voice, "slumped over that stupid wheelbarrow behind the shed. And I wasn't sorry."

Naia's voice was subdued again, and tight with pain, "Why didn't you just sell some more stuff from the house? There was some great stuff there, I saw it tonight. And at least that didn't hurt anyone."

"I was going to. I was going to find that ring, but the girl moved in, and—"

"Don't hurt her," Naia said quickly. It moved Saffron to hear Naia speak up for her. She hated that Derek used Naia's natural desire to protect people against her.

"I will if I have to. You know that. If I knew where that money was, or that ring, I'd be gone already. But I been here a bunch of times, and all I've found is feathers and trouble. You'd better find it."

"I don't even know where to look. There's nothing in the house. I tried."

"You looked everywhere?"

"Everywhere. Even in the desk drawers, which I had no idea how to explain to anyone if they'd seen me."

"What about in the cupboards?"

"Yes! Derek, yes! I looked everywhere."

Saffron couldn't stand to watch anymore. She'd heard him as much as confess to Bud's death. It was not the grisly scene she had imagined, but if Derek had caused Bud's heart attack, then he was responsible for Bud's death. She had the who, the where, the how.

She backed away from the barn and ran for the lanai.

She was calling Bradley's name as she ran up the steps.

Bradley was just ending a call on his cell phone. He looked surprised to see Saffron coming toward him.

"You were right. The forensics are back, and that blood is Derek's." His voice was edgy.

Saffron's head spun. Even if he denied it now, there was proof that Derek had been here that morning.

There was concern in his eyes.

"I need you to come with me. Derek's here! Naia's in trouble!"

Bradley looked confused, but he didn't hesitate to follow her, using his powerful flashlight to cut through the darkness in front of them. On the way, she told him what she'd seen.

Saffron threw the egg house door open to reveal Derek gripping Naia's arms. He stepped away from his wife quickly, shaking his shoulders to look casual.

"Hey, can't a couple get some privacy around here?" Derek was straining to make his voice light.

"I've been looking for you, Derek. You've been AWOL for a few days—ever since I got a call that you broke in here." Bradley waved a hand toward the farmhouse.

"Not me," Derek said, edging backward.

Saffron looked at Naia. She walked forward, putting herself between the girl and Derek. His sneer had returned.

"I just heard you threatening her. And Nik. And I know what else you did."

Derek's eyes narrowed.

"Naia, Bradley and I aren't going to let anything happen to you. You may not ever get another chance like this to take back your life from him."

Naia considered a minute, then stepped toward Bradley, speaking fast.

"You can't let him hurt my brother," she said. "He says he's going to kill him if I don't give him my inheritance. And you'd better believe him because there are at least two people dead back in Vegas that didn't believe him. I'm only alive because I went into state protection before he could kill me." Her voice sounded suddenly small, "I thought he couldn't reach me there, but he came here, and I didn't realize until Grandpa died that he might hurt people I love." She wrung her thin hands. "I should have come back sooner, it killed me to miss the funeral. But I was too scared."

Bradley seemed to consider this, then moved forward. "Derek, I've got a warrant for your arrest. Seems you were out here on the morning Bud died, and you left behind some DNA," Bradley stepped toward Naia. "Are you all right?"

Naia, not looking at her husband, nodded.

"Well, then, we're gonna keep it that way. We've given you lots of chances, Derek, but no more. I'm arresting you. We'll look into the Vegas stuff once we get back to town." Derek looked for a moment as if he might fight, but Bradley unsnapped his holster as he advanced. Once the cuffs were on, Saffron couldn't keep herself from speaking.

"And I heard you. You killed Bud, didn't you?" she said. "He wouldn't give you his money, so you were bullying him like you were bullying Naia. But then he had a heart attack, and you knew you had to get rid of the body. But I came along and scared you off, didn't I?"

Derek smiled. "I'll guarantee you can't prove that."

"We can prove you were here," Bradley said, "you left your DNA all over the shed."

"I didn't kill nobody!" Derek protested.

"Let's go," Bradley said, heading for the house where his squad car was parked.

"He was alive when I left!"

"I'll guarantee you can't prove *that*," Bradley said with a smirk.

Saffron took Naia back to the house, too. As they walked in the back door, she saw how the girl glanced around, still looking.

"I heard what he said," Saffron said. "You were supposed to find something for him?"

"I guess," Naia said. "There was a ring."

"I found them," Saffron said bluntly. "One was my aunt's, and one your grandpa gave to Lani."

"Lani!" Naia said, her eyes widening. "I should have guessed she was the one."

Saffron gave her a puzzled look.

"He's loved her forever," Naia said, "but she wouldn't have anything to do with him. Some kind of old hurt there, I think. I guess they reconciled."

Saffron would tell her about the complexity of Bud and Lani's past. She would, someday, get out the ring and show it to Naia, but tonight she would feel better with the girl safe and protected by her brother. "Let's get you to Nik," she said.

Nik looked relieved to see them. He'd been looking for his sister. He gave Saffron a genuine smile of thanks as Naia recounted what had happened in the egg house. Afterward, he helped Naia into the car, and when they pulled away, he gave Saffron a warm wave that suggested maybe their story wasn't over just yet.

Mano's music still wafted over the lanai, and she wondered if he'd ever taken a break. She got a plate of food and a cup of punch and delivered it to him before wandering back into the house. The Wonders were in the kitchen, still abuzz about Lani's revelations. Saffron glanced up toward the top cupboard, thinking about the ring in the hidden compartment. Had Bud hidden his nest egg here? If so, it may never be found. With all the secrets this place held, it could be in a wall, a book, inside a carved chicken. Saffron shivered to think that she may even have packed it off to Tiki Thrift and Trade, to be discovered by a bargain shopper when they got back to the dreary Midwestern town they'd been visiting from.

It made sense, though, for Bud to hide it here. Especially

once Derek had moved into his house. His treasure—whatever it was, wouldn't be safe there. The thought had crossed her mind that there was no justification for Derek to kill Bud at the farm when Derek had a million chances at home to do it. But Saffron could see it now. Derek had been out here looking for valuables, and when he'd stumbled onto Bud, the old man had pushed the confrontation to protect his nest egg—all he had left to give to his grandkids. Bud had tried to scare Derek out of the area of the shed, had protected the little building as fiercely as Tikka protected her own nest that first day that Saffron found her in the kitchen. Saffron knew then. She knew immediately. Bud's nest egg *was* here.

Rose, the real estate agent, was at her elbow with a trendy young couple so obviously fresh from the mainland that they made Saffron's eyes hurt. He was wearing a tailored blue suit and dripping sweat onto his lapels. The girl was wearing a fitted pencil skirt with a button-up blouse and heels. Saffron blinked. The girl's outfit was a match to one she herself had brought from the mainland. She smiled as she felt the soft, flowing fabric of her beachy wrap dress. Hawaii had changed her.

"Would you like to tell these folks about the charming mountain view from the cottages?" There was a prodding tone in Rose's voice.

"Oh, it's wonderful," Saffron said absently, edging toward the door, "Rose can describe it to you." She patted Rose on the arm and turned.

The agent caught her and towed her to the railing. "Saffron, you have to take this seriously. Sal's pulled his lowball offer. He's out. We need to find a buyer tonight."

"There seems to be a lot of interest," Saffron waved her hand.

Rose tipped her head in agreement, "yes, I think we'll get a few offers."

"Then let's focus on others. I don't think those two are interested in chickens. They'd probably put a sauna in the egg house."

She patted Rose and left the frustrated real estate agent to handle the prospective buyers while she slipped inside. Honestly, selling the place was less interesting to her right now than confirming her suspicion.

She opened the closet by the back door and pulled out her work boots and blacklight.

She was just lacing the second boot when she heard a deep voice behind her.

"Just saw Derek arrested," he said, "you know what that was all about?"

"It looks like I was right," she said, with no small amount of satisfaction, "he basically admitted that he killed Bud."

"Where you going?" Keahi asked.

"Back to the shed," she said.

"Mind if I tag along?"

"I don't know if you want to," she answered, "Our last visit out there was a little grisly."

"Still, I'd like to come," he said, holding the door.

"Sure," honestly, Saffron was glad for the company.

"There's a lot of strange things going on here at the farm tonight," Keahi followed her down the back steps.

The shed was stuffy, and when she reached back behind the barrels toward the wild nest, she tried not to think about rats.

"I really should have thought of it earlier," Saffron said.

"Thought of what?"

"This nest. It's always been an anomaly in here where it would be so hard for a chicken to get to, and the eggs are this beautiful cotton color. None of my hens lay white eggs. Did you know that a hen has to have white earlobes to lay white eggs? I read that in my chicken book."

She pulled one of the cool objects forward and took it to

the workbench. Scooting the teacup aside, Saffron studied it in the beam of light.

"Hold on," Keahi said, his voice tentative, "How long have those been down here?"

"Probably a long time. At least since I came here. I saw that nest early on."

"Then be careful. Don't drop it. Rotten eggs are nothing to play with." He kept talking, though she was only half-listening, "I know. We found a wild nest once when I was a kid. Tried to play egg baseball."

In spite of the stress of the day, Saffron laughed. "That sounds horrible."

"You have no idea. I smelled like it for a week, and the thought of it still makes me sick." He had eased back toward the door, though he held the beam steady on the egg. "Go back to your party smelling like that, and you can be sure you won't be getting any offers."

The egg was cool and heavy in her hand. Saffron couldn't see anything unusual. Its eburnean sheen was so bright in the flashlight's beam that it hurt her eyes. It was just the color of the moon over the water, just the color of the Empress' chicken. Bright, luminescent. She closed her eyes and rapped it sharply against the edge of the bench.

"Hey!" Keahi said, and the beam of the flashlight dipped down as he backed out the door. But there was no smell. Saffron couldn't feel any goo. He stepped back in, smiling sheepishly.

The beam from the flashlight swept across the broken egg in her hand. Inside, in a neat roll, were several hundred dollar bills.

Chapter Nineteen

Three offers came out of the open house, but Saffron was too excited to deal with them. Rose left, shaking her head and making an exasperated growl that sounded just like Tikka.

But Saffron couldn't worry about her Realtor just then. She and Keahi kept tossing looks at each other across the heads of the visitors, waiting for them to leave so they could open the rest of the eggs.

Everyone had a lot to say about Derek's arrest, and Saffron admitted that it was a relief to have him in jail. At least he wouldn't be prowling around here again. Nik and Naia weren't answering their phones. They were probably still giving their statements, and with Naia as a witness, Derek would definitely have plenty to answer for.

Finally, the last taillights turned onto the main road back to Maika'i. Saffron sent lots of food and flowers home with the Wonders, Mano let Bernadette from the diner give him a ride home, and the house was quiet again. Keahi and Saffron cleaned up the lanai to keep the rats away. Saffron threw some leftovers out in the yard to thank Curry for his alarm services. He scratched at them in the pale glow of the party lights.

She had sent cake home with everyone who would take it, and she stacked the leftover kababs in the fridge.

They sat at the kitchen table with a basket of powder-white eggs between them.

Exchanging a glance, they each cracked one at the same time. Saffron saw Keahi's grin out of the corner of her eye as he pulled a roll of bills out of his egg at the same time as she did.

The bills unfurled like flags, waving in the breeze from the overhead fan. They cracked another and another.

The shells in the center of the table sounded hollow as they knocked together. When they'd all been opened, there were nearly fifty thousand dollars. Saffron could see how Bud had folded each bill in half, then stacked the folded bills, then rolled them tight before inserting them into each egg. The rolls relaxed against the sides as if they were made to fit there.

"Look at this!" she pointed to the eggs, where Bud had carefully cut the wide end off each egg to insert the bills. He had then glued them back together, and the cut was nearly invisible.

Keahi whistled. "That's amazing. If I didn't know it was there, I'd never have seen it."

It seemed Bud was more of an artist than he had known.

Saffron sent the cash with Keahi, who would deliver it to Nik and Naia in town. She couldn't stand to have that much money in the house, especially after all the break-ins.

Curry had settled down outside, and Saffron was just switching off the lights when she noticed one of Sandy's woven grocery baskets was still on the counter. She'd have to take it into town tomorrow and return it. She decided to set it by the door, so she didn't forget. As she moved the basket, a fine shower of dust fell out through its woven bands.

The dust looked like sand on the Formica countertop. Saffron felt a sudden spark of remembrance. Tikka, clucking beside the toaster, scratching at the sand like she wanted someone to take notice. Now Saffron moved the toaster, and underneath found the same substance. That hadn't been sand after all. It was this same white powder.

Carefully, she put a finger in and tasted it. Just like she'd thought: pineapple powder. But why was it on her counter, too? And why had Tikka taken such care to show it to her?

Saffron breathed. She knew where she had tasted it before. The soup, on the night Sandy had cooked for them.

The powder had caught Saffron's mind alight like a tiki torch.

The screen door banged behind her as Saffron ran to the shed. She snatched the teacup and saucer and ran back, barely thinking about scorpions.

In the unsteady light of the kitchen fan, Saffron peered into the teacup and saw what she'd suspected.

More fine white powder lay in the bottom of the cup. She dipped in a fingertip and tasted it.

Pineapple.

Nik couldn't eat pineapple. Allergies are often hereditary, Saffron knew, and Nik had inherited more than his great grandfather's charisma and the nest egg. He'd also inherited Bud's pineapple allergy.

All the pieces finally slid into place. The strange powder on the counter, the teacup. The tracks with the jagged sneaker tread. Bud's asphyxiation had not been caused by a heart attack due to a fright or a threat. It had been caused by anaphylactic shock: an allergic reaction to his poisoned tea.

But of course, he would never put pineapple powder in his own tea. Bud hadn't been alone that morning. Sandy had been with him.

Sandy. Why had Saffron never put Sandy on her list? Sandy had been involved with Bud, too. But she'd never shown any real passion for him. Certainly no jealousy like Lani had.

But she was passionate about jewelry. Could she have known about the rings? And would she have killed for one?

It was their voices she'd heard on the beach, while Bud set up a morning picnic to share with Lani. Sandy must have feigned helpfulness, while Bud planned a date with Lani, his new fiancé. Saffron had found the invitation, streaked with rain, that he'd never gotten to deliver.

He was going to let Lani sleep in, and thought he'd work on the feeders a while. And ever-helpful Sandy had made him some morning brew while he worked. She'd missed walking club that morning because she was out here with Bud. And she'd played the gentle caretaker so well, running groceries to everyone, bringing food.

Bringing food. Saffron's mind reeled. What had Sandy said to Lani as she left?

"I'll drop by and bring you some of the leftovers."

Whatever had made Sandy go after Bud could very well involve Lani, too.

Saffron called the police as she drove toward Lani's little beach house. Bradley was unavailable, but the dispatcher promised that she'd have him drop by Lani's as soon as he could. Saffron tried to make them understand that he needed to go there *now*, that Sandy was there and Lani was in danger, but the dispatcher sounded a little tired of her calls, and the department didn't have a good track record of understanding urgency.

The night was dark, and Saffron wished that the moonlight would come back and light the water beside the road. The headlights of the rental car seemed small and ineffective against the thick darkness of the foliage outside.

The lights were off at the Oceanside Café and at Lani's little house next to it. Saffron saw no sign of Sandy's car, and she considered for a moment whether she was overreacting. But if Sandy had killed Bud, if she had been looking for the pearl ring, if she, like everyone else at the open house, had seen Lani wearing it . . . Saffron got out and went up to the peeling brown door.

A little breeze brought her the sound of muffled voices inside. Slowly, Saffron tried the doorknob. It was open.

She slipped into the dark entryway. From there, she could see a faint light in the hallway ahead. Saffron made her way forward, trying to catch what the voices were saying as she pressed herself to the wall and slipped along toward an open door and the little light.

There were two voices. One, bold and confident, was clearly Sandy's. The other, Lani's, was as quiet as the murmuring breeze outside.

Sandy was speaking, "Because Bud had something I'd looked for my whole life. Something that was like oxygen to me. You don't know how that feels, not being able to breathe."

Lani responded, but Saffron couldn't make out the words.

"I suppose you do have some idea."

Saffron moved silently forward.

Lani spoke again, her words forced and slurred, "You didn't love him. Don't try to pretend now, after what you've done. Why are you here?"

"Because I saw him the next morning at the cafe, picking up a breakfast basket. And when I asked him about it, he said he was making a surprise picnic for his *fiancé*" she said the word with disdain, "can you imagine him using that word like a teenager, with him almost a hundred years old? Ridiculous. And ridiculous that he would choose you over me." Sandy sniffed. "I went with him out to the farm, and he told me all about proposing to you, the old fool.

"After all I'd put into this project, do you think I was letting him out of it that easily? I nearly had it. It was mine."

"Bud never belonged to anyone," Lani said, "not his whole life. Except to those kids. Not even his own kids, or theirs, but the twins—his great-grandchildren. That's what it took to make him know love."

"That's a nice sentiment, but it was never Bud I was after. He should have just given me what I wanted. I tried a million ways to get it without anyone knowing. Now I'm done pretending. I'm here for my ring."

"Your ring?" Lani gasped.

"My ring. My father owned those pearls, all of them. He gambled them away to a fisherman, who apparently brought them here. I've been following them all my life. I wanted to get them honestly. I tried. After I heard the lore around here about how they gave those to the women they loved, I thought maybe I could get him to give it to me. But he said he'd have to be true to the girl who'd stolen his heart forty years ago. Of course, I didn't know who that was until that morning he told me he'd proposed to you."

"Why didn't you just ask me?" Lani's voice was trembling.

"I know you. Stubborn, vengeful. You didn't like any of us in the walking club. You wouldn't have given it to me for any price."

"I would have given it to you to save Bud."

"But then I would have had to tell you what I planned to do, and we'd be back where we are now, with you knowing what I was willing to do, and probably turning me in for it."

"Take it now, then," Lani said.

"I will. But there's something else I have to do, too."

"You don't have to," Lani begged. Her voice was growing fainter. Saffron tried to guess if Sandy had a weapon. She needed to see more.

"But I do. See, you know now, and though you don't have long to live anyway, I do, and I'm not taking any chances of spending the rest of my life in jail."

"I won't tell."

"Yes you will, you'll tell your brother, and he'll be at my place like an attack dog."

Lani's gasping words shushed through the room, "Just tell me how you did it. Did he suffer?" A little sob broke her words, "tell me he didn't suffer."

Saffron couldn't stand not being able to see what was happening. She edged around the corner just in time to see Sandy pressing a button on a machine near Lani's bed. The button was one of three: an up arrow and a down arrow flanking a "reset" button. Sandy was pushing the up arrow. Tubes ran from it to an IV in Lani's arm. It looked like a usual fixture in the room, and if Saffron had to guess, she'd have said it was for pain medication. In the dim light of a ruffled bedside lamp, Saffron could make out Lani's inert form on the bed. She wished she had brought a weapon.

She glanced around the darkened hallway. There wasn't even a vase or a picture frame she could use. But she did have a weapon. Her presence. Sandy didn't want anyone to know what she was or what she had done. Saffron could show the woman that she knew. Saffron straightened and walked directly into the room.

"I know how she did it," Saffron said, "Would you like me to tell you?"

Sandy looked up with dismay in her eyes.

"She poisoned him. Made him a cup of tea—those three elemākule loved their tea, didn't they, Sandy?" Even as she spoke, Saffron was trying to think how to get Sandy away from the machine. Whatever was in it was flowing freely into Lani's veins as they spoke. She thought, peripherally, about how she was going to get out of here alive herself. She kept talking, "and Sandy put her amazing homemade pineapple powder in it."

"No, Bud was allergic to pineapple!" Lani cried. One fragile hand fluttered up and then back to the quilt like a falling feather.

"Right. So he went into anaphylactic shock."

"Was he allergic?" Sandy made her eyes wide. "I had no idea."

And then Saffron realized. It was a straightforward defense: if Sandy feigned ignorance of Bud's allergy, then all the evidence was for nothing. How could they prove she'd done it on purpose? All these weeks of hunting only to find the killer and then have her slip out of the charge like an eel.

But then Sandy made a mistake. "If I were looking for a murderer, I'd keep my eye on Derek. And that should be easy since Bradley already has him in custody."

Derek. A memory fluttered through Saffron's mind. *Derek.*

He had been there that morning. The blood proved it. Why? He'd admitted that he was looking for the ring because he was going to get half of the money from it. Saffron had assumed that meant he'd be splitting it with the pawnbroker, but now she saw it was much more likely that he would have been splitting it with Sandy.

She bluffed a little, "Derek says that you hired him to kill Bud."

This shook Sandy. She blinked rapidly. She had no way of knowing what Derek had actually said. Her words were clipped and defensive when she spoke, "That's ridiculous! I hired him to find my ring. That's all. If he killed Bud that was his own doing." Sandy leaped on that detail, "and you know what? He did. He did kill Bud. I saw him at the egg farm that morning—he ran into the woods!"

She was obviously concocting a defense. Saffron tried to interrupt her train of thought, "You did hire him, though? To break into my house?"

Sandy shook her head, "Honey, you've told me often enough that you just wanted to get that thing sold. And you've carted a metric ton of junk to the thrift store yourself. Don't tell me you were attached to that stuff?"

"I'm beginning to be." Sandy was rattled. Saffron took a gamble. "So, where were you taking Bud in the wheelbarrow?"

Sandy admitted it before she saw the trap, "to get help, of course. I had to get him in there so I could take him to get help."

"You weren't taking him to help. You were trying to hide his body."

Sandy closed her mouth quickly. Saffron felt a rush. There was evidence. Plenty of it. She just had to keep Sandy talking until the police came. "Anyway, what's so special about this ring that you couldn't just buy it honestly?"

Sandy waved an erratic hand through the air. She was

getting less stable as they stood there, "You obviously have no idea what those rings are worth. I couldn't afford it. And anyway, they're not just any rings. They're special."

"How?" Saffron needed to keep them talking.

When Sandy answered, she spoke reverently. "My father was a dreamer. He always had new schemes to make his fortune. Once he bought this defunct pearl farm off the coast in Australia, and we moved there to harvest pearls.

"He had this grand scheme to grow pearls around gold nuggets. Pearls made from a grain of gold as the irritant, South Seas Gold pearls. And he did. He grew half a dozen out of over a thousand oysters he implanted. He sold three to pay off the farm, then the other three to a fisherman in trade for a boat. We lived on that boat for four years. But those three pearls were supposed to be mine. He wasn't supposed to squander them like he did everything else. I was supposed to have them. Years later, after my father died, I found the papers from the sale of that boat and found the name of the fisherman. I followed his paper trail here, and I've been looking for those pearls ever since."

"All this time?" Saffron said, "just for those?" It was hard for her to understand how someone could be so focused on a single goal for so long. She supposed that was called obsession.

"I didn't know that," Lani said, her voice like falling leaves. "I did know that they were perfect pearls," she said softly, "and that those rings meant something. They meant something deep. The three men who bought them promised they'd give them only to the girls they wanted to spend the rest of their lives with. Bud's was the most prized of all because after his first wife left, it disappeared. He dated a lot of women, and everybody thought they were the one he'd give it to, but he didn't. He gave it to me. And they saw it tonight." Her voice was drowsy, dreamy. "They were all talking about it." Lani smiled gently, her words soft and slurred.

"Oh, I know!" Sandy burst in, "it was like a firework went off in that room, everyone oohing and aahing. But I wasn't surprised. They've all been wanting that ring for ages. The Wonders talked about it nonstop," Sandy said, waving a disgusted hand. "They didn't know if Ila had been buried with hers, but they saw Glenda's on her at the funeral. I was about to go gravedigging when I found out from Rose that there were two of them in the house somewhere. She saw them on the paperwork."

Lani didn't react to this. Saffron looked at her and saw her eyelids fluttering closed.

"Honestly, I didn't think it would be so hard to get it. Bud asked me out the first day I got into town, and I figured he would fall for me sooner or later." She shifted her shoulders arrogantly, "Let's face it. The women around here weren't much competition. But those kids of his had so much of his attention, and I never thought to look at the egg farm until Beau was sick and I went with Bud to visit. I saw those mountains of junk and knew it must be in there somewhere. Then he died, and I kept waiting for an estate sale. I even volunteered to run it! But I found out that he'd left everything to some mysterious niece on the mainland."

"And Rose confirmed your suspicion, so you hired Derek to break in and find it?"

"I looked, too. Why do you think I came to cook for you? I looked all over that house. But it was hard to find anything there. And, to be fair to me, Derek was supposed to get in there *before* you came—but the idiot got distracted by cockfighting and got himself thrown in jail, so he didn't break in until you were already there, and he never did find it. I guess because Bud had already taken it to give it to *her*."

Saffron saw her opening. "Derek didn't find the other one, either."

Sandy narrowed her eyes, "What do you know about the other one?"

"I found my Aunt Ila's ring. Leave Lani alone, and you can have it."

Sandy narrowed her eyes. "You're a little gumshoe, aren't you? Just popping into our sleepy little town and uncovering all sorts of intrigue. Well, I do want that ring. I want both of them. But Lani still can't be trusted. Especially now that you've told her about Bud. She's going to want to turn me in."

"So am I."

"I'll have to take care of you both, then."

Saffron honestly wondered which of them would win in a scuffle. The woman was wiry and athletic, even at her age. Saffron watched her slowly reach down and open the drawer of the bedside table under the ruffled lamp. Saffron flinched when she saw Sandy withdraw Lani's ring.

"Predictable," she said, sliding it onto her finger.

While she was distracted, Saffron lunged. She moved across the room, reaching over the bed and pressing the reset button on the machine. She prayed that would work.

Sandy backed away as Saffron moved to the end of the bed. She was between the murderer and the unconscious woman now, and between Sandy and the door to the hall.

"You won't see me again," Sandy said, backing slowly. "I got what I came for."

"I'll tell the police what you did," Saffron said.

Sandy scoffed. "By the time Bradley gets here, I could have made it to India."

It was at that moment, though, that they heard a banging on the front door.

Sandy didn't run for the door like Saffron had expected. Instead, she spun to her right and grasped the heavy curtains, jerking them back to reveal the sleek surface of two glass doors.

The curtains fell closed behind her as she pulled the door open and disappeared into the night.

Saffron heard, simultaneously, the sound of a distant scream and a deep voice calling from the hall, "Police!" just before Bradley walked in.

She was frozen, her mind replaying what Bernadette had told her in the café. The king tide.

Bradley looked at her quizzically. "You called to say Sandy was here?"

Saffron pointed wordlessly at the billowing curtains.

"Be careful," she managed.

Bradley pulled the curtain back and peered out. He unsnapped a flashlight from his belt and shone it out the door. It revealed a few inches of concrete and then was lost in blackness. He let out a low whistle.

"Did she go out there?"

Saffron nodded.

"There's a dropoff," he said.

Saffron nodded again. Bradley pulled the door closed and raised a hand to the radio on his shoulder. "Annie," he said into it, "call up to Laie and get a recovery crew down here as quick as you can."

He moved to the bed and began to check Lani's pulse.

"Is she alive?" Saffron asked.

"She's alive," Bradley said, then spoke into his radio again, "better get me an ambulance over here, too."

"I got a lot of questions for you," Bradley said.

Saffron nodded numbly. She'd answer any questions he had. She leaned against the footboard of the bed, relieved, and breathed out a sigh. Lani was alive.

Chapter Twenty

The air was sweet, and the ocean was gentle. Saffron lay on a towel at the secret beach with her eyes closed, listening to the rush of water against the lava points.

She opened her eyes to see Keahi's topaz skin against the golden sand. He was sitting up, watching the waves.

"What are you thinking about?" She asked him.

"You don't give up," Keahi said. "I was thinking that I admire that."

Saffron was quiet.

"Sometimes I do," she said.

"I haven't seen it. You knew Bud was murdered, and you didn't give up until you proved it."

Saffron tried not to think about the whole event, from Bud's ashen face to Sandy's broken body the recovery team brought up from the bottom of the cliff outside Lani's house. She didn't mind thinking of Lani, though, who was due to get out of the hospital any day. She had her ring back, and her brother said she was doing fine. Nik and Naia were fine, too. Now that Derek was in jail and the sale of their house was complete, they were going on a surfing trip around the islands to put the whole thing behind them.

"Have you decided which offer to accept yet?" Keahi said, a strange tightness in his voice.

Saffron shook her head. "They're all good money. I just can't decide who would be best to pass it on to."

"Do you think any of them will keep the egg farm going?"

She shook her head and sat up, "not really. One couple says they will, but I think that's just because Rose is pressuring them to say so." Saffron thought a moment. "I had another offer, too," she said.

Keahi glanced at her. "Oh?"

"It was from Trish and Clark."

"Your assistants?" Keahi's voice revealed his confusion.

She nodded. "They want to buy the business."

"Your event business? Back home?" Keahi's voice was lighter, more animated. Saffron tried not to read too much into that.

"*Every Detail Events*," she said, "They seem to think they can run it."

Keahi was quiet as one wave rolled in, then two. A mynah bird cried somewhere behind them. "What could you do back there if you sold it? Start a new company?" He turned to face her, his amber eyes locked on hers.

She shrugged. "I don't know what I could do," she said.

He leaned close, and his voice was soft as he said, "You could stay here," He brushed her cheek with his hand, "that would be an adventure."

He smiled, and she tilted her face up to his. His kiss was as gentle as the little running waves that washed up the beach.

Saffron tucked her hand under his. "Every day is an adventure in Hawaii."

Sneak Peek: Book 2 Hen Party

Saffron hefted the chicken in her arms, trying to settle Tikka's protests. Tikka was not a car chicken. She did not enjoy car rides, and though the Empress insisted that a chicken could be trained to like civilized living, Saffron was not seeing much evidence of that with Tikka.

She carried the black and orange hen up the expansive

steps of the Empress' estate house, juggling it in one arm and a package in the other. In the paper-wrapped package was a gift for the Empress, a large fish called a kūmū. Saffron had bought it from Oke, the fisherman who showed up sometimes along the shoreline with his deep-bottomed canoe filled with fish. Saffron was always happy to see him, as his fish were fresh and delicious. Today she'd picked up some for herself and some to take to the Empress.

The Empress' home was an old plantation house built into the side of the mountain behind the little Hawaiian town of Maika'i, which Saffron had called home for several months now. She knocked and turned to take in the rugged palms that surrounded the estate, and beyond them, the gleam of the teal ocean striped with whitecaps.

The colors of Hawaii dazzled Saffron. The rich greens and bright floral accents, the golden sun and sand, the crystalline blue water, all of it fed her in a way she'd never experienced.

Saffron knew color differently than other people did. Color was a special experience for her. She seemed to see color more intensely and to see more colors than anyone else. When she looked at a red hibiscus blossom, for example, it was not just red. It was red with soft yellow hues, with the palest of blue cast over the curved surface of each petal. She had stopped trying to explain this to people, since to them a red flower was a red flower.

Today, the pale pink of the plantation house was shaded with yellow reflections from the brilliant sunlight, making it a cheery peach color. The subtlety was not something Saffron often thought of, but occasionally, when something stood out, she wondered about the strange ability.

She also had a perfect memory for color. In her mind was an extensive catalog of every color she'd ever seen, and the information her eyes sent her brain was constantly being cross-checked against that catalog. For example, the bronze sheen on the doorknob was exactly the color of the drawer pulls on the oak cabinets in the shabby Washington DC apartment where she'd grown up and the perfect match to the arms of a park bench in the U.S. National Arboretum. She toyed with the shade in her mind as the door swung open.

Carlo, one of the two strong middle-aged men employed by the Empress, opened the door, invited her in, and took the fish to the kitchen.

Coming here always felt like going back in time. The interior was decorated with lavish wood antiques from Europe, gilded mirrors, and Renaissance paintings. It smelled cool and dusty, and the crystal chandeliers were kept dim. Carlo returned to show Saffron through the vast entry and back into the drawing room.

The Empress sat, as always, at the window, gazing out at the immaculate garden and stroking Princess, her pet chicken. The Empress carried her everywhere on special pillows or lap quilts. Princess was a silkie, a breed of chicken known for its soft, fluffy feathers, blue earlobes, and devotion to its owners.

The third trait was evident now, as the little bird's eyelids drooped in contentment at the Empress' attentions.

"Saffron!" the Empress exclaimed, and Princess jumped at the sound of her voice. Rex, the assistant behind the Empress, moved without command to turn the Empress' chair and wheeled her over to greet her guest.

The Empress was a vast woman, colossal in friendliness as well as size. She enveloped the room with her genuine interest in and affection for all living things within it. Her warm skin was the color of sable orchids, and the silver hair piled atop her head was secured with carved koa wood combs. She spoke with the soft accent of her first language—Samoan—draped over each English word. Saffron smiled as the Empress exclaimed over Tikka.

"What a beauty! What a regal beauty you are!" Tikka

arched her neck in response, and Saffron could almost believe that she knew what the Empress was saying.

The Empress waved a hand, and Carlo swept Princess from her lap and held the chicken. The Empress waved Saffron closer and gathered Tikka out of her grasp. Tikka was much larger than Princess, but the difference was slight on the Empress' ample lap. Saffron tensed. Tikka generally spent her days out in the pen with the other hens, laying an egg nearly every day, scratching for bugs, and bathing in the sand. She was not a house chicken like Princess. Saffron wasn't entirely sure what Tikka would do. One look at the vases, rugs, and delicate carvings surrounding them brought an image of Tikka flapping and scratching her way around the pristine drawing room.

But the Empress' warm personality seemed to have the same effect on chickens as it did on people. As she stroked Tikka's head, the chicken stilled, then settled, laying down with her soft underfeathers spread around her like a skirt. She gazed placidly over at Saffron, who breathed a sigh of relief.

"This is a very special chicken," the Empress gushed. Saffron shrugged. She thought so, too, as Tikka had been her first friend when she'd moved here and taken over her late uncle's egg farm last fall, but she wasn't quite as demonstrative about her sentiments. The Empress went on, "she is a Wyandotte. Gold-laced, see?" she indicated Tikka's brassy feathers, each outlined in with a sharp black point, "they are very docile, generally, and make wonderful mothers." Here, the Empress' eyes flicked up to the clock and rested a moment on a silver frame on the marble mantel over the fireplace. She turned to Rex, "Check the window, will you? He should be here any time."

Saffron raised her eyebrows in an unspoken question.

"Oh, my dear, when I asked you over, I didn't know that my boy—my Davis—was coming to visit me today! He's in the

Navy, you know, and I don't always know when he is near his home port. But he is coming, and I can't wait to see him. I didn't call off our playdate because Princess is so looking forward to spending time with Tikka, and because—who knows?—you and my Davis may find something in common."

Saffron tried not to smile. So that was it. Since she'd moved here, everyone in town who had an eligible bachelor relative from 21 to 50 had been subtly and not subtly trying to set her up. She didn't mind, but she had been spending a lot of time with her favorite bachelor—Keahi Kekoa—lately, and he might mind her being set up with someone else.

Rex came back into the room and shook his head. "No one yet, ma'am."

The Empress waved a dismissive hand, "Thank you, Rex. Never mind." To Saffron, she said, "Oh, but that's not really why you're here. Let's go out to the garden so the children can play."

Again, Rex moved without instruction to wheel her toward the tall glass doors, and Carlo, cradling Princess in one arm, threw them open to let her pass.

Outside, Carlo put Princess down in "the chicken garden," a sunny spot where Saffron had seen her play before. It had been planted with chicken-friendly shrubs and sported a feeder, a small pond, and a nice sandy stretch for dirtbathing. Princess immediately set to work pecking at bugs in the grass below her. The Empress waved to Rex, and he gathered Tikka and set her down on the lawn next to Princess. Again Saffron tensed. She had seen displays of dominance in her flock at home, and she'd tried to talk the Empress out of the idea of this hen party, but the Empress had insisted that Princess was lonely for her kind and must have a visitor. Saffron had chosen Tikka to bring along because she was the most docile of the flock at Hau'oli ka Moa Egg Farm, and because she had recently raised several chicks, so she was more tolerant than many of the other hens.

Princess went immediately to the newcomer, watching her with one eye. Tikka didn't seem to notice the little ball of fluff. Saffron could only assume that because of the silkie's strange appearance, Tikka didn't realize Princess was another chicken, and so didn't feel threatened by her. Princess mimicked Tikka's movements and followed her around contentedly as they both scratched for bugs and pecked at seeds on the bushes nearby.

The Empress watched for a while, a look of pure satisfaction on her face. "This is what she has been needing. They are flock animals, you know?"

Saffron nodded.

"Humans need each other," the Empress stated, "and so do other creatures."

"I think you may be right," Saffron said, watching the birds as they dipped their beaks and raised their heads, drinking from the pond. She had struggled with loneliness herself, back in Washington DC, before she came here. Since arriving in the islands, she had learned to value friends.

In the still of the moment, a loud call broke the heavy Hawaiian spring air. It was half battlecry, half victory whoop, and it made the Empress' head swivel, and her hands flutter. Rex and Carlo scrambled to spin her around just as a handsome sailor strode out of the house.

"Mama!" His resonant voice filled the backyard, and he crossed the garden in three steps to throw himself to his knees beside the Empress' wheelchair. He wrapped his arms around her, and Saffron looked away as the Empress buried her face in his short black hair, tears streaming down her cheeks.

"Six months is too long for me to not see you!" she said, her voice soft with tenderness.

"Too long for me, too," he smiled.

The Empress seemed to suddenly remember Saffron.

"Oh, my Davis!" she said as he stood, "I have got a girl for you to meet! This is Saffron. She's come all the way from Washington DC to take over Beau's old egg farm!"

Davis smiled, a grin full of warmth and humor. Saffron saw in his eyes that his mother had also set him up plenty of times, "Nice to meet you," he said, "Mama's sent me lots of interesting tidbits about you while I was at sea."

Saffron felt her cheeks flush. Davis smiled and turned back to his mother.

"Guess what?"

"What?" The Empress' tone was light and playful.

"*I've* got a girl for *you* to meet."

Saffron felt a rush of both relief and disappointment.

Davis turned toward the house, and Saffron looked up to see a willowy girl with light brown hair drifting out the doors like a petal on the wind.

"My fiancé!" Davis' impossibly wide grin grew even more expansive. The girl slipped up to him and settled into the curve of his uniformed arm.

The Empress squealed like she was on a roller coaster. "What? My baby's getting married? When? How? Why haven't I heard of this lovely girl? What's her name? Davis! Introduce me to my new daughter-in-law this instant!"

Saffron squirmed. A confirmed neat freak, she did not like for things to be out of place, and that's exactly what she was now. This was an intimate moment between the Empress and her son, and Saffron felt conspicuous and awkward being there. She glanced at Carlo and Rex, both of whom stood calm and detached. They seemed more a part of the garden than part of the event: two stately topiaries whose only movement was the flick of an eye in the general direction of the now-forgotten chickens.

Saffron was glad to have the chickens to direct her attention to as she heard Davis say, "Mama, this is Lyza Carelli."

"Where in the world did you meet her? Was it in a port of

call? Did you see each other across a crowded marketplace?" The Empress had an affinity for exotic historical romance novels, and it was showing now.

"No, nothing so exciting as that," Lyza said, her voice soft and musical. Saffron couldn't help but glance back at the striking couple.

"We met through my bunkmate, Logan Prentice. He's another seaman from Lyza's hometown. She was vacationing in Spain when we came into port at Rota. She came to visit him in port, and she and I hit it off. Logan was on duty, so I took her to dinner."

"The rest is history," Lyza chimed in.

"And last night, when we came into port, she met me here and I asked her to marry me," Davis' face was shining, his eyes dancing with the news.

That's what it looks like to be in love, Saffron thought. Watching them together, she felt a stab of jealousy for the first time in a long time.

"Well, this is just the most exciting news!" The Empress beckoned the couple closer. "When's the big day?"

Davis laughed, "We haven't decided yet. But you'll be the first to know. I just wanted to bring her here, to introduce her to you, and show her where I grew up."

"Ah," the Empress said, "you're going to love it here, and my grandchildren will be close to me," She gazed lovingly at Davis and Lyza. Saffron noticed that it was their turn to squirm. No wonder, they had just gotten engaged, and now there was talk of grandchildren.

The Empress looked suddenly upset, "But you don't take her to the diving rock!"

Davis waved her away, "Aw, Mama, the accident was twenty-five years ago, and I can swim now! I'm a sailor!"

Lyza's blue eyes were wide, "What happened?"

"I was seven, a little too brave for my own good. We used

to hike from the beach up to the top of this cliff and look down on the diving rock and the bay. We were up there, and I saw people jumping off the diving rock, so I decided I needed to do it, too. Us boys went back down, and as soon as we got there, I climbed the diving rock like the teenagers were doing and threw myself off. Of course, I didn't know how to hit the water, and I belly-flopped. Got the air knocked out of me, that's all."

The Empress' eyes were closed, "He sunk like a stone. I couldn't get to him. I was screaming and screaming for someone to get him out of the water."

"When I could kick, I pulled in a big lungful of water," he was shaking his head, "If Uncle Mano hadn't been there, I would have drowned. He dived right in and hauled me up, pumped the water out of me on the beach. Saved my life."

"You know Mano?" Saffron blurted. The three of them looked at her as if they'd just remembered she was there.

"Oh, yeah. His grandson and I hung around a lot."

"Keahi?" Saffron still couldn't say the name without smiling.

"That's right. You've met him?" Davis shook his head, "Of course. I forgot he was back around here." Speaking to Lyza, he said, "You'll have to meet him. He's a great guy."

"And his grandfather saved your life. I'll have to thank him for that," Lyza gave Davis a squeeze and smiled up at him.

"That was a terrible day," the Empress said. "Terrible. I still have nightmares about it." A little shiver ran through her voice on the word *nightmares*.

Davis reached for his mother's hand, "Mama, I told you, I can swim now. I'm on the water all the time."

The Empress' hand trembled as she gripped her son's, "That's not the problem, atali'i, you mustn't go to the bay because the manōs have returned." Her voice was low.

"Your friend's grandfather?" Lyza asked.

"No, though that is his name, too," the Empress said

patiently, "manōs are sharks."

"Sharks?" Lyza's blue eyes were bright with alarm.

"She's from Massachusetts," Davis said, as if this explained her reaction, "don't worry, baby. They're just coming in to feed and mate."

"Ch," The Empress chided Davis, "You simplify. These are not just sea animals doing animal things. They are ʻaumakua. And they have gathered for a purpose. They sense something. They have not been to Maikaʻi all together like this for many years," the Empress said, "Of course, they individually have visited their families, but not as a group. The researchers, they say that the manōs have not been gathering because of currents or tourists or because there is not enough food, but we know. They have not all been needed at once. But they are needed now. Something is coming, and they need to protect their families from it."

Saffron had not been in Hawaii long, but the time she had spent with Keahi, and his grandfather had taught her that there were deep traditions here that she respected and was continually trying to better understand.

Lyza blinked rapidly, tipping her head up at Davis in a question. Saffron could see a struggle in him, between, she supposed, his traditions and his modern life, his mother and his fiancé. Finally, he closed his eyes and nodded, "Many families here have deities in the form of animals that watch over them and protect their families."

The empress smiled warmly as she explained further, "these are our ancestors, their spirits return in the form of these animals to warn us or protect us. Some families have ancestors that appear as honu—sea turtles. Others have geckos or eels or birds like the pueo—the owl." The Empress' words were reverent. "We know our own ʻaumakua, and we take care of them."

"Oh," was all Lyza said. Saffron thought she could be

more enthusiastic. It was a powerful and beautiful belief.

Davis went on, "For many families, their 'aumakua is a shark, and there's a legend—"

"An account," the Empress corrected crisply, and she went on from there, "of a gathering of 'aumakua: sharks that came to the beach at the diving rock and waited. Their families knew them, and they went and fed them. And when a huge jellyfish bloom came, the sharks stood guard and turned the tides and fed on the jellyfish to keep them away from the beach, and no one here was stung. The towns around Maika'i suffered, but no one in Maika'i was hurt because the 'aumakua protected their families."

There was a long pause, and Lyza cleared her throat, "that's amazing," she managed.

"And now they have returned, and they have work to do," the Empress chided, "so don't bother them at the diving rock."

"And if it keeps me away from there, then the 'aumakua are doing you a favor, too, huh, Mama?" Davis was teasing, but there was a gentle reverence in his voice.

"I give them an offering now and again," the Empress returned. "And they've kept you safe at sea, haven't they?"

Davis looked closely at his mother, "Hey, speaking of offerings to the sharks, where is Princess?"

The Empress' hands flew to her lap in a burst of momentary panic before she spied the two hens curled together, resting in the shade of an oleander bush. "We're having a little hen party, aren't we, manamea?" She used a Samoan term of endearment, a word that Saffron had gathered meant something like *sweetheart*. Princess looked up at her. "Come here, come here, then and see your big brother." She reached into a bag hanging from her wheelchair arm and extracted a small can, which she shook. The rattling made Princess leap to her feet and lumber over in an awkward canter to flap her way into the Empress' arms.

Tikka, disturbed from her nap, also stood, shook her feathers, and meandered over. The Empress rewarded each of them with a few golden treats of dried grains from the can.

Saffron reached down and collected Tikka.

"I'd really better be on my way," she said, grateful that a smooth segue had presented itself, "I've got customers coming for eggs soon."

The Empress bade her a cheerful goodbye, and Carlo saw her out. Saffron left the Empress and her guests cooing over Princess.

***

Join Saffron and the hens on their next adventure in Hen Party: Book 2 in the Aloha Chicken Mysteries!

DEAR READER,

Thank you for visiting Maika'i and the Hau'oli ka Moa Egg Farm! I hope you enjoyed Walking on Eggshells, and I hope you'll read more of Saffron's adventures in Book 17: Fly the Coop. If you did enjoy the book, please consider writing a review on Amazon and Goodreads. I love hearing from my readers and your reviews help other readers find my novels! I truly appreciate every review and every reader who spends time with Saffron, the hens, and me!

-Josi Avari